GORDON ZUCKERMAN

THE SENTINELS

CRUDE DECEPTION

This book is a work of fiction. Names, characters, businesses, organizations, places, events, and incidents are either a product of the author's imagination or are used fictitiously. Any resemblance to actual persons, living or dead, events, or locales is entirely coincidental.

Published by Greenleaf Book Group Press
Austin, Texas
www.gbgpress.com

Copyright ©2011 Gordon Zuckerman

All rights reserved.

No part of this book may be reproduced, stored in a retrieval system, or transmitted by any means, electronic, mechanical, photocopying, recording, or otherwise, without written permission from the copyright holder.

Distributed by Greenleaf Book Group LLC

For ordering information or special discounts for bulk purchases, please contact Greenleaf Book Group LLC at PO Box 91869, Austin, TX 78709, 512.891.6100.

Design and composition by Greenleaf Book Group LLC
Cover design by Greenleaf Book Group LLC

Publisher's Cataloging-In-Publication Data
(Prepared by The Donohue Group, Inc.)
Zuckerman, Gordon.
  The Sentinels. Crude deception / Gordon Zuckerman.—1st ed.
  p. ; cm.—(The Sentinels ; [bk. 2])
  ISBN: 978-1-60832-143-8
  1. Industrialists—Fiction. 2. Petroleum industry and trade—Corrupt practices—Fiction. 3. Conspiracy—Fiction. 4. United States—Politics and government—Fiction. 5. Great Britain—Politics and government—Fiction. I. Title. II. Title: Crude deception
PS3626.U25 S46 2011
813/.6   2011927094

Part of the Tree Neutral® program, which offsets the number of trees consumed in the production and printing of this book by taking proactive steps, such as planting trees in direct proportion to the number of trees used: www.treeneutral.com

Printed in the United States of America on acid-free paper

11 12 13 14 15 16   10 9 8 7 6 5 4 3 2 1

First Edition

List of Characters

Ainsworth, Henry (Treasury Secretary)

Armstrong, William (Senator, Indiana)

Arnof, Cecil (French banker)

Arnold, Bob (banker)

Cerreta, Don (alias Mr. Smith, lawyer, along with Mr. Jones)

Chang, Cecelia (a Sentinel)

Chang, Ivan (Tai-Pan, House of Chang)

Clarke, Sam (Samson)

Connors, Steve (ranch foreman for Bill Dean)

Cumberledge, Denise (friend of Claudine's)

Cumberledge, Lady Margarite (Denise's mother)

Cummins, Natalie (actress)

Dean, William (Bill) (Mike's boss, ranch owner)

Demaureux, Henri (banker, Claudine's father)

Demaureux-Roth, Claudine (a Sentinel)

Duits, Victor (Dutch advisor)

Dupree, Benjamin (Arnof protégé)

Ferrari, Pete (banker)

Garibaldi, Tony (a Sentinel)

Habib, Prince (House of Saud)

Hardy, Jack (Titus Oil)

Hess, John (Senator, Penn.)

Lee, Ted (Asian banker)

Lucas, Jordan (Senator, Calif.)

Mai Li (tea house owner)

Malone, Roger (chairman, Federal Reserve)

Marcus, Sir David

Matthews, Walter (journalist)
McLain, Jim (Big Oil bank pres.)
Meyer, Ian (a Sentinel)
Muirhead, Sir Desmond (chairman, London Bank of Commerce)
Oh, Lawrence (Indonesian businessman)
Perez, Juan Pablo (oil minister, Venezuela)
Roth, Jacques (a Sentinel)
Roth, Pierre (banker, Jacques' father)
Schmidt, Erhart (investor)
Stone, Mike (a Sentinel)
Stone, Morgan (Mike's father)
Tolles, Ray (banker)
Von Heusen, John (VP, Berlin bank)
Wan, K. Kai (Indonesian general)
Wang, C. K. Chairman
Warner, Phil (Times editor)

APRIL 1946

Less than four months since the six Sentinels had formed their new organization and capitalized it with their 25-million-dollar wine investment and 75-million-dollar cash balances that remained after the sale of their last remaining German gold bearer bonds.

Following three difficult years of challenge, personal danger, and tireless efforts to prevent German industrialists from using their two-billion-dollar "Fortunes of War" to start another Reich, each of the Sentinels was looking forward to resuming a career, returning to a more normal and peaceful life, and pursuing life's more personal aspects.

Jacques and Claudine Demaureux-Roth were settling into their new lives in New York City following their honeymoon in Sun Valley, Jacques was concentrating on developing Stone City Bank's International Banking Department, and Claudine was helping interface American financial and governmental interests with the emerging industrial community of postwar Europe.

In San Francisco, Mike Stone was determined to complete all the study and planning needed to help his new employer, Dean Securities, establish a worldwide market for the trading of petroleum futures contracts. Cecelia Chang was expanding America West Bank's efforts to better service the vacuum left in the many different Asian markets at the end of Japan's occupation.

With the defeat of the Japanese in the Pacific and the Germans in Europe, seven American and British oil companies were left in control of 92 percent of the world's oil production. For more than a year, respected economists had been predicting a dramatic postwar industrial revolution. They all agreed the combined effect of the pent-up consumer demand in the United States and the resurgence of reconstructed economies of Asia and Europe would create new economic prosperity. The demand for petroleum was expected to rise at an exponential rate for many years. Although the various prognostications differed in magnitude and duration, they all forecast exponential expansion in the demand for oil.

Rumors of the Oil Club's efforts to control future oil productions were beginning to circulate. The Sentinels were asking themselves, Was a new concentration of wealth and influence being organized to pursue a new agenda of self-interest that could conflict with the public's longer-term best interests? Did they need to become involved?

Prologue
A GATHERING IN WYOMING

Wearing bulky waders, Jacques Roth felt exposed and defenseless standing in the knee-deep riffles of Wyoming's North Platte River. It wasn't fishing that had brought Jacques to the Platte. His assignment was to record the make, model, and N number of each of the chartered planes that would be landing at the remote airstrip next to Wyoming's Rocky Mountain Club, a private and very exclusive hunting and fishing club. He needed to prove that the chief executive from each of the United States' seven largest oil companies had met here, all at the same time.

Jacques's presence in Wyoming was the result of an offhand comment made by a senior oil executive at a bankers' meeting attended by Morgan Stone, chairman of New York City's prestigious Stone City Bank. Based on the comment, Morgan had become concerned that this oil executive—and the executives of the other major oil companies—were arranging a private meeting, probably out of interest in extending their control over the nation's oil supply, which was needed to meet increasing postwar demand. He immediately alerted his son, Mike Stone, who was a longtime friend and associate of Jacques.

It was 1946; both Mike and Jacques had worked for Stone

City Bank for more than seven years following their graduation from the University of California at Berkeley's doctoral program. They were also two of the six Sentinels, a group that had been instrumental in preventing the German industrialists from using their war fortunes to fund another Reich. Though that mission was over, the core members of the Sentinels were still very much concerned with the corruption that results from too much power becoming concentrated in too few hands. And that's exactly what Morgan Stone suspected was about to happen in the oil industry.

Morgan had called Mike and Jacques together to discuss his growing worry over the situation. "As a result of Japan's defeat in the East and Germany's defeat in the West," he said to them, "seven American and British oil companies have found themselves in control of a large portion of the world's oil production. If these seven members of a self-styled 'Oil Club' are planning to extend their control of the world's future oil production, the concentration of so much power and wealth could eventually lead to their control of the world's economic and political future."

Mike and Jacques sat silently in the boardroom of Stone City Bank, eager to find out what they could do to help.

"Believe me when I tell you, their interest is driven as much by a hunger for power as it is by their desire to develop new supplies of oil," Morgan continued. "Given the Sentinels' concern with this type of situation, I thought you might want to learn more about what I suspect is happening."

As Jacques and Mike listened intently and scribbled notes, Morgan went on to explain that, his interest piqued by the oil executive's mention of an upcoming meeting, he'd obtained information that two executives from two different American oil companies were scheduled to make trips to the Rocky Mountain Club in Wyoming. He suspected that representatives from the five other Oil Club companies would be there for the same meeting—a clear violation of antitrust legislation. And he had a pretty good idea of what would be on their agenda.

———

Jacques had chosen his fishing garb carefully so he would blend in with the other anglers taking advantage of the early mayfly hatch that occurred every April. Since daylight he had been wading upstream toward the airstrip, pursuing the large rainbow and brown trout known to inhabit this stretch of the Platte.

Although his main objective was recording the planes' arrival, Jacques was determined to unlock the fishing secrets of the river as well. His best casts had failed to attract fish, so he decided to switch flies. He opened his small aluminum fly box and selected one of the two flies he had purchased from the local tackle shop on the recommendation of the clerk, a self-professed fishing expert. The "Stimulator" had an orange body and a large elk-hair hackle. A San Juan worm served as the drop fly. He cut about eighteen inches of light leader material off one of the small spools he kept in the side pocket of his fishing vest. Using an improved clinch knot, he attached one end of the leader to the hook portion of the Stimulator. Next, he tied the other end through the eye of the dropper.

Busy working on his tackle, Jacques didn't hear the approaching plane over the roar of the rushing water until it was almost upon him. The plane, flaps fully extended, was on its final approach. As quickly and discreetly as he could, he retrieved a stub of a pencil and a small notebook from one of his vest pockets and meticulously recorded the aircraft's make, model, N number, and time of landing. *One down, six to go*, he thought.

Armed with his new flies, he dropped his next cast near the bank, between two large overhanging willow trees. Mending his line upstream with a quick flick of his wrist, Jacques watched with excited anticipation as he saw the top fly suddenly begin to disappear below the surface. On one end of the line, a powerful, wily fish fought to free itself, waiting for any slackening of the line to throw off the hook. On the other end, the fisherman was determined to land his prey.

Worried that the combination of the fast water and the strength of what was obviously a big fish might break his line, Jacques began to move downstream with the fish. Several times he slipped on the smooth, rocky stream bottom. Thrusting his heels into the streambed, he righted himself each time, always making sure to hold the tip of his rod well above his head. Slowly, he reeled the fish toward him, a few inches at a time. When he had managed to work it close enough, he saw that it was at least two feet long and probably weighed more than five pounds. Just when he thought it was tiring, he watched with admiration as his prey turned and made another run. After its third attempt at escape, the fish turned over on its side, allowing Jacques to reel it toward him and his waiting net. The sight of the net and Jacques's shadow spooked the fish. With new life, it darted in the opposite direction, catching an unprepared Jacques off guard. He sighed as he watched his trophy fish break the line and swim away.

Deeply disappointed, he turned toward the sound of the next low-flying plane. He carefully recorded all the data, and watched as one plane after another approached the airfield. The six planes were bunched so closely together he was having trouble recording the crucial details about each one. When the last plane had passed overhead, Jacques took one final look around before resuming his quest for a big fish.

He watched the two anglers who had been fishing upstream from him abruptly leave the river. Glancing downstream, he saw a third fisherman leave the stream and begin walking toward the trees that lined the bank. *That's strange*, he thought. *Why would all three of them decide to stop fishing at the same time? Could it have anything to do with the arrival of the last plane?*

Within minutes, Jacques had spotted two other men standing at the edge of the tree line upriver. They weren't wearing waders or carrying fishing rods. Downstream, he saw two other similarly dressed men emerge from the trees.

Pretending not to notice the four men who were now slowly moving toward him, Jacques continued to concentrate on his fishing, all the while realizing that if they got too close, they would be able to rush him. A few more yards and any opportunity to make some kind of a surprise move would be lost.

Jacques felt a tug on his rod and reflexively jerked his hand, setting the hook in a second fish. Tightening the belt he wore on the outside of his chest waders, he began to follow the fish downstream. He held the rod over his head and continued to revolve and palm the reel, doing his best to maintain a firm line. Lowering himself into the water, he raised his feet off the streambed. Trusting the trapped air in his waders to act like a flotation device, he allowed the fish and the fast-flowing water to carry him downstream. He glided along, passing the two men downstream from him and continuing until he rounded a bend and passed out of sight. None of the men had tried to run after him.

Jacques worked his way to the side of the stream and righted himself. After releasing the fish, he wasted no time in retreating to the cover of the trees. *I must be at least two miles from where I parked my pickup*, he thought. *They probably have it staked out, anyway.*

He sat on a fallen tree and considered his situation. After a moment, he took out his knife and cut off the legs of the waders so he could use the bottom portion as hiking boots. Though the rubber soles weren't designed for walking long distances over rough surfaces, they'd have to do. He then quickly buried his fishing vest, waders, hat, fishing gear, and coat and headed deeper into the forest in search of a road that would lead him out of the area.

Jacques had been walking for half an hour when he discovered a narrow dirt road. Judging by the large and relatively well-defined tire tracks on it, he decided that it must be an active logging road.

To distract himself from his weariness, Jacques thought about Claudine, his lovely wife of less than a month, as he trudged up the winding road. Soon, he heard the sound of a car approaching from behind. Moving quickly to the cover of the trees, he waited until he could see the approaching vehicle. It was an old red pickup badly in need of some long-overdue body and fender work. Reasonably certain that this was not the kind of truck his adversaries would be driving, Jacques moved to the shoulder of the road and motioned for the driver to stop.

The driver, a local cowboy in need of conversation, stopped and rolled down the passenger-side window. "Hey, stranger, what are you doing walking around clear out here?"

"I'm trying to get back to Casper."

"Going that way myself, climb aboard."

Thinking of his pursuers, Jacques feared that he might find someone waiting for him at his hotel. *Did I leave anything in my room they could use to identify me?*

He made a split-second decision to abandon the personal belongings he had left in the room and asked his new friend to drop him off at the train station in Casper. The local depot was small enough that he could easily spot any of the four men who had been at the river. Jacques paid for his ticket and then anxiously awaited his eastbound train in the virtually deserted station.

At the train's first stop, Jacques disembarked and, after asking directions, walked several blocks to a men's clothing store, where he bought new attire. He then spent the next few days transferring from train to train in a cross-country journey that would eventually deliver him to New York. For most of the time, he remained sequestered in the private compartment he had reserved. Sitting quietly for long periods of time gave Jacques a lot of uninterrupted time to think.

Those seven executives have to be aware of all the laws they were breaking and the risks they're taking if their presence at the Rocky Mountain Club were to be discovered. Just the fact that seven competitors were secretly meeting would violate more than a handful of antitrust laws.

It's difficult to imagine how formidable the Oil Club would become if these men combine their financial reserves, their management expertise, their production, technology, and distribution capabilities, and their experience to deliver the oil needed to supply the postwar industrial boom everyone's expecting. Who would be left to compete with them? If we thought the world might be threatened by the German industrialists using their war profits to start another Reich, what's at stake if the Oil Club succeeds in controlling 90 percent of the world's oil supply?

What can the Sentinels possibly do to oppose the concentration of so much power? Each of the companies is a big and influential corporation in its own right.

If they were to cooperate on a collective basis, their power could be overwhelming.

Chapter 1

WELCOME HOME, JACQUES ROTH

Claudine Demaureux-Roth was sitting on the couch in front of the fireplace of her New York apartment. With the aid of a warm fire, her second glass of wine, and a good book, she was trying not to think about Jacques. She had not heard from him in four days. His last call had been the night before his trip to Wyoming. *Why hasn't he called me?* she thought. *Has something gone wrong?*

The sudden sound of the ringing phone jarred her out of her thoughts. *Who would be calling at this hour other than Jacques?* Claudine was relieved to hear his voice, but she barely had time to speak; he delivered a short message: "My train arrives late tomorrow night. Please don't meet me at the station. I'll grab a cab and come to the apartment. Once I get there, I'll explain everything. Right now, I've got to go." And with that the line went dead.

Claudine knew something must be very wrong. It wasn't like Jacques not to call for four days and then be so brief.

It was 9:30 the next night when Jacques's train finally pulled into Grand Central Station. The platform leading to the station was virtually deserted. Jacques watched the last passengers disembark, waiting until they had proceeded well along the platform before he stepped from the train. *So far so good. Nobody seems to be following me. But could someone be waiting in the station?*

Taking his time to make his way through the lightly populated depot, he slowly walked toward the exit to Forty-Seventh Street, hailed a cab, and watched to see whether anyone appeared to be tailing him. He instructed the cabdriver to make several turns, only giving him the address of his final destination once he was convinced none of the cars behind them were following his path.

Standing near the opening of an alley across the street from the entrance to his apartment building, Jacques spent another half hour making certain that no one was watching him or the apartment. The weather had turned cold and it had begun to rain. By the time he proceeded across the street, he was soaked through and half frozen. For the first time in several days he allowed himself the luxury of thinking about his warm, beautiful, sensuous new wife.

Not having a key and not absolutely clear on the number of their new apartment, Jacques selected a number that seemed familiar, pushed the button, and hoped it was the right one. Almost immediately, the door buzzed.

Exiting the elevator on the fourth floor, he turned right and proceeded down the hallway, inspecting the numbers next to the doors he passed. Glancing ahead, he saw that the door of their apartment was ajar. When he pushed it open, he found Claudine standing in the entrance, dressed in three-inch spike heels, a fur coat, a long strand of pearls, and her most mischievous grin. Her silvery blonde hair was done up in a French twist, accentuating her height. Her turquoise eyes shone like bright spotlights out of her perfectly chiseled Nordic face.

With her left hand, she slowly opened the coat, revealing her nakedness. "Like the pearls?" she asked. With her right hand she handed him a glass of champagne. "How about giving your girl a big hug and a long kiss, getting out of those wet clothes, and taking a long hot shower with an old friend? Welcome home, cowboy."

Twenty minutes later, Jacques was totally immersed in the charms of his beautiful, affectionate wife, made all the more enjoyable by copious amounts of hot water and foamy soap. The cooling water signaled the rapidly approaching conclusion to what had been an amazing greeting. Not wanting to lose the moment, he brushed a strand of wet hair from her forehead and said, "The warmth of the hearth beckons."

After they'd dried off and returned to the living room, Jacques poured them a second glass of champagne and gently laid Claudine down in front of the fire.

Staring down at this magnificent woman, her skin glowing with the light of the fire, he asked, "Does this remind you of a certain night in a small cabin in the Swiss Alps?"

"How could it not?" Claudine answered, beckoning him toward her with an index finger.

As he carefully lowered himself onto her, he looked down into her blue-green eyes. *I've always heard that a woman's eyes were the window to her soul*, he thought. *Does she really feel what I am seeing?*

Half an hour later, he whispered into her ear, "Claudine, we have to make a choice. We can lie here and freeze to death, or I could put another log on the fire while you find us a blanket and pour us another glass of champagne."

"I know what kind of a log you want to put on the fire!" she said. "Let's sit on the couch and you can talk to me. While you've been traipsing around the Rocky Mountains catching fish, I've been here all by myself with nobody to talk to. I'll get us that blanket while you put a real log on the fire and open a bottle of the Bordeaux you left in your apartment."

Settled on the couch under the warm blanket and enjoying the fine wine, Jacques finally began to explain what had happened during his trip.

"It wasn't until mid-afternoon that it became evident the men in the river were interested in doing more than fishing. I was lucky to get away. The question is, were they able to identify me or follow me when I left Casper? I still don't know, but it took three days and five trains before I finally arrived at Grand Central."

Sensing her alarm, he continued, "Don't worry too much—even after I arrived at the station, I took every precaution to make certain that no one was waiting for me or followed me here. For a half an hour before I pushed the buzzer, I was standing across the street observing. But now that we know Big Oil has had their meeting, we have to assume their plans are under way. The Sentinels need to learn a lot more about what they're planning—and a whole lot more about the oil industry. We have a lot of ground to cover before we can formulate a plan of our own."

Chapter 2

SIR DAVID MARCUS

When he woke up the next morning in a strange apartment, Jacques was at first unsure of where he was. Gaining his bearings, he realized two things: Claudine was lying next to him.

Moving slowly to avoid waking her, he eased his way out of the bed. On his way back from the bathroom, he thought, *Now if I can just get back into bed without disturbing her, maybe we can continue where we left off last night.*

Jacques watched his wife and listened to her quiet breathing while he carefully climbed back in bed. Cuddled up behind her with his arms carefully wrapped around her, he was trying to decide what to do next when quite unexpectedly she said, "If you will give a girl a minute, I'm thinking about a hell of a way we can start the day!"

With a quick wink, she slid out of bed and disappeared into the bathroom. Jacques listened intently to the little noises she made, the same ones all women seemed to make. When she reappeared, her hair was combed, her face washed, and she was wearing nothing but a mischievous grin. As she slid back into bed her only words were, "Do you think breakfast can wait?"

It was almost noon by the time they finished breakfast. They had consumed two cups of coffee each and finished scanning both newspapers that had been delivered to the door of the apartment. He hated to destroy the moment, but Jacques knew he had no choice but to begin the discussion of Sentinel business with Claudine.

"All we know for certain," he said, "is that the chief executives of the seven major oil companies have conducted a secret meeting. It's obvious that we need to understand a lot more about what they discussed and what they are planning. Mike and I had planned, once I completed this trip to Wyoming, to begin preparing for the Allied Bankers Association meeting. As part of our preparation, we scheduled a trip to Washington to pay a call on the Fed chairman and some of our other government contacts. They need to know what's happening, and we need to hear what they have to say."

A weary look came across Claudine's face. He knew she didn't want to be away from him again this soon.

"This process could take a few days," said Jacques. "Why don't you schedule a trip to Europe while I'm in Washington? You could visit your father in Geneva and discuss our concerns with some of his banker friends. On your way through London, you might also consider paying a call on my old friend Sir David Marcus.

"David Marcus?" said Claudine. "Have you told me about him?"

"You've heard me speak about David on several occasions. We attended the London School of Economics at the same time and became quite good friends. If there is anyone who can help us develop a better understanding of the Middle Eastern oil world, it's David. Outside the Sentinels, he's one of the few people I have learned to respect and trust—as long as it involves business. When it comes to women, it's an entirely different matter. If it was anybody else but you, I would be worried."

Claudine laughed. "Oh, Jacques, you know you have nothing to worry about; I learned a long time ago how to handle men like him."

"Well, when you meet him, be prepared for a shock. In addition to having the title of Duke of Trafalgar bestowed on him, he's one of the most unusual men you will ever meet. He's short, maybe only five feet four, and he's powerfully built, with shocking red hair and penetrating blue eyes. But it's not his physical presence that you will remember. David is one of the hardest-working, brightest, and most completely trustworthy men I've ever had the chance to know. At least until the next attractive woman enters the room."

"Perhaps you would like to explain how it is that you know so much about his interest in women? And while you're at it, you might want tell me why you think I'm so trustworthy."

Claudine enjoyed watching Jacques squirm for a few moments. Finally she said, "Why don't you pour us another cup of coffee and relax? If I hadn't learned to deal with your former ways, I wouldn't be sitting here. Now tell me about Sir David Marcus—is he really a duke?"

Relieved at the change of subject, Jacques said, "Yes, and he's the grandson of one of the founders of English Oil, Limited. From the day he joined English Oil, it was always assumed that he would be the third member of the Marcus family to become English Oil's president.

"But then, three years ago, without warning, David resigned. He sold his shares and used the money to organize his own oil investment advisory firm. When I had the opportunity to ask him why he did it, he gave me a very illuminating answer. He told me that the center of the petroleum universe is going to be domiciled in the Middle East. Without gaining the trust and respect of a small number of sovereign leaders, he said, it will become almost impossible to do business in that region. As a high-profile executive representative of English Oil, it was only natural that David was expected to implement the policies of his family's company. Accordingly, he was finding there wasn't very much he could do to break down Middle Eastern leaders' suspicions.

"He told me he felt, over time, that he could be a more effective deal-maker if he renounced his allegiance to English Oil, created his own independent research and investment company, and began to practice the kinds of things that would clearly suggest he was anxious to win these leaders' trust and respect."

With the assistance of the Federal Aviation Administration, Jacques used his list of the planes' makes, models, and N numbers to learn where each of the chartered aircraft had originated. A few FAA calls to the local fixed-base operators were all that was required to have the planes' logs released. The logs identified each of the executives, placed them at the Rocky Mountain Club, and established that they were all there at the same time.

As soon as the affidavits were drawn and signed, Jacques had the information he would need to prove that the seven executives had indeed met together in private. And it was a good thing: Morgan Stone had asked him if he would make himself available at the Allied Bankers Association meeting the next day, before he and Mike left for Washington.

Chapter 3

THE BANKERS CONVENE

As Mike Stone entered the Stone City Bank's executive quarters on the thirty-fifth floor, he couldn't help but stop, stand in front of the big plate-glass window, and look at the view of the East River, the Brooklyn Bridge, the Statue of Liberty, and Ellis Island. No matter how many times he saw the view, it always reminded him of the burden of trust people like him must assume.

Before joining his father at the annual meeting of the Allied Bankers Association in the bank's boardroom, he stopped for a moment to inspect the size of the group assembled. As he looked through the open door, he saw forty of the world's leading bankers, who had convened to discuss the anticipated funding requirements of the world's petroleum industry. Mike couldn't remember when so many of the prominent members of the ABA had attended the same meeting. He walked in and took a seat toward the head of the table.

"Gentlemen," Morgan Stone said after giving the bankers a few more minutes to talk among themselves, "thank you for coming. As has been previously announced, I have asked my son, Mike, to join us today. Mike has recently joined the Dean

Securities firm in San Francisco where he serves as the President of International Operations. In his new capacity, he has been asked to establish a worldwide futures market for petroleum. His work has required him to make a careful study of the world's sources of supply, both current and future. He has talked with the most highly regarded economists who are studying the future demand for oil, and he has met with local government officials, oil company executives, exploration experts, and many of you who represent the Oil Club's banking interests.

"Today, Mike will be talking to us about some of the broader economic and political issues related to the credit requests we are being asked to consider. Mike, if you please?"

Mike cleared his throat and stood. "Good day, gentlemen. Perhaps it would be best if I begin by quantifying the world's demand for petroleum. The best experts all seem to agree that the world's daily demand for oil will increase from the wartime demand of approximately four point five million barrels per day to five million barrels by 1950. Thereafter, as a result of anticipated postwar industrial expansion, consumption is expected to double every ten years. Thus, if the experts' forecasts are correct, ten million barrels per day will be consumed by 1960, twenty million barrels by 1970, or a net increase in daily demand of fifteen million barrels between 1950 and 1970.

"At an estimated total cost of approximately one billion dollars per million barrels of increased capacity, we are talking about total development costs of approximately fifteen billion dollars. Since a ten-year lead time is required from the time development of a new oil field is first considered until the new facility comes on line, we will be asked to commit to this level of funding within the next three years. The bottom line is that the oil industry needs to know that it has reliable access to fifteen billion dollars of developmental capital."

Ignoring the startled coughs and nervous glances among the crowd of bankers, Mike continued. "One of the questions I have been asked to answer is where we are going to find all this new supply. By 1950, the United States will become a net importer of oil. In fewer than ten years, the center of oil production will shift from the Gulf of Mexico to the Middle East. According to our reports, much of the more accessible, higher-quality oil will be developed in smaller, undeveloped countries in the Middle East, North Africa, and Southeast Asia.

"Each of these countries has vastly different cultural and religious backgrounds—from each other as well as from us. These are not countries with histories of modern governments, free enterprise, and sophisticated legal systems.

"It is not a question of whether we need to invest fifteen billion dollars into these uncharted waters. About that we have little choice. It's a question of how we are going to do it. Until now, we have relied on the capital, the technologies, the management, and the marketing networks of the seven oil companies that presently control the vast majority of the world's developed petroleum supplies. In my opinion, these seven companies are members of an oligopolistic organization intent on perpetuating their control over the world's future oil requirements.

"One of the first basic questions we need to ask ourselves is this: Are we comfortable with the idea of remaining dependent on these seven companies to meet our future needs, or do we believe it's important to encourage the introduction of a more diversified and competitive industry?"

Jim McLain, president of Big Oil's largest bank, rose to speak. "Mr. Stone, are you suggesting that we, as bankers, should interfere with the efforts of the major oil companies to solve this problem that you have so eloquently described? Are you suggesting that the ABA and its member banks create some new financing vehicle that will fund the developmental efforts of independent oil companies just to create competition for our own clients?"

Silence settled over the room. Morgan Stone's principal competitor had just challenged the mighty banker's son, in the sanctity of the Stone City Bank boardroom. Curious as to how the Stones would react, the other bankers sat back in their chairs, waiting with more than mild curiosity to see what was going to happen next.

Mike glanced at his father and noted his slight smile.

"No, Mr. McLain, that is not what I am suggesting," Mike said congenially. "I am asserting that the oil industry, as we know it, is a closed, highly incestuous group of seven companies that want to do everything they can to control the production of the new oil reserves for themselves. They didn't earn the name 'Oil Club' by accident. Their stated policy of protecting the future of oil development for themselves possesses all the earmarks of eighteenth-century British Liberalism, which some feel is the source of twentieth-century oligopolistic economic policies, more commonly referred to as cartels.

"If you remember, under British Liberalism, industrialists, acting in concert with the government and the financial community, used their combined influence to provide themselves with greater market control, prevent new products from competing with their established product lines, and inhibit new organizations from entering their marketplace.

"Therefore, I'm asking you, sir, whether you *seriously* believe that the Allied Bankers Association should consider reverting to a two-hundred-year-old economic ideology and agree to limit its extension of credit to these companies alone. Shouldn't our goal be to encourage the growth of a larger, more diverse industry capable of ensuring the world that it has an adequate and reliable supply of affordable oil? Shouldn't we as financiers be concentrating on how we can use our financial resources to encourage the entry of all qualified companies to help achieve this goal?"

Mike had barely sat down in his chair before McLain was on his feet. "Morgan, I'm sure you understand that the major oil companies have already met and informed us they are interested in establishing new lines of credit for their exclusive use. At the bank level, it's not a question of how we feel; it's an issue of our having to respect the interests of such important clients."

Motioning for Mike to stay seated, Morgan slowly rose, focusing his full attention on his challenger.

"You said they 'have already met and informed us,' Jim. Think about what that means. Your choice of words implies that these companies have already met in private—perhaps secretly—to discuss how they plan to control the development of the world's oil supply. I can't even begin to count the number of antitrust laws the executives of these companies have already broken by meeting secretly. Are you suggesting we join them in their illegal quest?"

"Morgan, my choice of phrase doesn't mean a thing, and you know it!" Jim replied.

Smiling at his adversary, Morgan continued. "Knowing that this subject might come up, I asked Jacques Roth to stand by. He's in the next room. If you don't mind, I think we should invite him to join us; you may be interested to hear what he has to say."

The bankers were silent. Morgan left and soon reappeared with Jacques at his side. "To those of you who haven't had the pleasure of meeting him," said Morgan, "I would like to introduce Jacques Roth. He is Pierre's oldest son and the heir to his family's banking empire."

Turning toward the revered banker sitting next to him, Morgan asked, "Pierre, is there anything you would like to add?" The older man smiled and shook his head, so Morgan continued. "In case you didn't know, for the last seven years Jacques has been responsible for Stone City Bank's international banking operations. Jacques, if you please."

Jacques confidently looked out over the gathered bankers before he spoke. "Several weeks ago, gentlemen, I was alerted to the possibility that the seven chief executive officers of the Oil Club were scheduled to hold a private meeting. In response, I made arrangements to record the landing of each of their aircraft at the Rocky Mountain Club near Casper, Wyoming.

"Subsequently, I turned my notes over to the FAA. They have obtained access to logs of the seven privately chartered airplanes and have confirmed that the passengers on board those particular aircraft were the Oil Club executives. What I am passing out to you now are copies of the affidavits executed by the local fixed-base operators and the responsible FAA officials that support my contention. Experienced antitrust legal counsel has opined that this information will satisfy the Attorney General's requirements to authorize a follow-up investigation."

Jacques took a seat, and Morgan waited for the murmuring of the bankers to quiet down before he spoke again. "I can appreciate why the Oil Club believes such a union would be consistent with their orderly development of new reserves, but have we really stopped to think about what the political and economic consequences could be if ninety percent of the world's oil supply is controlled by these seven oil companies?"

The room was silent.

"No one is questioning the world's need for their help and cooperation," Morgan continued. "That is not in dispute. The question being raised here is what kind of an oil industry do we envision for the future?

"If we don't stop the Oil Club's efforts to extend its control of the new supplies today, the day will come when both the oil-producing countries and the oil-consuming nations will wake up to a world that is politically and economically controlled by a handful of corporations. When that time comes, I can assure you that more drastic remedies will be required to undo what they are considering doing today.

"Have we forgotten that the federal government of the United States was forced to break up the monopolistic control of Standard Oil in the early nineteen hundreds? Have we forgotten that our government was forced to stand by and tolerate the shipping of domestic oil to Germany after war had been declared? Have we forgotten the lessons of what can happen when excessive concentrations of wealth and influence are allowed to proceed without the constraints required to protect the public interest? Haven't we just finished fighting a very costly war to stop the expansion of unbridled greed and ambition?"

McLain interrupted him. "Morgan, I strongly object to your highly inflammatory statements. There are those of us who believe the world is fortunate to have the services of such capable and financially worthy companies, whose resources can be directed to solving the world's burgeoning demand for oil. These companies are not the villains; they should be regarded as saviors! Our efforts should be directed toward *helping* them, not opposing them. If you insist on pursuing this course of diversification and new competition, you and your friends could be responsible for creating a permanent split within the ABA. Is that something you really want to do?"

Morgan was quick to respond. "Call it what you want, Jim, but I would like to remind you and the others gathered here today that it's neither the function nor the responsibility of the ABA to dictate operating policy to any of its member banks. For thirty years, this has always been a forum where reasonable men could gather, identify problems, and, hopefully, seek solutions that allow us—individually and collectively—to better serve the free world's banking needs."

Morgan delivered his next line with enough conviction to make many of the bankers seated at the table squirm in their chairs: "It is my hope that someday the ABA will once again become such a responsible forum!"

Chapter 4

A DIFFERENT APPROACH

Incensed by the outcome of the meeting, Morgan retired to the small conference room adjacent to the boardroom. Joining him were four of the original Sentinels: Jacques, Claudine, Mike, and Cecelia Chang. Morgan's closest ABA friends were sitting around the table—Claudine's father Henri Demaureux, the respected Swiss banker, Pierre Roth, and Pete Ferrari, Chairman and President of San Francisco's American West National Bank.

"Make no mistake," said Morgan, "the big money-center bankers are planning to restrict their lending activities in the petroleum industry to only the seven major oil companies. Unless we can come up with some alternative financing plan, their threat of creating an international financial blockade will be more than capable of restricting any serious competition for a very long time!"

Pierre Roth was the first to respond. "The incremental economics of developing new oil fields clearly favor the existing oil companies. I have it on good authority that the big investment banking houses needed to lead syndicated financings have also come under the influence of the Oil Club. Together, the commercial banks and the investment banks stand a very good chance of accomplishing exactly what they are expected to do."

"I think there are other things the Oil Club members can do which could be equally difficult to overcome," added Henri. "The Oil Club will not permit competitors access to or the use of its members' refineries, pipelines, shipping, or retail distribution outlets. The independent oil company will be required to build one hundred percent of the infrastructure required to process and bring its oil to market. The full costs of vertically integrated capital improvements will have to be absorbed by the newly developed oil production. Conversely, the established oil companies will be able to use their new production to spread their fixed costs over a much larger base."

"Vertically integrated?" Claudine interrupted.

"Yes, referring to consolidated ownership of the pipelines, refining plants, ships, pumping and storage equipment, and retail distribution facilities necessary to convert crude into the end product that the customer uses at a gas station in his local neighborhood."

Pete Ferrari was the next to speak. "Regardless of the short-term incremental economics, in the absence of any viable financial alternative, what is there to stop the Oil Club from perpetuating their ninety-percent control over both existing and to-be-developed oil fields? Such extensive control will provide the Oil Club with the unrestricted ability to manage production quotas and prices on a global basis."

"I'm not so certain that's necessarily true," Jacques said. "What you've just described might appear to be the case, but only if we look at the capital formation process through conventional eyes. Claudine has been doing her homework, and she thinks she's discovered a way to create an alternate source for funding new oil development."

Mike couldn't resist the opportunity to tease his friend. "Whose money are we going to steal this time, Claudine?"

Ignoring the comment, Claudine turned to Morgan. "If I

owned an oil field with proven and certifiable production of a million barrels per day, and I needed to install all the remaining facilities required to process and bring my production to market, would your bank lend me the money I would need to do it?"

"Providing that you were prepared to put up your ownership in the oil field as collateral, we would be happy to make you the loan," said Morgan.

Claudine pursued the subject. "Conceptually, what's the difference between using deposited gold bullion and using proven oil-generating revenues as collateral?"

"That works well once the productivity of a new oil field has been established," said Ferrari, "but where does the capital come from to arrive at that point?"

"From private investors willing to accept the development risk once they have the take-out commitment needed to fund all the remaining vertical development costs," said Claudine.

Morgan asked the obvious question. "And where does the capital to fund those commitments come from? You are talking about billions of dollars!"

Smiling at the formidable banker, Claudine said, "From an international bond fund we're going to organize."

"And who is going to raise the fifteen billion dollars required to capitalize such a fund?" Morgan asked.

"We are. Once the domestic and foreign members of the financial community understand the importance of diversifying the oil industry, why can't we draw upon our relationships with them to secure the needed funds? Morgan, I don't mean to be disrespectful, but once we start thinking internationally, how do you know there isn't a sizable market seeking a secure and liquid bond that carries an attractive rate of interest? We know there is a plethora of prewar, pent-up capital needing to be warehoused on an accretive basis until it is needed for some other purpose."

The diminutive Cecelia Chang rose from her chair to speak.

The simple gesture of her standing up was more than adequate to attract everyone's attention. "Perhaps it might be wise for us to assume there are influential people, outside the United States, who are also threatened by seven oil companies' control of the world's oil supply," said Cecelia. "Given the opportunity to consider an alternative, they might see the value in Claudine's idea."

Jacques, who had been listening carefully, said, "Fifteen billion could represent a very high percentage of the total size of the market. Before we try to access that amount of money, we need to make sure we know how to ask and answer the right questions."

"I agree with Jacques," said Mike. "For example, when you consider the fact that no single independent oil company is capable of satisfying all the necessary criteria, creating a suitable consortium of motivated and qualified independent oil companies could be one of our biggest challenges."

"I'm back at square one," said Cecelia. "Knowing the limitations we are going to face in postwar European economies, and from the Oil Club's domestic resistance, to have any chance of fulfilling our requirements, we are going to need investors' maximum commitments. It's critical we understand what terms and conditions the final agreement needs to reflect. We *have* to know what we're doing before we do anything!"

Chapter 5

WALTER MATTHEWS

After the group's discussion following the ABA meeting had drawn to a close, Morgan Stone suggested that Jacques meet with Walter Matthews, the celebrated *New York Times* journalist whose column was syndicated in thirty-two newspapers nationwide. Eager to learn more about the oil industry before he and Mike headed to Washington, Jacques had welcomed the suggestion. After driving Claudine to New York Municipal Airport for her flight to London, he made his way back toward Manhattan for his meeting with the reporter.

Jacques and Walter had just seated themselves at one of the smaller tables in the back of P.J. Clarke's, an after-work gathering place long favored by members of the working press.

"Thank you for agreeing to meet with me, Mr. Matthews," Jacques said to open the conversation. "I've been reading your column ever since I moved to New York eight years ago. Your ideas and your superb way of expressing them make me proud to be living in a country of free speech."

After the waiter came and took their order for two beers, Walter said, "Ever since I heard you present your doctoral thesis at Berkeley in 1938, supported by the rest of the Sentinels, I've been a great fan. You may recall that I was the reporter who wrote the article describing your presentation. I have often thought about how different things might have been had the American, British, and French governments heeded your prediction that the German industrialists were leading the world to war."

"That's very kind of you," said Jacques. "And it is upsetting that so few would listen to us."

"So, Morgan says you folks are studying the oil industry now," said Walter. "Perhaps I should warn you, I'm no friend of the Oil Club. For as long as I can remember, I've been a longtime student and loyal disciple of Ida Tarbell, the reporter whose work eventually led to the breakup of the Standard Oil monopoly a few decades back. All of which means I don't trust the motives of the major oil companies. I'm completely convinced that when they argue about the importance of supplying the world with oil, they are using their rhetoric to mask their private agendas of strengthening their own economic and political power."

"Walter—may I call you Walter?" said Jacques.

"Of course," he replied. "But most of my friends call me Walt."

"Well, Walt, maybe I should explain the purpose of my call. You may be interested to know we have recently learned of events that suggest a new power cycle may be forming in the oil industry."

For the next few minutes, Jacques explained the Sentinels' concerns and their mission while Walt took notes, interrupting him only to ask for clarification on certain points.

When Jacques was done, Walt spoke. "Coincidently, Jacques, I've been hearing some very interesting rumors about recent events in Venezuela. It's been said that Juan Pablo Perez, Venezuela's minister of oil, has been quietly building a file to show that the two major oil companies operating in Venezuela—both members of the Oil Club, of course—have been fraudulently manipulating their charges for transporting and refining oil. Should those rumors prove to be accurate, the associated damages over the last five years alone could be enormous. Can you imagine what would happen if fraud can be proven and treble damages were to be imposed?"

"It would obviously be devastating to the oil companies," said Jacques.

"And that's not all," Walt continued. "Venezuela is in the final stages of renegotiating its operating agreement with these two major oil partners. I checked the prevailing agreements. They contain clauses enabling either party to vacate the contract if fraudulent behavior by the other party can be proven. Just imagine the added leverage the Venezuelan government will enjoy over its operating oil partners."

"The Venezuelan government would have most of the power," Jacques agreed. "Not to mention how the revelation would affect the other oil companies' relationships with their operating oil partners."

"Exactly," said Walt. "Similar to the situation in Venezuela, the value of sovereign oil reserves in the Middle East and Southeast Asia has dramatically changed since the original contracts were negotiated in the thirties. All these other governments are waiting for Señor Perez to complete his negotiations before initiating a new dialogue of their own. There are no secrets in the oil industry. Everyone is closely watching the events in Venezuela. If Perez's files contain concrete proof of fraud, they could create the risk of exposure the oil companies will do almost anything to avoid."

"Well, we don't really need more evidence to demonstrate precisely why an oligopolistic oil industry dominated by seven companies can't be allowed to continue, but that certainly would be a compelling reason for sovereign nations to think twice before trusting the major oil companies," said Jacques.

"Well, there's still more. Do you know anything about the foreign profits tax provision in the Internal Revenue Service's tax code?"

"Nope, that's new to me."

"During the thirties, our country was awash in domestic oil. When nobody was looking, the oil lobby in Washington introduced a bill that allowed the American oil companies to use the royalties paid on the production of foreign oil to offset taxes due on profits made from transporting, refining, distributing, and selling the same oil in the United States."

Jacques looked shocked. "Are you suggesting that once the United States becomes dependent on foreign oil, in 1950 or so, the American taxpayer will begin subsidizing the oil companies' cost of importing petroleum?"

"Exactly. If you don't believe me, have your accountants research the tax code and obtain a current copy of any of the major oil companies' annual financial reports. Tell them to pay particular interest to the footnotes. If that's not enough, have your friends at the Treasury Department check their tax returns."

Jacques thought hard about what Walt had just told him before asking his next question. "If your research proves to be accurate, what are you planning to do with the information?"

"Not *if*, Jacques. I've already completed most of my research. And though I don't have enough data to help me calculate the extent of the damages in Venezuela, I do have some indication of what the annual American taxpayers' subsidy of imported oil could be. My rough calculations still need to be refined, but they indicate that over the next ten years, the annual cost to the American taxpayer could reach approximately five billion dollars. That's a lot of lost tax revenue."

"If you already know all this," said Jacques, "why are you waiting to write your articles?"

"Writing an article is one thing; making people believe it and motivating them to take action is another. If my articles could be associated with some newsworthy event, they would have a much greater impact."

"Like the disclosure of premeditated fraud in Venezuela?"

"Exactly," said Walt. "If there is any way we can get our hands on those Perez files, it would be very helpful. Blow the cover off that can of worms, and we have a whole new ball game."

Chapter 6

MEETING IN WASHINGTON

Without the input of Roger Malone, the Federal Reserve chairman, Mike and Jacques recognized that it would be extremely difficult for the Sentinels to organize any kind of a plan to oppose the plans of the Oil Club. On June 13, 1946, they arrived at the nation's capital to consult with the Fed chairman, knowing full well how crucial his support was.

When Chairman Malone's secretary announced Jacques and Mike's arrival, the chairman rose from behind his desk and walked forward to greet the two young men. The four other men who had been sitting with the chairman rose to greet them as well.

"Jacques, Mike, it's so good to see you," said the chairman. "And if you'll excuse me, I've taken the liberty of inviting some of your old friends to join us. I'm sure you remember the Secretary of the Treasury, Henry Ainsworth, and Senator John Hess of Pennsylvania. And this is Senator William Armstrong of Indiana—we just call him Bill—and Senator Jordan Lucas of California. Knowing how helpful they were in leading the congressional charge the last time around, when you needed to obtain their support to create the gold bearer bonds, I thought it would be good to have them here."

"Thank you, Mr. Chairman," said Jacques. "We believe the significance of what we are planning has some very serious implications for the future of the oil industry and could represent the start of the next great power cycle. If you don't mind, I would prefer that Mike explain our problem with the Oil Club and our concerns about the safety of Señor Perez in Venezuela."

"Certainly," said Roger. "Go right ahead, Mike."

"Thank you, Mr. Chairman," said Mike. "We began to suspect the intentions of the seven major oil companies as we were preparing for the most recent annual ABA meeting. And, as my father has informed you, the explosive exchanges during that meeting with bankers—whose clients are the members of the Oil Club—confirmed our suspicions. It seems evident that a new power cycle is in the making."

While Mike was speaking, Jacques had reached into his briefcase and extracted a file, which he handed to Roger. "Inside that file," Jacques explained, "are affidavits from the FAA certifying the attendance of the executives of each of the seven major oil companies at a secret meeting in Wyoming. And as I collected data on the meeting for the FAA, I was pursued by four men, who I suspect were Samson operatives."

Noticeably shaken, Senator Hess said, "Okay, I understand the first part, but why do you believe a ruthless paramilitary company such as Samson was hired to provide security at that meeting? I thought we got rid of them after they caused you so much trouble during the war."

"Apparently not," Jacques answered immediately. "I spent the better part of one afternoon escaping them, and I purposely took three days to cross the country via a circuitous route to make certain I wasn't followed."

"Secret meetings, Samson, power cycles, controlling of the world's oil supply—this is all pretty wild stuff," Senator Lucas said. "What exactly are you asking us to do?"

"Nothing, for the moment," Mike said. "We just wanted you to know about the possibility of a new pocket of corruption that, left unattended, could cause a lot of trouble. We also wanted to make you aware that we are working on it.

"In addition, there is the problem of the Venezuelan minister of oil. My father had requested that I invite Juan Pablo Perez to the ABA's April meeting. I called Señor Perez to explain the importance of our invitation, and he seemed flattered by our interest in him and his negotiations. He asked me some pertinent questions, and he verbally accepted my invitation. Then, as a matter of protocol, we sent him an official invitation. Three days before the meeting, we received his handwritten response, declining our invitation."

Handing the note to the chairman, Mike added, "I think you will agree, upon close examination, that his response is confusing, and perhaps alarming."

Roger Malone read the letter aloud for the benefit of the senators.

Mike,

I regret that I cannot accept your kind invitation. Our oil concessionaires believe that the sensitivity of our current negotiations prohibits any interruption caused by my absence at this time. I have also received similar suggestions from the banks that support the opinion of the oil companies.

Respectfully,
J.P. Perez

"What is it that you find so unusual about his letter?" asked the chairman. "His role in those sensitive oil-rate negotiations is well known."

"That was my first impression too," Mike said. "Upon more careful examination, however, I became convinced that the minister may have been trying to send us a message within his message. The first thing I found curious was his failure to mention our former discussion and his initial agreement to attend the meeting. The second thing is that he works for the Venezuelan government, so if his temporary absence were problematic, why wouldn't the government, not the oil companies, be the ones announcing their concern?"

"He could be trying to tell us that he is being watched and can't leave the country," volunteered Jacques. "Walt Matthews of the *New York Times* recently informed me that Señor Perez is assembling a file, the contents of which could prove that British and American oil companies have been fraudulently overcharging their sovereign oil partners."

"Knowing the oil companies, nothing they do would surprise me," Chairman Malone said. "But why would Señor Perez fear his own government?"

"It may not be the Venezuelan government that he fears," said Secretary Ainsworth. "As we've just heard from Jacques, the Samson group is alive and well. They could be the real cause of the oil minister's concern. As you may recall, Samson was originally organized in Venezuela to protect Big Oil's interests in case the coup in the thirties resulted in the nationalization of the country's oil."

Jacques nodded. "Exactly, Secretary Ainsworth. After hearing about these rumors, I asked Dr. Tom Burdick, our friend and professor at Berkeley, to see if he could find a secure way to communicate with Señor Perez. Tom has pen pals all over the world. It turns out that Señor Perez's wife's brother is a big sugar cane grower in Venezuela and one of Tom's correspondents. According to Señor Perez's brother-in-law's most recent letter, our hunch about the minister's motives may be accurate. To say that he is under house arrest would be a little too strong, but he is being watched very carefully."

Chairman Malone looked troubled. He was silent for a few moments before saying, "Gentlemen, it appears that any plan to thwart the Oil Club must involve securing the safety of the oil minister, his family, and his files. Does anybody have any suggestions?"

Mike spoke first. "If Perez can't come to see us, why can't I go to see him?"

Chapter 7

DANCING WITH THE DEVIL

Claudine was standing outside Sir David Marcus's London office. She was early for the meeting. The sandbags placed in front of the old brownstone building during wartime were still there. The damaged nearby buildings were somber reminders of the bombings. Somehow, the building that housed David's office had managed to escape unscathed.

After carefully descending the seven steps leading to the building entrance, located a half a story below street level, she entered a no-frills office environment not unlike the spaces that housed Britain's war rooms. The huge room was well lit, efficiently organized, and very clean. Secretaries and office administrators, heads down, were hard at work. It was only after Claudine had been standing patiently just inside the door for a few moments that one of the girls looked up and saw her.

"Excuse me, ma'am, I didn't see you at first. May I be of assistance?" she asked.

At almost the same moment, a man matching Jacques's description of his former classmate entered the room just behind where Claudine stood.

"Hello, you must be Claudine," he said as he extended his

hand in greeting. "So you are the woman who tamed the rogue of two continents. I've always wondered who she would be. Ever since I heard Jacques got married, I've been looking forward to meeting you. You are more beautiful in person than you have been described. You can tell him for me he's lucky he saw you first."

Claudine didn't speak as David led her through the rows of workers to his small office. Once they were seated, she immediately expressed what had been bothering her: "Sir David, naturally, I am pleased by your compliment, but I need to warn you. Over the years, I've worked very hard to be recognized for my intelligence, creativity, and business accomplishments. I haven't come all this way *not* to be treated as a person of professional skill and accomplishment!"

Not offended by her directness, David smiled. "Not to worry, Claudine—if I may call you by your first name. For several years I've been following your career. I watched with great interest as you developed the gold bearer bond program. When you discovered the means for allowing the business community to transfer the ownership of gold instead of the physical gold, it changed international commerce. It was truly an outstanding piece of work. During the war, we and the Americans used your bonds to pay a lot of bills."

After smiling and settling a little deeper into her chair, Claudine said, "Thank you, David. You would be very pleased to hear how Jacques described you. Not only does he respect your intelligence and your work habits, but he believes you to be one of the most trustworthy men he has had the pleasure of knowing. In fact, he said we could learn a lot from you, and that he doubted there was anyone more trusted by the Middle Eastern governments."

"I'm flattered to have earned Jacques's high opinion," said David, looking momentarily embarrassed. "He may have told you that I am the grandson of one of the founders of English Oil, Limited. It was always assumed that I would be the third member of the lineage of Marcus to become president of English Oil."

"Yes, he did mention that," said Claudine.

"Ah, then he probably also told you that I resigned three years ago. Sold my shares and used the money to organize my own oil research and investment advisory firm. Perhaps that unexpected turn of events caught Jacques's attention. You see, I'm sure that the center of the petroleum universe is going to shift from the Gulf of Mexico to the Middle East, and unless we earn the trust and respect of a small number of sovereign leaders there, it will become almost impossible to do business in that region.

"If I had remained a high-profile executive for English Oil, I would have been expected to implement the policies of the company that employed me. Now that I've established my independence, I'm a far more effective businessman and leader. I practice the kinds of things that clearly suggest to Middle Easterners I am eager to win their trust and respect.

"Claudine," he continued, "it's important we don't underestimate the importance of trust, but without the money needed to complete the development of a new oil field, trust will never become an issue. It's all about money. Any serious plan has to include reliable access to the kind of money required to develop new oil fields on a vertically integrated basis."

"Am I correct in assuming that the aggregate cost of all these elements is approximately a billion dollars per million barrels of added daily capacity?" asked Claudine.

"You've done your homework, I see; that's a fairly accurate number. The enormity of the amount of capital and the complexity of constructing all the facilities represents a big part of the reason why the major companies feel so secure in constructing an economic blockade around the independent oil companies."

David paused and asked Claudine if she would like a cup of tea. When she said yes, he called in his secretary and asked for two cups.

"*Economic blockade*," she said once the secretary had left. "I think that's the phrase I remember reading in the reports from the ABA conference."

Noticing the strained look on Claudine's face, David hastened to say, "I wouldn't allow that threat to throw you off stride. No matter how much the Middle Eastern rulers distrust Big Oil, there are those of us who are allowed inside the 'oil tent.' One of the first things you learn is how much they resent having to do business with the British government and any of the major oil companies. In the Middle East they have a saying: becoming involved with the Oil Club is like dancing with the devil. Should the right kind of plan evolve, you might be surprised who will be motivated to help you break the Oil Club's grip.

"Suppose a Middle Eastern country has large, undeveloped oil reserves and is uncomfortable with the idea of having to dance with one of these seven oil companies. In addition to Iraq, Iran, Saudi Arabia, and Kuwait, think about the smaller countries that surround Saudi Arabia and comprise the balance of the Persian Peninsula. In addition, there are at least six large countries in North Africa where substantial reserves are believed to exist. Then there's Southeast Asia. According to my people, the British and the Dutch haven't scratched the surface there. Closer to home, you have to include Venezuela and Mexico."

David paused when the secretary returned and set down their cups of tea. When the door closed behind her, he continued his explanation. "Any analysis of future oil supplies must take into consideration offshore reserves that lie beneath the ocean. Deep-water drilling technology, while in its infancy, is developing rapidly. It's only a question of time before they start drilling off the coasts of Texas, Louisiana, Florida, California, Mexico,

Venezuela, and the north coast of Scotland. And that doesn't count the suspected oil fields of Central Asia that are believed to lie between the Caucasus Mountains and the Caspian Sea.

"My point being, there is a lot of oil waiting to be developed, in a lot of different places, with many different local governments, cultures, and economic issues in each area. Given the choice, do you really believe that these sovereign mineral rights–owners won't prefer to form long-term relationships with someone other than these seven arrogant oil companies?"

Listening to David reel off all this information reminded Claudine of watching Jacques at work. No wonder her husband felt so much admiration for his old friend.

"David," she said, "when I hear you talk about the future production side of the problem, I think of all the developed and emerging countries that don't have a captive energy supply. When you realize they are going to be forced to purchase most, if not all, of their petroleum on the open market, you can't help but appreciate how they have to worry about the oligopolistic tendencies of the major oil companies.

"When you realize that the list of those dependent countries includes most of Western Europe, Japan, India, China, and the United States, how can one help but conclude that the day is coming when we must think of the global oil industry as if it were one big pot into which all developed oil is delivered and from which all consumptive needs are supplied? When viewed in those terms, it's difficult to conclude why any net-importing nation would be relaxed about having to fulfill its requirements from a market controlled by the Oil Club."

Grinning, David said, "For a beginner, you catch on pretty fast!"

Before she could say anything, he continued, "We still need to talk about the source of capital. I understand that we would have to raise about fifteen billion dollars. In a market made smaller by

Big Oil's domination, I've been wondering about what kind of a plan you and your friends have dreamed up. What will enable you to raise that kind of money?"

"The honest answer is we're not sure," Claudine replied. "We have some ideas, but we're a long way from having any concrete solutions."

"Well, tell me about your ideas," said David. "Maybe I can be of some help."

"The solution, as we see it, involves the creation of a new source of capital that would replace the balance sheets of the big oil companies. To make matters more complicated, the American government's sources of credit are already being stretched to the limit by postwar reconstruction commitments. The pervasive influence of the Oil Club will substantially reduce the availability of capital in the United States. All of which means we are left with no alternative other than appealing to private pools of equity capital. Fortunately, these pools of capital, for the most part, are independent of the long arm of the Oil Club."

"It seems that the problem facing us," said David, "is how we produce the money necessary to bridge the gap between the start of the exploration process and the time when the reserves can be measured. Without proven production, how do you raise the money?"

Claudine paused a moment and then smiled broadly. "You know how persistent Jacques can be. Once he puts his mind to it, everything seems to start and stop with those diagrams of sequential logic he's so famous for drawing. Have you noticed how he sketches through the process by breaking each element into its component parts? And how he then breaks down each of the component parts into its own component parts, and continues the process until he is satisfied he has peeled enough skin off the onion?"

"Yes, I'm quite familiar," said David.

"Well, when he began to assign estimated costs to each segment, he quickly realized that the really big dollars required to fund the total costs of a new, vertically integrated oil field are only required after the productivity of the new field is proven. That's when he came up with the idea of the two-stage financial commitment."

"A two-stage financial commitment?" said David.

"Let's suppose you, for whatever reason, wanted to make a deal with a qualified independent oil company. Would it bother you to provide two financial commitments? The first would finance the exploration and drilling of new wells and whatever else was necessary to reliably determine the productivity of the new oil field. Once the production was proven, the second commitment would fund the remaining costs of all the capital improvements necessary to transport, refine, and bring the oil to market."

"Well," David replied, "two financial commitments would be fine, as long as we were convinced that we had an enforceable contract, subject only to our demonstrating that the productivity of the wells exceeds a prenegotiated minimum requirement. But, even so, who is going to provide you with those kinds of commitments?"

Claudine sat back and let David's question remain momentarily unanswered. Finally, when she thought his curiosity was going to boil over, she said, "From a fifteen-billion-dollar pool of U.S. government–guaranteed debt we are planning to create and fund from private investment sources."

David looked shocked, but after a moment of thinking nodded approvingly. "That is a remarkable, simple, and obvious solution," he said. "I think it might just work. It's been right in front of us all this time and nobody could see it. Do you mind telling me how you came up with that idea? And why do you think the American government is prepared to cooperate and provide the necessary credit support?"

"It's not so original," Claudine replied nonchalantly. "When you think about it, it's the same concept that we used in developing the gold bearer bond. All I did was substitute proven oil-well production for the 'gold in the vault' for collateralization purposes. Other than that the oil bond is interest-bearing, the two financial instruments are the same. Also, plans are under way in the United States for mortgage-backed securities to be used to fund the capital required to finance the exploding demand for single-family homes. We're simply adapting that plan to our needs and expanding the funding to include the international investment community."

"What makes you believe that the U.S. government will cooperate?" David asked. "If memory serves, the American government would have to be willing to create a special agency to create and issue the bonds and provide the guarantees. Both actions would require legislative action. Normally, passing those kinds of regulations would be considered very difficult. In this instance, in which you are going to incur the wrath of the oil companies, their commercial banks, and their investment bankers, you will be making your job exponentially more difficult."

"Well," said Claudine, "Jacques believes there is a high level of White House motivation to make this happen. According to Fed Chairman Malone, the President is prepared to lend the behind-the-scenes support of the White House to the 'right people with the right plan.'"

David sat back in his chair, crossing his arms over his chest. "Bravo! I thought you were going to run a few ideas by me, but it seems that you've come up with a solution already. What can I say?"

"You can say that you would like to be a part of our team, that you'll help us accomplish the trust we need to develop in the Middle East and raise all that money."

"Claudine, why don't we discuss it over a couple of drinks at the French Club? There's an old friend of yours who would love to see you."

Maggie, the famous wartime proprietress of the French Club, was waiting to greet them when they walked through the front door. Claudine stood to the side as Maggie gave out a warning whoop and embraced Sir David Marcus, kissing him on the lips. After giving her best imitation of a polite curtsy, the five-foot-ten woman with broad shoulders and enormous breasts said, "Welcome back, Miss Demaureux. You've been gone far too long!"

"Is that the best you can do, Maggie?" said Claudine. "I don't know about the kiss, but I think I do deserve at least one whoop and a hug!"

Beaming, Maggie stepped forward and, after giving Claudine her best hug, picked her up from under the shoulders and turned her around so the other patrons could see her. "Look who's here, everyone! I'm sure you remember Claudine Demaureux, Jacques Roth's girlfriend."

"Actually," Claudine said, addressing the familiar crowd of regulars, "I'm not Jacques's girlfriend anymore, I'm his wife. We were married in January at a ski resort in Idaho." Claudine watched as Maggie glanced at David for a confirming nod.

"Well, I'll be damned," Maggie said. "The old buck finally met his match. This deserves a celebration."

Drink after drink, story after story—it didn't take long before any thought of serious conversation was long forgotten. Claudine welcomed the chance to relax and forget the details of oil refineries and high finance as she and her friends talked and drank into the evening. It had been one hell of a day.

Chapter 8

SAVING PEREZ

Mike arrived at the office of Señor Juan Pablo Perez just before noon on June 16, 1946. The office was in a remodeled older building that served as the headquarters of Venezuela's oil ministry. Located on the main plaza in the center of the commercial district of Caracas, the building contrasted with the newer and taller modern buildings that housed the executive offices of the American and British oil companies.

At the time appointed for the meeting, Mike crossed the busy street and entered the dark, musty lobby of the oil ministry. The guard, waiting behind a small desk, rose and approached him, asking for identification, the name of the official he was meeting, and the purpose of his visit. Satisfied with Mike's credentials, the guard picked up the phone on his desk, dialed a two-digit number, and waited for someone to answer.

"Minister Perez is expecting you," the guard said to Mike after a brief phone conversation. "You will find his office on the third floor. Turn left out of the elevator; his office is the second door on the right."

Compared to the sleek machines in New York's downtown office towers, this building's elevator was truly an antiquated relic. For a brief moment Mike considered taking the stairs, but he decided against it and stepped onto the platform. The young operator closed the outer door and then pulled the expandable metal inner door closed before turning the circular handle that raised and lowered the car. When they reached the third floor, the young man jiggled the handle back and forth until the elevator floor lined up within a few inches of the hallway floor. Mike exited and walked left down the hall. Knocking first, he opened the door to the office of Venezuela's minister of oil. Inside, fans attached to the high ceiling were slowly spinning in an attempt to cool the warm, humid room. The windows were open. Dust-covered piles of folders were stacked everywhere. Clerks were busy studying the documents, sorting them into new piles. The room was poorly lit, and the soft whirring of the fans and the shuffling of paper were the only sounds. A pretty young secretary dressed in a brightly colored dress contrasted sharply with the rest of the room.

"Good morning, Mr. Stone," she said with a heavy accent. "Minister Perez is expecting you. May I show you to his office?"

As Mike entered the room, Señor Juan Pablo Perez, already standing, moved toward him and extended his hand. "Please be seated, Mr. Stone," he said in perfect English. "I've been looking forward to your visit."

After exchanging some preliminary pleasantries, Mike was about to ask his first serious question when the minister put his finger to his lips, signaling for Mike to remain silent. Before Mike could react, the minister asked, "Do you like our local cooking? Why don't we walk across the plaza to one of my favorite restaurants? They know me well and make an extra effort to prepare local, same-day fish in some very unusual ways."

Mike agreed, and they walked down the three flights of stairs and exited the building. Perez led Mike across a busy street and into a flowered park, where a band of six musicians was playing in one of the gazebos. People everywhere were smiling and talking. Stopping to light a cigarette, the minister turned and looked behind him. Noticing the look of concern on Perez's face, Mike turned around as well. Two men following close behind them immediately turned away, as if trying to look as inconspicuous as possible. They were the same two he had seen near his hotel earlier that morning. He couldn't help but wonder, *Could I have added to Señor Perez's problems by calling on him?*

The park was about a quarter of a mile across. Walking slowly, Perez said, "We won't be able to talk over lunch. I never know who is sitting next to me, but out here in the park, it's safe to talk. We've got no more than ten minutes. While we walk we need to discuss what I hope is the real purpose of your visit."

Encouraged by Mike's nod, Perez continued. "I have in my possession documents that contain a lot of information on the transactions between my country and our oil partners. If we can find a way to organize all the bits and pieces, we may be able to prove the oil companies have been dealing in bad faith with the Venezuelan government. I have hidden the evidence in a safe place, and the files will fit into a set of suitcases. Everything is ready to go. My family and I are prepared to leave Caracas at any time."

Mike was surprised by the directness of the minister's statements, but he tried his best not to react.

Continuing to look straight ahead and listen as if they were conducting a normal conversation, Mike continued to match Perez's leisurely pace as they slowly made their way across the park.

Mike's call from his hotel room in Caracas to his home in San Francisco took several minutes to be put through. "Cecelia," he said when she picked up, "I'm leaving Venezuela tomorrow morning and should be in San Francisco late the following night. Don't worry about picking me up. I'll take a cab."

As soon as he hung up the phone, he felt awful. It was the first time he had lied to the woman he loved. *I know she'll be worried when I don't show up in San Francisco, but what choice do I have? I have to believe my phone has been tapped and that the content of any cables or telegrams I send would be checked.*

Understanding the importance of Samson's believing the official purpose of his visit was as reported, Mike had followed the same routine he'd followed on his prior trip. The first day he had met with representatives of the oil companies. The second day he had called on certain high government officials, and finally, on the third day, he had lunched with Señor Perez. Mike hadn't veered from his schedule in any way.

Early in the morning on the fourth day of his trip, Mike checked out of his hotel, took a taxi to the main terminal of Caracas International Airport, and checked in at the Pan American ticket counter. His ticket in hand, Mike walked toward the designated gate. About halfway down the long corridor, he abruptly turned right and exited the terminal through an unmarked side door. He was met by a uniformed American customs official and transported by jeep a short distance to a clearly marked United States customs DC-6 aircraft. Its engines were running and the wheel blocks had already been removed. Mike quickly ascended the stairs and entered the plane.

Greeting him with warm smiles were Señor Perez, his wife, and their two sons. Their luggage, along with the suitcases containing the files, had been neatly stowed in the rear of the plane.

As soon as the door was closed, the plane began to taxi toward the main runway. Once airborne, the plane adjusted course to a northwesterly direction. Their route would take them across Central America to Mexico City, and after refueling there, they would continue on to Douglas, Arizona, a small town located on the Mexican border.

Bill Dean, the owner of the Castle Dome Ranch, and Mike's employer at Dean Securities, was waiting to meet them as they disembarked into the dry, warm, windy desert air of southern Arizona. "Welcome to Arizona, Mr. and Mrs. Perez," he said, clasping their hands enthusiastically as they stood on the tarmac. "I'm William Dean, owner of the Castle Dome Ranch. It's such a privilege to have you as my guests. Everything has been arranged for your comfort and safety. You and your family are welcome to stay as long as you like."

The drive from Douglas, Arizona, to Castle Dome Ranch was long, hot, and dusty. To the outsider, Arizona's high desert seemed like a remote, gently undulating, endless, arid land of dry streambeds and strange-looking bushes, trees, and exotic plants.

To make the time pass more quickly, Bill pointed out interesting features of the landscape as he drove. "The ecological balance in our high desert country is very different from other areas," he said at one point. "Certain types of plants grow only at specific elevations. In fact, it is said that an educated botanist can look at the vegetation and determine the elevation of where he is standing to within five hundred feet."

Señor Perez and his family listened politely but were more interested in watching the passing desert.

At last Bill proudly announced, "See that high archway? It marks the entrance to our ranch. In the distance beyond it you can make out our headquarters. And see that steep red mountain with the rounded top in the background? We call it Castle Dome; that's where the ranch's name comes from."

As they traveled closer they could see a small group of buildings clustered on the mountain's dome-like surface. Mike asked Bill to explain to the Perez family what they were seeing.

"The dome is an extinct volcano," said Bill. "If you look closely, you can see one of the lava tubes at the base. It's one of three that connect to a large cone-shaped hole inside that leads up to the top, about six hundred feet high. The only way you can get up there is by following one of those tubes into the center and then hiking up a spiral path that's been carved out of the inside walls. One of the tubes leads into Mexico and the other two can be entered from the American side.

"The ranch itself is part of an old Spanish land grant purchased by an earlier generation of my family who settled here. Those were lawless times. Apache Indians roamed freely.

"The family lived in the ranch compound, except when they could sense trouble approaching. Lookouts on top of the dome could spot anyone coming from a long way away. Can you see the big old bell on the mountaintop from here? Three rings of that bell meant trouble was approaching. Hearing the signal, my ancestors would retreat to the Castle Dome. It served as the family sanctuary from the Indians, Santa Ana and his Mexican troops, and bandits from both sides of the border.

"We haven't used the compound up there for years, but knowing that you were coming, we stocked it with fresh water and all the supplies you will need should it become necessary to use it."

The family was fascinated by their new surroundings. They had heard stories about the American Southwest, but they never expected to see it, much less be forced to live there.

"You should be quite comfortable staying in our guesthouse," Bill continued. "It has all the facilities of a regular home. No one will disturb you, and you are welcome to join us in the main house for meals whenever you wish. Señor Perez, you and your family should be safe here since the ranch is in such an isolated part of the state. Everyone in Douglas knows everyone else. If visitors come through, we will be informed in plenty of time and can make whatever arrangements are necessary. Tomorrow, I'll take you up to the top of Castle Dome and you'll be able to see for yourselves how we can protect you from uninvited intruders."

"I can't thank you enough for your hospitality," said Juan Pablo, his wife smiling in agreement.

"After you get settled in and finish your unpacking, why don't you come up to the main house?" said Bill. "We usually gather at about six-thirty for cocktails. Dinner is served at seven-thirty."

After dinner on the second night following their arrival, Mike, Bill, and the Perez family were sitting around the big circular oak table when Mike said, "All hell has to have broken loose." He turned to Señor Perez. "By now the oil companies and Samson must know that you, your family, and I have disappeared, along with the files. I bet we have Samson working overtime."

"Samson? What is Samson?" Bill asked.

Mike glanced at Juan Pablo. All it took was one glance for him to realize that Venezuela's Oil Minister knew all too well about the organization. Next, he proceeded to explain to Bill how it operated. After listening to what Mike had to say, the rancher responded by describing all the precautions they should be taking. "As long as we're careful, everybody should be okay," he said. "Over the course of a century, members of our family have had to defend themselves against far greater threats."

Mike looked at Bill, his expression somber. "Bill, I don't want you to overreact, but Samson might suspect where we are, and they have very drastic ways of going about their business. They were originally organized as a clandestine paramilitary organization to protect British and American oil interests in Venezuela against a military coup in the 1930s. They've remained in business as a mercenary 'security' organization despite the efforts of the U.S. government to eradicate them.

"During World War II, when my five friends and I were involved in prohibiting German industrialists from using their private wealth to start a Fourth Reich, we were forced to survive Samson's threat if we were to complete our mission. Knowing I am involved will alert them to the possibility that the U.S. Secret Service and the rest of the Sentinels are involved. Not only do we need to make the necessary arrangements here, but I need to find some way to alert our friends."

"In that case," said Bill, "there are some additional precautions we should be taking. To be on the safe side, I'll ask some of the vaqueros to ride the perimeter of the ranch each day. I can also ask Steve Connors, our ranch foreman, to alert the Douglas locals. If anyone suspicious arrives in town asking questions, they'll let us know."

Chapter 9

CECELIA CHANG

Cecelia sat at her desk on the executive level of the American West National Bank building, staring out at the San Francisco Bay. A ship was being unloaded at Pier 8 down at the Embarcadero. A large tugboat was gently guiding another ship into its berth at Pier 10, and two more heavily laden ships were headed toward the Golden Gate Bridge. Normally, she would watch the ships and think of life in Hong Kong. Today, her mind was preoccupied with worry over Mike.

It had been four days since the night he was supposed to have arrived at the San Francisco airport. *Perhaps I should call Pan American operations and give them his name and flight information*, she thought. *They might have some record of him.*

When she called, a ticket agent in Caracas remembered a Mr. Stone checking in at the ticket counter and then walking toward the gate. Further checking revealed there were no unclaimed bags at the lost and found either in Caracas or San Francisco. "Judging from our records," said the agent, "we have no reason to believe he didn't complete his flight as planned."

After saying she was sorry that they couldn't be of more assistance, the representative paused and added almost as an afterthought, "It's strange, but you are the second person today who has called to inquire about Mr. Stone."

An alarm went off in Cecelia's mind. "What was that? Did I understand you correctly? Another person was checking on Mr. Stone? Do you have his name?"

"I'm sorry, but the man didn't give his name."

"I see. Thank you anyway," she said as she hung up.

If she was concerned before, now Cecelia was really scared. She was startled out of her thoughts by the ringing of her telephone. She snatched it off its cradle, hoping it would be Mike. Instead, she recognized Pete Ferrari's gravelly voice. "Cecelia, excuse me for bothering you, but I was wondering, could you join me for an early lunch in my private dining room?"

Why would the president of the bank be inviting me to lunch? she wondered. *Could it have something to do with Mike?*

Stepping out of the elevator on the eighth floor, she was greeted by Mr. Ferrari's personal secretary. "Good morning, Miss Chang. I've been asked to escort you to the boss's private dining room."

As they entered the small but elegant room, Pete Ferrari and Bill Dean rose to greet her. "Good morning, Cecelia. Thank you for coming right up. I think you know William Dean." He gestured to the man standing next to him.

Now her mind was really racing. Why would her boss and Mike's boss both want to see her? Something must have happened to Mike. *Get ahold of yourself, girl*, she said to herself. *Don't let them see how scared you are.*

As soon as they were seated at the table, Bill Dean handed her an envelope. "Cecelia, Mike asked me to give this to you. He's deeply sorry he couldn't call you. I left him yesterday and I can assure you that he's fine, and not in any immediate danger. Pete and I will excuse ourselves for a few minutes to give you some privacy while you read what's inside the packet. When you're done, we can all have a pleasant lunch and enjoy some of Pete's best wine."

Shaken but nonetheless relieved to know Mike was alive and safe, Cecelia thanked Bill and began trying to open the letter as the men left the room. She had considerable trouble unsealing the envelope. *Maybe I don't want to know what it says*, she thought.

She laid it on the table as if it had burned her hand. After staring at the envelope for several minutes, she used one of the knives from the table to slit open one of its ends. She shook the letter out of the envelope, allowing the folded paper to fall on the table. Leaving it there, she lowered herself into the nearest seat and continued to watch it. *What am I afraid of? What's stopping me from seeing what it says?*

Holding it by the edges, pinched between the forefingers of each hand, she began to read, the dread building inside her.

My dearest Cecelia,

I'm concerned that by the time you receive this note my unexplained absence will have scared you half to death. I'm so sorry for any worry that I may have caused you. My actions were necessary to protect Señor Perez, his family, and myself. As you predicted, things got a bit sticky in Caracas. Thanks to Bill Dean, my dad, and Roger Malone, I was able to rescue Perez and his family before Samson could catch up with us.

There's no longer any question that our old enemies are after me, and if they know about me, they know about you and the rest of the Sentinels. Roger has already asked the Secret Service to provide 24-hour protection for each of us. I don't want to alarm you any more than necessary, but I think it's extremely important that you not try to contact me or any of the others, no matter how important you might think it is.

I am sure a full court press is being applied to find Perez and recover his files. In trying to find us, they are probably watching everyone we might contact, monitoring all calls and communications, and checking all public transportation.

For the time being, I think you are all quite safe. Samson needs you free to lead them to us. The best thing you and the other Sentinels can do is continue with the normal, everyday activity of your lives.

Unfortunately, I can't tell you where I am or how long it will be before I can return. Maybe the time has come for you to take that long-overdue trip to Hong Kong. It's been more than ten years since you've seen your family. I'm sure they would love to see you. By the way, you might consider talking to your father about us. I love you very much and I still hope we can someday be married.

Please don't worry, Cecelia. I'm perfectly safe.

Love,
Mike

When Bill and Pete knocked and reentered the dining room a few minutes later, they could immediately see that Cecelia had been moved by the contents of the letter. She had paled, her eyes were watering, and her lips were trembling.

"Cecelia, are you all right?" Ferrari asked gently. "Shall we continue with lunch, or would you prefer to be excused? We can continue our discussion at some other time."

"No, thank you," she replied. "I'll be all right. I just need a minute to collect myself."

The waiter was called in and food orders were placed. Pete and Bill kept the conversation light until the main course was served.

"Cecelia, there is something else besides news of Mike we need to talk about," Ferrari said. "Now that the war is over, things in the Orient are beginning to change. It's not just a question of the countries that were occupied by the Japanese returning to their prewar status. There are issues of local desires to achieve sovereign independence being challenged by the recolonization efforts of certain European governments. Protection of prior investment interests is being translated into the need to reestablish political control. There is a nasty political revolution being resumed in China. Communist and Nationalist Chinese forces are no longer united in their common defense of China against the Japanese.

"Reports from our best experts indicate that, contingent upon receiving assistance from America, many of these Asian countries will start positioning themselves to participate in the postwar economic explosion that is expected to occur. These countries are beginning to formulate strong feelings regarding their future independence.

"We need you to help us develop an understanding of what is happening. As you know better than most," Ferrari continued, "a lot of personal and national wealth was put beyond the reach of the Japanese before and during the outbreak of hostilities. These monies will start flowing back into their countries of origin. When that occurs, new and modern systems of banking services are going to be needed.

"American West National Bank is desirous of becoming involved in this process. Correspondingly, the bank has decided to form a new operating division, Asian Banking, and we want you to be in charge, Cecelia, you are both the first female vice president of the bank and—should you accept—its first female president of an operating division. Both Bill and I couldn't be more pleased."

Caught completely by surprise, all Cecelia could do was stare at the two men. Her mind was seven thousand miles away. *I only wish my father could be here*, she thought. *He would be so proud.*

Taking Cecelia's broad smile as an acceptance of the promotion, Ferrari eagerly continued. "As a first step, we would appreciate it if you would organize an extended trip to the Orient. We think it would be a good idea for you to meet the new players, introduce the bank, and learn more about their regional banking needs. You remember Ted Lee, the former head of the Bank of Hong Kong's operations here in San Francisco? Ted has been transferred back to Hong Kong to assume the responsibility of running the entire bank. I've talked to Ted and he is eager to meet with you, and to personally introduce you to his friends and clients."

About the same time, three thousand miles to the east, Jacques was back in his New York office, wondering how Claudine's trip was progressing. A knock on the door broke his train of thought. "Mr. Roth, a messenger from Christie's has just given us a special-delivery package for you," a delivery boy said. Opening the large envelope, which displayed no return address, Jacques saw that there was a second package inside that had been opened and resealed. The address on the smaller package read:

From: Mr. Mickey. P.O. Box 2302, Dallas, Texas

**To: F. Time. C/o Christie's Auction House,
20 Rockefeller Center, New York, New York**

This has to be from Mike, Jacques thought to himself. He recognized "Mr. Mickey" as the nickname Cecelia used when she wanted Mike's undivided attention. F. Time, a.k.a. Father Time, was the nickname they had affectionately used when they referred to Ian Meyer, their fellow Sentinel. Even as a student, Ian wore both belts and suspenders, drove old cars, and was fascinated by anything old.

"Ian Meyer," Jacques said to himself. *I've always regretted that he felt it necessary to retire from active participation in our Sentinel activities. How can the original forger of a hundred million dollars' worth of duplicated gold bearer bonds be fully absorbed by his daily art auction activities? Ah, well, Mike must have deliberately sent this package to Ian at Christie's to confuse anyone who might be watching me.*

Opening the package, Jacques saw several sheets of notes and calculations and two one-page letters, with a handwritten note attached by a paper clip.

He immediately recognized Ian's almost illegible handwriting on the note: "*Jacques, it looks like Mike may have hit the jackpot.*"

The first letter was a copy of the note Mike had sent to Cecelia. The second letter was addressed to him.

Jacques,

You need to contact my Dad, show him these briefs, and ask him to send attorneys Smith and Jones to Dallas. He'll know whom I'm talking about. We need them to talk with Perez, review his files, and determine if we can develop this information into the kind of evidence needed to produce the ironclad case required to challenge the big oil companies either directly or in court.

Don't try to call me or attempt to locate us. Just have those lawyers at Union Station on the morning of July 12th. I'll check the schedule and be there to meet them when they arrive.

Mike

Chapter 10

BREAKING THE CODE

Each morning after breakfast, Mike and Juan Pablo would excuse themselves, walk across the ranch compound, and enter an old deserted warehouse. Taking time out only for lunch, they would remain there all day, studying the contents of the oil minister's files, which contained thousands of invoices, revenue receipts, market reports, bills of lading, transport schedules, and refining reports. They involved shipments over a span of five years from Venezuela, Mexico, and the United States to customers located throughout the Allied world.

By themselves, the thousands of individual pieces of paper meant nothing. Somehow, the two men had to discover some pattern that would enable them to understand what had actually happened and prove their conclusions in a court of law. The work was detailed and time-consuming. It quickly became obvious that weeks, not days, were going to be required before they would finish their task.

Mike and Juan Pablo first focused on the revenue receipts for oil purchased from Venezuela, sorting them chronologically and laying them out on the floor in a long line. Invoices for oil purchased from suppliers affiliated with the Oil Club were sorted by date and placed in a second line parallel to the first. The bills of lading for oil purchased from the nationalized Mexican sources were similarly sorted and placed by date in a third line.

The two men would walk around the warehouse and study the information, intently looking for some pattern that might solve the puzzle. One afternoon Juan Pablo decided to randomly select same-date invoices and compare their gross selling prices, refining charges, and transportation costs. The gross selling prices paid per barrel of oil purchased from each of the three sources, when adjusted for sulfur and British Thermal Unit content, coincided with published market data.

He did notice, however, that refining expenses appeared to vary. Comparing these costs was complicated. Different sources of oil contained varying levels of sulfur content, viscosity, wax, and BTUs. To make matters even more complicated, Juan Pablo explained to Mike that oil was not always "cracked" into the same mix of distillated products.

Based on the variations in refining expenses, they re-sorted all the invoices by mix of distillates. By working backward from the distillated end products, they began to see a relationship emerge between the identifiable distillates and charges made for refining. To test their theory, they began to apply their provisional formula against oil of similar mix from the same sources and different customers. The formula withstood the test. Extra charges of twelve to eighteen cents per barrel were routinely charged against the oil shipped from Venezuela and Mexico by their two Oil Club partners.

Next, they started looking for variations in transportation charges. Once again they re-sorted the invoices. As with refining charges, it took a good deal of detailed analysis before they could begin to understand the differing transportation costs charged by shipping lines on oil purchased in Mexico and Venezuela. Once they understood the formula, they could calculate the loss to the oil-producing countries. Over the previous five years, the variation was again remarkably consistent: an overcharge of ten to twenty cents per barrel by the two major oil companies.

When added to the refining charges, the total averaged overcharges amounted to about thirty cents per barrel. The formula was so precise and the amounts so consistent that there was no doubt as to the premeditated nature of the swindle.

To calculate the loss in revenue, Mike and Juan Pablo began to add up the total volume for just the Venezuelan shipments over the previous five years. It totaled 1.8 billion barrels. At thirty cents per barrel, the overcharges amounted to $540 million.

Letting out a low whistle, Mike said, "That's a lot of lost revenue, particularly when you multiply it by a factor of three to take into account the awarding of treble punitive damages. Add interest and penalty fees and we're talking about a total exposure of approximately three billion dollars! Juan Pablo, what do you think the Venezuelan government is going to say when you give them this information?"

Smiling, Juan Pablo replied, "I think they are going to tell the oil companies that they owe Venezuela a lot of money, and that material changes need to be made in our agreements if they expect us to extend their contracts. I'm sure the Mexican government will follow suit once they hear about this."

"And if the oil companies don't agree?"

"It appears that they are going to have to make a choice," said Juan Pablo. "It will be my pleasure to inform them they can accede to our terms or face the possibility that we will not renew our contracts and sue them in court, but not before we have made full disclosure of the bad faith practices to the press. It will be very interesting to determine what Venezuela's production value is on the open market."

Mike couldn't help but express his excitement. "Juan Pablo, you are truly a lovely, crazy man. I know you've been primarily trying to improve Venezuela's leverage in your negotiations, but do you have any idea what kind of problems this evidence could create for the major oil companies on an international basis? You may have just provided the lever we need to pry open the Oil Club's grip on the oil-rich nations."

For the next three days, the two men spent their time summarizing their data, explaining how they were able to arrive at their conclusions, and calculating damages. Finally, when they were finished, Juan Pablo asked, "Now that we have confirmation, what are we going to do with it?"

"Despite the fact that we have been able to organize all these little pieces of data into a mosaic that clearly supports our conclusion," said Mike, "the information only becomes useful once it is converted into the appropriate legal format. When the information is in the form needed to satisfy the requirements of the court and can be used for negotiation purposes, we're in business."

Mike looked off into the distance as he thought something over. "Somehow, I need to get word to my father," he said. "Perhaps we need to talk to Steve Connors. He should be able to get a package out for us without attracting too much attention."

Chapter 11

THE CORK LOOSENS

New York Times, June 20, 1946

SHOULD THE AMERICAN TAXPAYER SUBSIDIZE THE PRODUCTION OF FOREIGN OIL?

By Walter Matthews

In the 1930s, an obscure bill was passed into law providing American oil companies the privilege of offsetting any royalties paid on the production of foreign oil against taxes due on profits generated from the refining, distribution, and sale of the same oil in the United States.

Historically, the United States has been a self-sufficient producer of its own energy needs and a net exporter of oil. Experts are now forecasting that by the year 1950, the combination of level domestic production and increasing consumption will convert our country into a net importer of oil.

By that time, the "foreign profits tax" provision of the Internal Revenue Service tax code established by this bill is expected to have become a material burden on the

American taxpayer. Preliminary estimates indicated that over the ten years following 1950, the tax relief offered the largest oil companies could be approximately $5 billion annually.

Three new public opinion polls are being designed to measure the public's attitude about this foreign profits tax provision.

The key question being tested by these polls is this: Is the public interest better served by preserving the foreign profits tax and incentivizing the consumption of foreign oil, or by eliminating the provision and using the savings to reduce taxes?

To ensure the reliability of the results, three of the nation's leading market survey companies have been retained. These surveys will be conducted in the six states that produce over 90 percent of America's oil and in six states that are the highest consumers of petroleum products. The states of California, Pennsylvania, and Texas will appear in both polls.

The normally unflappable personal secretary of Phil Warner, senior editor of the *New York Times*, rushed into her boss's office without knocking.

"Mr. Warner? Jack Hardy of Titus Oil is on the phone. By the way he's talking, he seems very upset."

The senior editor hardly had time to place the phone next to his ear before a voice shouted, "Phil, what the hell is going on?"

"Calm down, Jack," he replied. "I'm sure these surveys won't reveal anything you can't handle!"

"How the hell did this thing get started, Phil? I thought we had it stopped!"

"So did I. Several weeks ago Walter Matthews approached me with the idea about polling voters. After we talked, I thought it best for the *Times* to decline from funding the research project. I just assumed that would be the end of the matter. Apparently some other private party has funded Walt's surveys."

"Where could Walter be getting the financial support to conduct these surveys?" said Jack. "They have to be very expensive."

"Jack, I honestly don't know. When I asked him to reveal the source of his funding, he refused."

For the rest of the day, calls from irate senators, congressmen, and oil company executives jammed the newspaper's switchboard. Phil couldn't remember when anything the paper had done had caused such a furor. Smiling, he leaned back in his chair, clasping his hands behind his neck. *Well, this time it's going to be really interesting to see where the chips fall! The genie isn't out of the bottle yet, but the cork is real loose. If he ever gets loose, putting him back in will be harder than putting toothpaste back into the tube.*

News of the pending survey quickly spread throughout the oil industry. In Caracas, Houston, San Francisco, New York, New Jersey, London, Teheran, Baghdad, and Riyadh, oil-company executives with tense, drawn faces met to assess the implications of the study and to formulate plans to minimize the damage.

In Washington, the congressmen and senators aligned with the oil lobby were being asked questions they didn't want to answer. In their casual meetings in the halls, in the privacy of their offices, or in their clubs, they continually asked one another who was behind the surveys, and how they could be stopped.

But the senators from the more populous but non-oil-producing states were smiling. The letters were pouring in, in a ratio of nine to one favoring the repeal of the foreign profits tax provision.

The senators from the oil-producing states were not smiling. Domestic oil producers were already applying pressure toward repeal. Big Oil was pushing them hard in the opposite direction. And the majority of the people, even in these oil states, were favoring repeal. Transparency was becoming a very real issue. Local voters and campaign contributors were becoming a loud and articulate voice against the foreign profits tax provision.

In Washington, the national contributors were calling their lobbyists. Lobbyists were calling congressmen. Dinner parties, golf games, hunting and fishing trips were being arranged. Nobody was amused.

The President of the United States was smiling. Might this struggle over the foreign profits tax be the start of a long-overdue reform movement directed at eliminating the tax preference for foreign oil? Was it the work of Jacques Roth and his friends? It certainly looked like something they might do.

Roger Malone, too, was smiling. *This time Jacques has really shaken the tree!* the chairman thought. *I wonder how he plans to use the information . . .*

———

At the Castle Dome Ranch, Señor Juan Pablo Perez was also smiling, and not only because he and Mike had come up with the proof they were looking for. The newspaper article indicated to him that someone else had taken up the cause of bringing fairness and honesty to the industry. He briefly wondered if his new American friends had anything to do with the organization of the polling surveys.

———

In his London office, Sir David Marcus sat at his desk, smiling. "The industry's historical tree of order is about to be shaken," he said aloud. "And with change comes new opportunity."

Chapter 12

CLAUDINE AND NATALIE

Claudine had forgotten how glorious an English breakfast could be. Eggs cooked to order, broiled kippers, freshly squeezed orange juice, toast, unsalted butter, and the finest of English marmalades were all set before her. Sir David Marcus was sitting opposite her at the brightly lit London restaurant enjoying his second cup of coffee. He was refreshed after an enjoyable night at the French Club and anxious to resume the previous day's conversation.

"Claudine, I've been thinking about the problem of raising so much money in a hostile environment," he said. He reached into his pocket and withdrew a world map, which he unfolded and spread across the table. "This morning, I placed marks on thirty separate locations where I believe we might be able to identify motivated sources of investment for our oil development bonds. The presence of a mark indicates an unusual regional need to create a more diversified and competitive petroleum market. You will note that there are three different types of mark. The round mark signifies that there are petroleum reserves waiting to be developed. The square mark indicates a market that supplies its petroleum needs by buying oil on the open market. The triangle represents a regional money center needing to warehouse surplus funds in liquid, investment-quality, interest-bearing bonds.

When he had finished giving her his rationale for marking each location, Claudine said, "David, as I listened to you I couldn't help but notice that each time you discussed one of those marks, you mentioned some overriding reason which would motivate that particular group of investors to become involved.

"And I'm beginning to see what you're saying—we have to help these investors solve their own unique problems as we try to raise funds. So many of them have compelling reasons to support what we're doing. When I look through your financial telescope, I see a much different picture of the oil companies. Perhaps the long arm of Big Oil isn't as long or intimidating as we originally thought."

"Yes, but I wouldn't underestimate the power of the Oil Club. No one has ever attempted to do what you are going to try, but I doubt that there has ever been a time when international investment cooperation was so needed. If anybody has a chance to pull it off, it has to be you and your Sentinel friends."

The work portion of their conversation completed, he asked Claudine, "How would you like to join me for opening night of London's newest musical? Afterwards, you are welcome to accompany the star, Miss Natalie Cummins, and me to dinner at one of London's newest private supper clubs. Natalie is a very interesting woman, and I'm sure you will enjoy meeting her."

Obviously, David has no idea that Natalie and Jacques had an affair during the war, Claudine reflected. *I'm not even sure Jacques knows I know about his relationship with Miss Cummins. This could turn out to be a very interesting evening. How often does a wife have the opportunity to meet one of her husband's former girlfriends, particularly someone as famous and talented as Natalie Cummins?*

"Thank you, David. I'm a great fan of Miss Cummins. I've

actually seen her current show in New York twice, but I'd love to see it again—especially if I get to meet her afterward!"

"Perhaps I should warn you—I have already invited a mystery guest who will be joining us. You may find him most interesting. He will meet us at Claridge's at seven o'clock, in time to have a drink and become acquainted and still have time to make the curtain."

Lost in thoughts of what she would wear, Claudine simply nodded and thanked David once more for his invitation.

Claudine rarely gave much thought to impressing new people. This night, however, was different; everything had to be just right.

Entering the ground-floor restaurant in Claridge's, Claudine could see that David had already spotted her and was moving in her direction. As they walked back to the table, she could tell he was proud to be escorting her between the tables, introducing her to some of his friends and enjoying the envious looks of all the other males.

She met a flurry of new people on the walk across the establishment, and it was only when they approached David's table that she recognized her old friend Prince Habib of the House of Saud.

"Claudine, what a pleasure it is to see you again after all these years," said the prince, standing to greet her. "Life in the world of international banking hasn't been the same since you moved to the United States and married that rogue French friend of ours."

Noticing David's confusion, the prince said, "Claudine, I hope you don't mind my little surprise of joining you this evening. I didn't tell David of our previous acquaintance because I didn't want to rob him of the pleasure of thinking he was introducing us. By the way, I was in Geneva this week meeting with your father. He is very excited about your forthcoming visit."

One look at David's face was all it took for both Claudine and Prince Habib to break out in laughter. "David," the prince said, "If I didn't know you better, I would have said you look like a little boy who just learned there is no Santa Claus!"

They sat down as a waiter poured Claudine a glass of wine, and at last David responded. "Habib, how many of the Sentinels do you know? I knew you and Mike had attended the Harvard Business School at the same time, but I never knew you were a friend of both Jacques and Claudine. You could have told me before I went to all that trouble of explaining who they were!"

"David, the banking relationships between my family and the Roths and the Demaureuxs date back to before I was born. You have no idea how many dinner parties Jacques, Claudine, and I were all required to sit through together, and never allowed to talk. I think I was thirteen years old when I first fell in love with Claudine. By the time she left for school in the United States, I was fully prepared to give up the Bedouin practice of multiple wives to marry just her, but she never gave me the chance."

The combination of the laudatory London reviews, the presence of London's homegrown star, and the excitement of an opening night's performance all served to make the show the hottest ticket in town. Every seat was filled, and there were standing-room-only patrons gathered in the rear of the theater.

Prince Habib and Claudine watched the show from their host's private box, the last one to the left of the stage, overlooking the orchestra pit. Engaged in quiet conversation as they waited for the overture to begin, the three friends were oblivious to the attention they were attracting from much of the audience. The sight of such a beautiful woman sitting between the celebrated Saudi prince and the much-reported-on Duke of Trafalgar was a difficult vision for people to ignore.

As the overture concluded, the lights dimmed, the curtains opened, and the celebrated star made her entrance. When she smiled, the audience erupted into appreciative applause.

Claudine could not help but be impressed. Without singing a single note, dancing a single step, or uttering a single word, she had captivated the audience.

By the time the final curtain had come down and the audience had given the last of their standing ovations, Claudine was exhausted from all the excitement of watching a true star dance and sing her way through three acts. Her hands were sore from clapping; she was relieved when David tugged slightly on her arm, motioning for her to follow him backstage.

Standing in the wings, Claudine, the prince, and David watched an excited Natalie comparing opening-night notes with the play's director and its two famous composers. When they'd finished talking, they turned and started walking toward the left wing of the stage. At almost the same time, all four of them appeared to notice David and his friends.

David stepped toward them and smiled. "Natalie, I would like to introduce my dear friend, Jacques Roth's new wife, Claudine Demaureux. Claudine is a highly respected member of the international banking community. In addition to perfecting a new financial instrument, she is here to organize a new oil-development fund. Don't be fooled by her appearance, she is a smart, accomplished lady."

David couldn't help but be puzzled by the two women's silent interaction as he introduced them. Both stood very still, assessing each other, as the director and composers took their leave.

After a long, awkward moment, Claudine finally broke the ice. "Miss Cummins, I am a great fan. I saw your show twice in New York before you left to return to England. I enjoyed both your performances, but tonight I noticed something even deeper in your interpretation of your character."

Flashing the warm smile that had made her an audience favorite, Natalie said, "Thank you for noticing. Ever since I returned to London, I have been taking more acting lessons. It's a personal goal of mine to someday be regarded as a serious actress."

"Natalie," said David, "this quiet, handsome man next to me—who, believe me, is not used to waiting so long to be introduced—is Prince Habib of the House of Saud. He is a great fan of yours and has insisted that I introduce you to him. But before I do, I want to make it quite clear that you are *my* date. I insisted that he behave himself."

"Thank you for the introduction, David," said Natalie as she shook the prince's hand. "Claudine, gentlemen, now if you will excuse me, I have to change. It may take a while. Why don't the three of you go ahead? I'll meet you at David's club."

Watching Natalie return to her dressing room, Claudine thought, *I can't believe how I'm reacting to her. I don't even resent her. In fact, I'm flattered that Jacques chose me. I think I could even grow to like her.*

Chapter 13

A RETURN TO HONG KONG

It was June 27, 1946, a good three days and two stops after Cecelia's takeoff from San Francisco. She was startled when the wheels of her plane touched down on the Hong Kong runway. *Can it really be more than ten years since I left home?* she thought.

Standing in the plane's doorway, she looked on the tarmac below and recognized her father immediately. Despite his graying hair and thicker waistline, his erect posture and penetrating eyes reminded her that he was still the proud and powerful Tai-Pan of the House of Chang. *Even at this distance, I can sense the aura of his power*, she mused. *He is still the Great Eagle of Hong Kong.*

She still remembered the day she first heard her father referred to by that name. One of her girlfriends at school was repeating what she'd heard her father say at home: "From the way that young Tai-Pan fellow is recruiting trade from all over the Orient, you would think he was the Great Eagle of Hong Kong!"

She watched as he made his way toward the bottom of the stairs that led up to the plane. Carefully descending, Cecelia was seized by a sudden fear. Was he still the soft, gentle, and caring father she loved so much? Was she still his little girl?

She didn't have to wait long for an answer. The Great Eagle

made his way forward, spread his wings, and enveloped his beloved daughter.

Safely inside the black Mercedes limousine, Cecelia sat close to her father. Leaning her weight against him, her head touching his shoulder, she held both his hands in hers.

It wasn't long before Cecelia noticed they were taking a different route home than the one she remembered.

Tai-Pan asked his chauffeur to stop at an old teahouse in the oldest part of Hong Kong, down by the wharf. Turning to his daughter he said, "I'd like to talk to you before we both become distracted by all the excitement waiting for you at home. Mai Li's Teahouse is the best place I know where we can sit quietly and speak of the many things that have passed since we were last together."

Mai Li had been Cecelia's nanny, raising her as if she were her own daughter. She had also been Tai-Pan's number-one mistress. When their relationship was over, he had purchased the teahouse for her and set her up in business. He would frequently visit his old friend, and his private booth was always available when he came to think and didn't want to be disturbed.

Consistent with her normal custom, Mai Li greeted Tai-Pan formally, bowing and expressing her honor at having him visit her humble teahouse. She was so intent on what she was doing, she at first failed to recognize Cecelia.

"Mai Li," said Tai-Pan, "say hello to Cecelia. Look how she has grown up. She is a very important banker in San Francisco who has just traveled seven thousand, five hundred miles—*to see you*."

"Oh, Tai-Pan, how you like to joke with me!" said Mai Li gleefully as she embraced Cecelia.

After Mai Li had gotten over her initial shock, she seated Tai-Pan and his daughter at his personal booth, the one in the back away from interfering chatter and eavesdroppers.

When the tea had been served, the father began to share what was in his heart. "Cecelia, I used to receive regular reports from the Bank of Hong Kong regarding your international banking activities during the war. That's when I learned of the local network you established to move the money, bonds, and gold of so many of our friends into and out of China and Hong Kong.

"Not knowing what risks were involved, I was never certain whether I should acknowledge what you were doing. Whenever possible, I tried to help you by lending my support behind the scenes. After you were kidnapped by those Samson operatives, all I could do was hold my breath and hope you would survive. Learning of your rescue was one of the happiest days of my life. Since then, however, I have been worrying about your health. I've heard many stories about a person's mind shutting down to protect it from overloading. I've been receiving your medical reports, but you have no idea how relieved I am to see you in person and observe your complete recovery. You were very lucky."

Cecelia patted her father's hand. "My doctors said if I feel any light-headedness or sudden loss of energy, I should immediately stop whatever I'm doing and get plenty of rest. But as long as I wait for twenty-four hours after the last of the symptoms have disappeared, I should be okay."

"If that is the case," said Tai-Pan, "why have you decided to return to Hong Kong now? Aren't you taking a big risk?"

"Not in my mind," she replied. "As long as I back off the minute I start to feel strange, this trip is an opportunity for me to test my capacity for added stress and take care of some timely and important work—and of course see my family."

"And you promise me you will follow your doctors' instructions?"

As the acknowledged leader of the Orient's most powerful trading company, Tai-Pan knew his industry's practices needed to adapt to the new ways of the fast-changing world. With the defeat of the Japanese, Hong Kong was rapidly reverting to its former state as a British colony. On the mainland, the withdrawal of the Japanese was being closely followed by Mao Tse-tung's resumption of his Communist revolution. It seemed to Tai-Pan it was only a matter of time before Communism would consume all of China, forcing Chiang Kai-shek's Nationalist government and its prominent families to relocate to the island of Taiwan.

Once that occurred, Hong Kong would become an even more important window to China. For the first time in its history, the House of Chang would require the assistance of high-level executives who understood the business climate and cultures of both the Orient and the United States.

As he rode in the limousine with his daughter, Tai-Pan wondered whether Cecelia, with her advanced degree from the University of California, Berkeley, and her executive-level business experience in America, would consider moving back to Hong Kong. *Could it be that after all these years she had returned home to evaluate such a possibility?*

"Cecelia, there are a lot of very grateful people who would like to meet you and express their appreciation for all you have done. The wealth you helped protect represents a significant portion of the private capital needed to rebuild postwar China. Your old friend Ted Lee from the Bank of Hong Kong and I have been hoping you wouldn't mind mixing a little bit of business with pleasure."

"Not at all, father," she replied. "My boss and mentor, Pete Ferrari, specifically asked me to visit with Ted in an effort to create a cooperative working arrangement between his bank and American West. I'm looking forward to seeing him. When we were both living in San Francisco, he was always one of my favorite friends."

"To be perfectly honest, my child, when I learned of your success with American West, I couldn't help but consider what someone with your credentials and connections could accomplish here in China."

"Father, at times I really would have considered coming home, but I think I was afraid of becoming trapped in China's parochial business environment. As limited as things are in the United States, there is some improvement in attitudes about women in the workplace. It's a problem I have to fight every day."

"Little daughter," said Tai-Pan, "if you could see the growing need for someone with your skills and experiences here in Hong Kong, I doubt you would give the matter of gender much thought. How many people do you think there are with your background, your connections, your track record, and your familiarity with both the Chinese and American business communities? Do you have any idea of the many options available to you? At a minimum, you should keep your eyes open while you are here."

"Father, I confess that leaving Hong Kong was never easy. Without your support, I never would have had the courage to leave. Surviving as a female foreign student was lonely at times, but never as difficult as taking that step of leaving home. In fact, upon occasion I was really tempted to leave the United States and return to you and mother. If it hadn't been for my fear of failing and dishonoring the House of Chang, and the thought of jeopardizing my relationship with Mike, I probably would have come home a long time ago."

Cecelia had been looking directly into her father's eyes as she spoke. His facial expression and body language didn't change.

I'd forgotten how inscrutable he is when he chooses to be, she thought. *I thought I'd at least get some sort of reaction when I brought up Mike.*

"Tell me about Mike Stone," her father said after a period of silence.

She was startled that he knew Mike's last name. "How did you know about Mike?" she asked guardedly. "I have always been careful to never talk of him or our life together."

"If it hadn't been for his call when you were kidnapped, your mother and I wouldn't have known he existed. I could tell by the concern in his voice that he must love you very much. His father, Morgan, and I have met on several occasions before the war. You can't do business on the scale we do without the assistance of the New York banking community."

"How come you've never asked me anything about him?"

"He asked me not to mention anything about his call, and I've continued to respect his wishes. Besides, I always assumed you would tell me about him when you were ready."

"Well, we met my first day at Berkeley," said Cecelia. "We were attracted to each other at first sight. We were in the same study group, so we were constantly together. He's a lot like you, father, both intense and intelligent. He's amazingly disciplined and organized, but Mike is also a sensitive and an affectionate man. He's been highly supportive of my career and never appears to be threatened by my independence. It's important to me that you understand there is no doubt in my mind how I feel about him."

"Have you considered marrying him?"

"Father, I could never marry a man without your consent, and I have always been afraid to ask. Allowing me to attend school and work in the United States was one thing, but consenting to my marrying a Caucasian male of Jewish descent is quite another.

I realized it would upset you, so I never asked. We have both always believed that you and Mike's parents would be opposed to our getting married and having children, so we decided that living together was our next-best alternative."

"How do Mike's parents feel about you?"

"For a long time we kept our relationship a secret from them as well. Mike wasn't prepared to take the risk of being forced to make a choice between his father's expectations and me."

"For a long time, you say? Has something changed?"

"When I was kidnapped, Mr. Stone, out of concern for his son, became involved. Then, this winter, when Mike and I were going to be in New York for business, the Stones invited Mike and me to stay in their home. While we were there, I was invited to join Mr. Stone and his international banking team for lunch. Gradually, we expanded our talks to personal interests. He is quite a student of Asian art and literature. We got along just fine."

"I'm impressed," said Tai-Pan. "It sounds as if Morgan treated you with dignity and respect, and his invitation to stay in his home must be regarded as a singular honor."

"Oh, I think it was even more than that," said Cecelia. "Dinners at the Stones always include a different group of influential men and women. I think Mike's parents have introduced me to most of their closest friends. It's been their way of expressing their approval and support of our relationship. And . . . Father, it would mean a great deal to me if you could come to San Francisco and meet Mike. I'm not asking you to consent to our getting married. It's just that I would prefer to continue my relationship with Mike knowing everything is out in the open."

Chapter 14

THE INSULT

Arriving at his club well before Natalie would make her grand entrance, David asked the maître d' to show the three of them to his table. As they passed among the other members already seated for dinner, there was nothing David could do but stop at almost every table, say hello to his friends, and introduce the prince and Claudine.

Even when they were seated at his private table, other members, breaching the club's code of privacy, approached the table to say hello and be introduced.

The three of them were so immersed in conversation, they almost missed Natalie's entrance into the club. Suddenly, there she was, standing under the light near the maître d's station. Her transformation from singer-dancer-actress to wholesome-looking woman, wearing a simple knee-length black cocktail dress, perfectly tailored to accentuate her hourglass figure, was remarkable. The three-inch heels made her appear taller than her usual five feet four. Her short curly hair, washed and combed, framed her smiling face with the perky nose and the large brown eyes. Wearing no jewelry and only a minimum of makeup, the healthy-looking farm girl from Sussex stood searching the room for David and the others.

Excited by Natalie's presence, the club's members and their guests rose to give the actress a standing ovation. Walking forward and clapping, David arrived in time to greet her before the applause subsided. He took one of her hands in his and stepped back so that he could enjoy the vision of her, up close, before saying, "Natalie, would you give me the distinct pleasure of joining my friends and me for dinner?"

David was enjoying the moment. *How often does a man have the opportunity to escort such a celebrated actress through a room filled with so many friends?* he thought.

Once they sat down, the chilled Dom Pérignon, the caviar and toast points, and all the other accoutrements were quickly served.

Natalie couldn't help but think, *Can this all be true, or am I dreaming? How is it that a tomboy from Sussex can star in an opening-night show, receive such a lovely welcoming ovation, and be joined at dinner by the Duke of Trafalgar, the Prince of Saud, and the beautiful and talented wife of my previous lover?*

With her adrenaline flowing, Natalie knew this was going to be a great opening night, one she would long remember.

After lifting up his freshly filled glass of champagne, David said, "Natalie, not only have we witnessed a rare night in the history of London theater, but my instincts tell me that Claudine and her friends are about to embark on a very important journey that could affect the world for a very long time. Here's to the success of all of you."

Shocked by David's toast, Claudine wondered, *Doesn't David understand this is Natalie's evening? Why would he include me in his toast? I hope Natalie doesn't mind!*

Wanting to steer the conversation in another direction, Claudine asked, "Natalie, what is it like to have to perform the same play, night after night? How do you keep from becoming bored?"

"Good question!" said Natalie. "Not many people ask me that. First of all, while it might seem that we are always performing the same play, in reality, that isn't the case. In our minds, each night's play is different. Before each performance, we are consciously or subconsciously thinking about some new twist that we can introduce to make the play better or our personal performance more convincing."

"How interesting!" said Claudine. She then took a sip of champagne and eyed the caviar. "I never am quite certain, do you put the caviar on the toast and then add the onions, capers, and the grated egg, or is it the other way around?"

"Here, let me help you," the prince offered.

Still impressed by Claudine's question, Natalie continued, "You might say that we use each performance to test fresh ideas on a new audience. As you can imagine, not all audiences are the same. The challenge of winning their approval never stops.

"One of the great things about the theater is that you are constantly being tested. The excitement you feel from an appreciative audience is like no other. The depression when things go badly can be devastating. Believe me, life in the theater can be just as cruel as it is rewarding."

"What an exciting life you must lead!" said Claudine. "I can't even begin to imagine what it must be like to be so talented, and to have so many people appreciate your work."

"In a way," said Natalie, "I often think those of us who are fortunate enough to have lives in the theater must be part of some very special cult. The work can be very demanding and exciting, but it is not a very realistic part of life. Often, I wonder how it would be to have a more normal kind of life, one more like yours."

The prince sensed that it was a good time to change the subject. "Tell us how you prepare for a new role, Natalie," he said.

"I understand a good actress frequently conducts a lot of personal research in an effort to learn more about the character she will be playing. Is that true?"

Without hesitating, Natalie reached into her cocktail purse and proudly extracted her library card. "Say hello to Mr. Dewey Decimal."

David laughed. "Come on, Natalie, are we to believe that you actually show up at a public library and check out real books and actually return them, like a regular person? You, our star of stage and screen? You're much too pretty for that."

What was supposed to be an amusing statement made the evening of celebration suddenly turn ugly. Before anyone could react, Natalie said, "Well, Mr. Know-It-All, who do you think I am? Do you really think of me as some brainless theater trophy to be shown off in public and pummeled in private?"

Natalie, now in tears, was halfway across the room before Claudine could react. *Whatever just happened must have been a long time coming*, she thought as she chased after her. *I don't blame Natalie—if someone had made a comment like that to me, I don't know how I would react. What a horrible way to end such an important evening!*

Catching up with her outside the restaurant, Claudia said, "Why don't you come back to the hotel with me, Natalie? I'm told Claridge's is an excellent place to have a cognac and conduct some good old-fashioned girl talk."

Seated in the back seat of the same limousine that had delivered Natalie to David's private club, Claudine put her arms around the sobbing actress, held her close, and gently patted her back on the way to Claridge's. By the time they reached the hotel, Natalie had stopped crying, content to remain quiet in the protective arms of her caring new friend.

Hoping not to be noticed, Claudine requested that the driver deliver them to the rear entrance of the hotel, where they could enter the restaurant through the service entrance. Choosing a table near the fireplace, she helped Natalie sit down before signaling to the bartender. Recognizing both Natalie, a regular customer, and Claudine, from earlier in the evening, and remembering both women's preference for vintage Napoleon cognac, he simply nodded to her before warming two snifters, pouring a generous portion of the clear brown liquid into each glass, and delivering them to the table.

Instinctively, both women leaned forward, picked up their glasses, and, looking into each other's eyes with a knowing expression, took a healthy swallow. Natalie reached into her purse, took out a hanky, wiped her eyes, and then let out a little laugh, surprising Claudine.

"Do you realize where we are sitting?" said Natalie. "This is the same table where Jacques and I were sitting the first night we met. I'm sure you wouldn't mind if we move over there." She pointed to a table on the other side of the room.

After settling down at their new location and taking the first taste of their second order of cognac, Natalie said, "Claudine, this is a difficult thing for me to admit, but I really, truly loved your husband. Naturally, I didn't know about you or anything about your relationship with him. The first time I heard about you was the afternoon when we were standing at the top of the Statue of Liberty. He had just returned from Geneva. It was in the fall of 1944. He was telling me about his love for you and his desire to marry you, providing you showed up in New York after the war to accept his offer.

"Comprehending what he was telling me, and not overreacting to it, was the most difficult thing I have ever had to do. It was at that moment that I realized the things I most cherished in life were not to be found in my world of the theater."

After draining the last of her cognac and asking for another, Natalie continued. "Tonight was supposed to be such a special evening. I was so excited. There have been other openings when I spent the night by myself in a strange hotel room. Tonight, I was looking forward to celebrating my return to the London stage with my friends. I even thought I was going to finally deal with the memory of that horrible afternoon atop the Statue of Liberty."

Claudine was still as she listened to Natalie and sipped her cognac. She could hardly believe the amount of sympathy she felt for the woman across the table from her.

"I understood that David was trying to be funny when he made that crack about the library card," Natalie continued, "but to me his remark represented further verification that I am regarded as nothing but a sexy musical star, someone to be conquered, bedded, and added to a personal trophy case of masculine conquest, not someone who is cherished or taken seriously. You have no idea how difficult it is to live with that kind of fear."

Pausing to thank the bartender for the next drink, Natalie said, "I regarded your earlier question as being very perceptive, and I was looking forward to answering it more fully, before David made that unfortunate remark."

"Natalie," said Claudine, "it's important that you not overreact to a careless remark. If it will make you feel any better, I have spent most of my life worrying that people will fail to recognize me for my intelligence and my professional accomplishments. You, better than most, can appreciate how many times I have wished they weren't focusing on my physical appearance or my family's banking background."

Glancing down at their drinks and winking at Natalie, Claudine then said, "I'd like to think by the time we finish this third cognac, we will have found a way to work through the situation."

Chapter 15

THE VOTER SPEAKS

Walter Matthews's *New York Times* articles on the foreign profits tax were being picked up by newspapers across the country. Supporting editorials regularly appeared in the same papers. The idea of the American taxpayer subsidizing the costs of foreign oil had hit a very sensitive nerve. Citizens were asking themselves why their taxes should support companies they didn't trust and that already possessed so much wealth. Surely there were better uses for their money.

The story just wouldn't die. Weekly news magazines were conducting their own polls and reporting the results. The results showed sharp upward trends favoring the repeal of the provision. Interviews were broadcast on radio and network television news channels. The voting records of key Republican and Democratic congressmen were dug up by America's best investigative journalists and published on the editorial pages of leading newspapers.

Frantic meetings were held behind big and powerful doors. Over the strongest possible protests of the oil lobby, a new bill was being prepared for the House Ways and Means Committee. What had been an obscure and small part of a very large and complex tax code was being fully displayed in the clear light of day.

For the first time ever, the pro-oil and the anti-oil lobbies would be squaring off against each other. Congressmen from the oil-producing states were pitted against their colleagues from rural America and the more populous states. Phones were ringing; the late-night poker games, long rounds of golf, and hunting and fishing trips were now commonplace. Campaign coffers were depleted and refilled. Past political favors were being called in. New political favors were being requested.

Congressional staffs were working overtime. Constituencies were being polled. The voters were talking at town meetings and on street corners. Straw votes in the House of Representatives indicated the vote was going to be close. The time had finally arrived for the President to begin exerting the full influence of the White House, behind the scenes, and away from the press.

It was becoming clear that the congressmen loyal to Big Oil were being squeezed, and they were finding it nearly impossible to explain anti-bill attitudes to informed and angry voters. In the final days, one by one, individual congressmen who opposed the bill reluctantly concluded that they couldn't take the risk of alienating their voter base or tarnishing their voting record in a losing cause. Slowly, they began to change their positions.

By the time the bill was ready to come to the floor, it was passed by acclamation and sent on to the Senate. The voters had spoken.

Chapter 16

CLEARING THE AIR

On the morning of June 19, 1946, Prince Habib, Claudine, and Sir David were sitting in David's somewhat cramped private office. Claudine had spent the previous few days enjoying the sights of London, and it was the first time she'd seen the prince and David since the unfortunate events after Natalie's show the previous week. The atmosphere was strained, and none of them could ignore it. The air had to be cleared before they could proceed with the day's business agenda.

Finally David said, "I hope you understand how badly I feel. Claudine, you and Natalie were out of there so quickly, I didn't realize how personally she took my careless remark. For hours, I kept calling her apartment, hoping I could explain and apologize. There was no answer."

In his best Oxford accent the prince said, "I must say, old man, you were a bit of a *prick*!"

"David," said Claudine, "there is a lot at stake here. Because of the importance of our task, I've decided to say what I have to say. If the circumstances were any different, I would have preferred to remain silent and quietly move away. The night of the show, after I finally put a heartbroken but proud woman to bed,

I spent the better part of what remained of the evening trying to decide how I felt. If, after hearing what I have to say, you would prefer to not work with me and my group, I will understand."

David nodded, and the prince took on the look of someone about to witness something very entertaining.

"David," said Claudine, "as brilliant a businessman as you obviously are, I am having a difficult time understanding how you can talk about trust and at the same time treat a very special woman as if she were some trophy to be added to your already considerable collection. You have no idea how much damage you have done to a sensitive woman whose only desire is to be respected by you as a serious and intelligent person."

David's face went pale as she continued. "My question is, how can I be comfortable being interdependent with someone who is capable of treating people in such a way?"

"Claudine, believe me," said David, "I feel as badly about what happened as you do. All I can say is that if I ever have the opportunity to set the record straight, I'll do whatever I can. I don't know what else I can say, and yes, I would prefer to proceed."

"David," asked the prince, "will you give us your word that you'll try harder to treat the people in your personal life with more dignity and respect—especially the females? You understand this issue has become one of trust?"

David looked down at his hands. "Yes, yes, of course. I'm terribly sorry it came to this."

Understanding that the prince had extracted a promise from David that couldn't be broken, at least not without severe consequences, Claudine said, "Well if that's settled, why don't we move on?"

"Saudi Arabia is rapidly becoming the leading member of the Middle East oil community," Claudine said confidently. "If you would give me a few minutes, I would like to explain our plan to the prince."

After concluding her remarks, she said, "It would be very helpful if the royal family would play an active and constructive role in assisting us in solving the problem of access to readily developed oil reserves."

"We already have long-term contracts with two of the major oil companies," said the prince. "Our involvement with Pan-Arabia Oil Company is well known. I don't understand how we can be of assistance."

"Well," said Claudine, "we want to talk to you about the future development of your other oil fields that aren't under contract to Pan-Arabia Oil."

The atmosphere in the room instantly changed. Shocked by Claudine's statement, all the prince could say was, "How is it that you believe we hold such interests?"

"Habib, my old friend," said Claudine, "think back to the years before the war when your country needed to borrow money. I had my father go into the Demaureux Bank archives and look at some of your old files. Prominently displayed in collateral agreements is the specific mention of those holdings."

Reaching toward her briefcase, she said, "My father sent copies of those files in the event I need them to refresh your memory."

"Thank you, Claudine, but that won't be necessary. I should have known better than to try to confuse you. You would think after all these years I would know you do your homework and are not shy about expressing your opinion."

In an attempt to break the tension that had suddenly permeated the room, the prince said, "Well, I guess this is your day for keeping David and me on track! You are to be congratulated!

But you have to understand, Claudine, that without access to at least one of the major oil companies' financial resources, technology, and management—not to mention their markets—we can't develop a single drop of oil. No one likes the idea of being forced to dance with the devil, as they say, but it's our only alternative."

"My dear friend, you have just described the importance of our mission," said Claudine, pressing the point further. "Subject to solving all the problems, we are committed to diversifying the oil industry to relieve the leverage the Oil Club has been asserting—and will continue to assert. We have not come empty-handed. We have a report indicating that Señor Juan Pablo Perez, Venezuela's oil minister, hopes to conclude his negotiations with his country's oil partners. He is requesting that royalties be increased to fifty percent of gross revenues and that Venezuela be allowed to participate in twenty-five percent of the peripheral service profits derived from its oil."

"I'm aware of those negotiations," conceded the prince. "But our people have been closely monitoring them and report that, without some outside leverage, they are doubtful of Venezuela's ability to achieve such dramatic changes."

"We think they will have all the leverage they will need. Your old friend Mike Stone and Señor Perez have recently smuggled certain files out of Venezuela. Perez believes their contents prove that two members of the Oil Club, the British and American companies, have overcharged their sovereign oil partners. You might be surprised by what those two oil companies are prepared to do."

"I must say, if the minister has concrete evidence, it certainly does bode well for your success," said the prince. "Just one more question, Claudine. Knowing the technical issues and the precedent-setting features of your plan, wouldn't it be more practical if you completed a more manageable prototype project before attempting to raise the full fifteen billion dollars?

"Obtaining the cooperation of Middle Eastern nations is going to be one of our greatest challenges. If we scaled the size of the prototype properly, I think I might be able to find a way to produce the undeveloped, yet proven, oil fields you will need," the prince explained.

Chapter 17

DEAN'S TRAP

Following the road toward Castle Dome Ranch until they could see the high-arched entrance, the two Samson operatives pulled off and parked behind a cluster of palo verde trees. After unloading the horses from the trailer they'd rented in Douglas, they checked their makeshift map, marked their starting point, and rode north along what they presumed to be the eastern boundary of the ranch. The land was flat. The dried winter grass, creosote bushes, cholla cacti, and an assortment of desert trees made it difficult, from ground level, to see any great distance.

Dismounting and proceeding on foot, they walked along the sandy bottom of a mesquite-lined arroyo until they were within several hundred yards of the ranch headquarters. "I think this is as close as we can go," said the smaller of the two men. "Any farther, and we take the risk of being seen."

With the aid of high-powered binoculars, the taller man, who had a pockmarked face, could see the buildings of the main compound, the big barn, the working corrals, and the nearby dome. But he still couldn't see the faces of the people clearly. "We need to move closer," he said.

"I'm afraid we might be seen. You remember our instructions.

Why don't we find a way to get up on top of the dome? From up there we'd be close enough to clearly see anybody who comes or goes. We could take some pictures and make a log of all the arrivals and departures. It shouldn't take us very long to determine if Stone, Perez, and his family are staying at the ranch."

They rode back to the trailer, loaded the horses, and headed back to the bridge that connected Douglas, Arizona, to Agua Prieta, Mexico. On the other side, the two operatives found a deeply rutted road that appeared to follow the perimeter of the ranch south of the border. They went along it until they were opposite the dome. Finding a secluded place to park the trailer, they unloaded and re-saddled the horses. Half an hour of careful searching yielded what appeared to be the southern entrance of the lava tube that led to the cylindrical mountain. The mine-like entrance was protected by a door made of heavy wood and wrought iron and was secured by a bulky iron lock.

After dismounting and studying the rusty old lock, the pock-marked agent took the heavy four-battery metal flashlight from his knapsack and, with one healthy blow, knocked open the well-rusted lock. With a flashlight held in one hand and a drawn revolver in the other, each of the two agents slowly made his way into the dark cave.

It had apparently been years since anyone had passed this way. Their progress was hindered by the occasional hissing of rattlesnakes resenting the invasion of their dark, cool domain. The two city-boy agents may have been paid killers, but in this strange environment, the thought of snakes terrified them. They moved slowly, focusing the beams of their flashlights on the trail ahead of them and on the cave walls on either side. Some of the snakes were frozen in place by the blinding light, some coiled to strike, and others slithered away. Standing very still, the two agents took careful aim and shot in the general direction of the slithering serpents.

After several hundred feet, they could see a light at the end of the cave. Arriving at its source, they found themselves in the center of a circle of light made by the sun shining through an opening above. A winding corkscrew path had been carved into the irregular inner surface of the conical walls.

Still mindful of snakes, the two men worked their way up the path until they emerged into the bright sunlight at the top of the dome. From the elevated site, it seemed as if they could see forever. They took up positions from behind the low walls constructed of piled rock that looked directly down on the ranch headquarters. From there they could carefully study everything happening in the compound below. Through their binoculars, they watched many people coming and going, but no one resembled Mike Stone, Señor Perez, or any members of his family.

A vigilant ranch hand, having noticed one of the men on top of the dome, reported his presence to the ranch manager. One of the vaqueros was dispatched to relock the heavy door. Satisfied their quarry wasn't there, the two men retreated down the path to the bottom of the dome and back through the cave toward Mexico. Reaching the end of the path, they found that the door at the end of the tunnel had been closed and wouldn't open. At first they thought it was just stuck, but after an hour's work they concluded that someone had relocked the heavy door from the outside. This time, their flashlights and guns were no match for the door's wrought-iron hinges.

Retreating back through the cave, they found two other tunnels whose entrances were also securely locked. With their flashlights running out of power, and still fearful of the hissing snakes, they made their way back to the top of the dome. Seated near the water storage tank, they began to realize they were trapped.

The larger man with the pockmarked face suggested, "Maybe we should stop for a few minutes and take stock of our situation. When we don't report or show up, someone in our organization is bound to become curious. It shouldn't take long before they send an operative to Douglas looking for us."

The smaller, more quick-witted man responded, "What good will that do? How will anybody find us clear out here in the desert and on top of this old dome? We could be here for a while!"

Searching around, they were surprised to discover the top of the dome was supplied with plenty of food, water, and heavy blankets—everything they would need.

Night fell on the two disgruntled men. Each man tried to cheer himself with the thought that, sooner or later, when they didn't show up, their fellow operatives would have to visit the ranch.

Finally, the smaller of the two men said, "Maybe our situation is not as precarious as it first appeared. Nobody at the ranch knows we are here; we have plenty of food and water; and from up here we will be able to see our guys when they arrive. Signaling for their attention shouldn't be so difficult."

More than once, one of the vaqueros had reported seeing two men on top of the dome. Their pale complexions, their manner of dress, and the fact they weren't recognized as previous guests all served to make them easy to spot. Adding the vaqueros' information to the report of the busted lock, Steve Connors surmised that two strange men must now be trapped inside the dome.

Chapter 18

TRIP TO DALLAS

Dressed as ranch workers, Mike and Juan Pablo boarded the afternoon bus that took the day laborers back to Douglas. No one—least of all the two Samson operatives glued to their binoculars—took notice of the two deeply tanned men shuffling along, stooped over, carrying old cardboard-like suitcases bound together by pieces of rope. They wore faded shirts, worn Levi's, old sandals, bleached serapes, and sombreros that had seen better days. The disguise was flawless.

Once the bus reached Douglas, Mike and Juan Pablo disembarked and, along with some of their fellow passengers, began their trek over the bridge that led toward Agua Prieta.

After purchasing tickets in the local bus station, the two men shuffled out to the waiting bus. *Is the added security of taking the Mexican bus worth riding 250 miles on this rusted hulk of what must have at one time been a school bus?* thought Mike.

The original yellow color was now covered by what looked like blue and yellow house paint that had been applied by hand with a worn brush. Spare tires hung from hooks along both sides. Water bags were suspended from the front and rear bumpers. Bailing wire held down the dented hood. All the passenger windows had been adjusted to their permanent position: down. The windshield was pitted and cracked. The rack on the roof had already begun to be loaded with the passengers' most cherished cargo, crates filled with live chickens.

Inside the bus, a caked layer of dust was the paint of choice. The wicker seats were ripped, the metal frames bent, the overhead racks jammed full of the passengers' personal cargo. Worst of all, the smell of perspiration, urine, and old vomit assaulted Mike and Juan Pablo and brought on waves of nausea.

No two adjacent seats were available, which Mike thought was probably a good thing; the companions wouldn't be able to talk together in English, guaranteeing that they wouldn't draw unwanted attention to themselves.

Periodically, the bus stopped for what seemed to be extra-long breaks at every small village. People would get off and others would get on. Loading and unloading their precious cargo took time. No one was in a hurry.

If the bus's scheduled stops didn't thoroughly irritate Mike, the unscheduled stops succeeded in doing so. First, they had to stop to refill the ancient, leaky, overheated radiator with water from the canvas bags. Next, they had to change a tire. After five hours, they had covered only the first hundred miles of their journey. Mike alternated between trying to nap and filling his mind with thoughts of Cecelia and what she was doing with her family in Hong Kong.

It was well after dark when the bus finally arrived in Ciudad Juarez. Tired, hungry, and thirsty, Mike couldn't wait until they crossed over the border into El Paso. The promise of a Coke, a hamburger, a shower, and clean sheets dominated his every thought.

The next morning, the two *gringos*, dressed in sport shirts, slacks, and shined shoes and carrying small canvas bags, appeared at the Greyhound bus station in El Paso. After purchasing two tickets to Dallas, they boarded the clean, luxurious bus, sat together, and spent time swapping stories about their recent escapade.

The next morning, after a night of restless sleep, the two tired and very hungry travelers found a coffee shop located across the street from Dallas's Union Station. After asking the waitress for the table in front of the big plate-glass window, they settled down to order huevos rancheros, an extra side of patty sausage, a tall glass of freshly squeezed orange juice, and a big pot of coffee. From their vantage point, they could watch anybody entering or leaving the train station.

The express from New York had just pulled in. It wasn't difficult for them to spot Smith and Jones among the arriving passengers. They were dressed in black pin-striped suits, white dress shirts, striped ties, and highly polished black dress shoes, and they were carrying large leather briefcases that appeared to be heavy.

Placing his hand on Juan Pablo's arm as he started to rise, Mike said, "Why don't we stay here for a moment and see who else might be getting off the train?"

Two more men, dressed in slacks, sport shirts, windbreakers, and heavy rubber-soled shoes were among the last to leave the station. They were clearly intent on following the black-suited lawyers.

After about fifteen minutes, Smith and Jones became noticeably irritated that they hadn't been met at the station. Seemingly oblivious to the two men in windbreakers lurking a few yards away, watching their every move, the attorneys climbed into a waiting taxi. The men in windbreakers motioned for the next yellow cab in line.

Mike and Juan Pablo were considering their next move when what appeared to be two cowboys approached their table. One of them said, "Mike Stone? Maybe I should introduce myself. My name is Don Cerreta, better known to you as Mr. Smith. My friend is Mr. Jones."

"Wait . . ." said Mike. "If you two are Smith and Jones, who are the two men dressed in dark suits who just got off the train?"

"They're two Secret Service agents assigned to act as decoys in the event the Samson people were smart enough to figure out our next move. They're going to their hotel to check in and wait to see what happens next."

"Designated decoys?" said Mike. "What made you think Samson could have possibly figured out our next move? We couldn't have been more careful in how we informed my father we needed your help."

"Relax," said Don. "You didn't make any mistakes. When the Samson operatives failed to find you at Castle Dome and retrieve those files, we assumed they would anticipate your needing our assistance. Without our conversion of your information into an appropriate legal format, the information would be useless."

"Even so, how were they able to learn which lawyers my father would select to come to Dallas?" asked Mike.

"We assumed, with all the resources available to an investigation firm as sophisticated as Samson, they wouldn't find it difficult to discover which outside law firms the Stone City Bank uses for different kinds of cases," said Don. "Once they identified the firm, it was only a question of waiting to determine which lawyers were selected to work on your case. All they had to do was wait for us to leave New York and follow us wherever we were going. Apparently, they failed to realize the two men they have been following are Secret Service agents."

"Even so, aren't you worried about your agents' safety?" Mike asked.

Smiling, Smith said, "Oh, they'll be all right. I doubt those two Samson operatives will try anything until you, Señor Perez, and the files appear on the scene. It's those files they are after."

"What if you're wrong?" asked Mike. "What happens when we don't show? How do you know they won't decide to seize the two men they believe to be the two of you and hold them hostage?"

"That's certainly a possibility," said Don, "but I doubt very much it will be a problem. Additional Secret Service agents are waiting in both the adjacent rooms and the one directly across the hall from the room reserved for our dark-suited friends."

Chapter 19

THE CHINA PLAN

Two weeks was a long time to spend traveling among China's many provincial capitals. Having her father's DC-3 at her disposal was making a long, arduous trip feel a little easier. Cecelia was also pleased to be accompanied by Ted Lee. At each stop, he would introduce her to the provincial leaders and businessmen, the men who played such prominent roles in China's national government and economy.

Despite the many stops and the long schedule, it seemed to Cecelia there was no sense of urgency on the part of her hosts to speed things along—in fact, quite the opposite. In addition to their traditional ways of greeting people of perceived prominence, each of her hosts appeared to be intent on demonstrating their gratitude by extending their best and most formal hospitality. They spent quite a bit of time on local tours, exquisite dining, and friendly conversation. They clearly wanted to become better acquainted with the charming representative of America's banking system. Any discussion of primary agenda items could only proceed once the traditional rituals had been fully observed.

However, once these formalities had been completed, it didn't take long for each of her new hosts to come right to the point.

"Miss Chang," said one, "much of our gold and our cash has already been transported to Hong Kong for safekeeping. Our problem is not that of transferring our wealth to safety, it's converting it into an equally secure, liquid, and income-producing investment. About half of our liquid wealth has been converted into gold bearer bonds and sent elsewhere for safekeeping. The remaining balance is still deposited in local vaults.

"Should the Communists succeed in occupying our province," the provincial leader continued, "we will lose the income regularly derived from our lands, local taxes, and other sources. It's entirely possible that we will have to rely on the income or profits generated from our exportable wealth."

Knowing she was expected to respond, Cecelia decided to be equally direct. "If the American government is receptive to your suggestion, would you be willing to invest a substantial amount of your remaining unconverted gold into interest-bearing government-guaranteed bonds, the proceeds of which will be used to finance the development of new oil reserves by independent operating oil companies?"

"Miss Chang," he said, "you have a saying in the United States: one hand washes the other. If we support your oil development bond program, will it be reasonable to assume we will be accorded the same respect and cooperation when the time comes to finance the growth of our local industries?"

Cecelia understood the relevance of the question and the implications of her response. "You are in reality asking two questions. First, will lenders accept the oil development bonds as alternate collateral for lending purposes? Clearly, the answer to that part of the question is yes. I assume you understand the nature of the loan request must necessarily provide supporting information required to document the economic feasibility of each request. The second question I understand you to be asking is, Is American

West prepared to provide you with access to the American capital markets? I can assure you that, subject to the satisfaction of established bank lending criteria, American West will not only make its funds available for such purposes but also, if necessary, will act as a lead bank and ask our correspondent banks to join us when your demands exceed our capacity."

―――

On the sixth day, almost halfway through her tour, a very tired Cecelia was back on board Tai-Pan's plane when she began to feel light-headed and weak. She told Ted Lee, and he immediately directed the pilot to adjust their course and head for Hong Kong. An ambulance was waiting to transport Cecelia to her family's preferred hospital.

The next morning, awake, refreshed, and clearheaded, she saw her nervous father sitting in one corner of the room and Ted, looking concerned, in the other. The subject of the unfinished tour didn't come up until Cecelia had finished her breakfast.

Moving to the end of her bed, Ted announced, "Ray Tolles and Bob Arnold are waiting outside. May I invite them to join us? I'm sure you remember meeting them here in Hong Kong. Ray Tolles is president of the Colonial Bank of Hong Kong, Arnold the president of the Bank of Shanghai."

Once all three bankers were standing around her bed, Ted continued. "Cecelia, we are here to talk about the balance of your tour. Rather than expose you to any further harm, we want you to go home, get well, and allow us the opportunity to finish the tour for you."

"But I feel fine," Cecelia insisted. "I appreciate what you are trying to do, but I don't think it will be necessary. Give me one more day's rest and I'll be ready to resume the tour. Besides, I'm afraid if my friends in China learn of my condition, it might affect how they feel about supporting our program."

"Cecelia, it's important you listen to the three of us," said Ted. "We were concerned you'd feel this way, but Ray, Bob, and I are here to assure you we can carry on with the introduction of your program. Between the materials you have developed and what you have taught us, we feel comfortable about completing the unfinished portion of your tour. After all, everyone on whom you would be calling is a customer of one of our three banks. It's much more important that you return a healthy woman with a complete collection of the information you've gathered."

Cecelia was silent, but the bankers could tell she was not convinced.

"You're going home," continued Ted, "even if we have to chain you to a wheelchair. All the arrangements have been made. In a little while, two of the biggest orderlies you have ever seen are going to appear in the room, and they have strict orders to deliver you to a plane we have standing by."

"Gentlemen, I appreciate what you are trying to do," said Cecelia. "I think the more appropriate course of action is to give it a couple of days before we make any drastic decisions."

Chapter 20

CLOSING THE TRAP

The Secret Service agents quickly notified Steve Connors. Early the next morning, the four of them appeared at the ranch. Concerned that their arrival might alert the two Samson operatives, they took extra care to dress so they would appear to be cattle buyers, similar to other men who regularly visited the ranch.

The four athletic-looking men—dressed in Levi's, checked, long-sleeved cotton shirts, and cowboy boots—were being conducted to the corrals containing the cattle that were for sale.

The lead agent talked to Steve while the other three made their independent assessments of the ranch and the dome. After making certain their conversation would appear as two men haggling over price, he asked, "Is there any way you can get my men into the dome without being noticed? We want to be in position before the Samson people decide they want to rescue their buddies."

Connors noticed that one of the other agents was looking in the direction of the lava tube, the one that was closest to the ranch compound and in clear sight.

"That entrance is not the one you want to use," Steve said. "It's longer and not as easy to pass through as the entrance around the other side, which is well hidden and out of sight of the two men on top of the dome. Unless you know what you're looking for, it's difficult to find. It's the one we use."

Connors went on to tell them exactly how to find the entrance, and the lead agent gave his men directions on how to carry out the operation. Before leaving, he turned back to Connors and asked, "Is there something you can do to remove the Perez family safely?"

Remaining inside, out of sight of the two Samson operatives, Señora Perez and her two sons waited until the sun had set and the moonless darkness of night had settled in before venturing out to the barn and the waiting saddled horses.

Led by one of the vaqueros, the family headed out on what during the day would have been a picturesque ride through the high Arizona desert. The guide, who was intimately familiar with the terrain, led them through the darkness, along an old and seldom-used path, until they reached a red Ford station wagon.

Brazenly, the four unsuspecting Samson operatives drove out to the ranch, crossed under the large archway, and pulled to a stop in front of the main house. Identifying themselves as federal immigration officials, they produced what appeared to be valid credentials and warrants. They entered the house with the permission of Steve, looked around, and asked a lot of questions. Convinced there was no one of interest in the main house, they extended their search to include the other buildings—the guesthouse, the barns, the bunkhouses, and even the working families' living quarters.

Watching what was happening below them, the two Samson operatives atop the dome built a fire and began to wave. The smoke did its job, attracting the attention of their fellow agents.

"What and who is that up there?" one of them asked the foreman.

"It's an old sanctuary that Mr. Dean's ancestors would use to protect themselves from Indian bands and Mexican troops," said Connors. "I have no idea who those two men are. They're certainly none of our people. We keep the gates to all the caves locked. It's a well-known rule that no one is allowed up there, and I have the only key."

Showing the agents the large brass key, he continued. "A few days ago, one of my men noticed that the lock on the Mexican entrance had been pried open. He reported replacing the lock, assuming whoever had broken in had long since departed. I'll be happy to open the door if you want to look inside."

Motioning for the men to follow him over to a large storage closet, he reached inside and said, "You might want these." He handed them each a flashlight and a long-handled broom.

Confused, one of the Samson operatives asked, "What do we do with these?"

"They're for the snakes," the foreman said as he walked away.

"For the snakes? What the hell are you talking about?"

"You'll find out."

―――

The four Secret Service agents were already inside the dome. Two of them had taken up positions behind two large boulders where they could train their rifles, loaded with high-impact shells, on the outcropping of rock that hung over the narrow trail leading to the top of the dome.

The other two Secret Service agents assumed positions from which they could get clear shots at anyone trying to proceed up or down from the point below the outcropping.

The reverberating noise from the tunnel alerted the Secret Service agents that the Samson operatives had entered the old volcano. It was hard for them not to laugh as they heard the curses about the snakes and the occasional gunshots.

Hearing voices, the two Samson operatives atop the dome leaned over the edge of the opening and peered down. Anxious to leave, they started down the path to meet their fellow agents, who were beginning to cautiously make their way up the steep corkscrew trail.

The Secret Service agents waited until the two groups met, about halfway up, in an exposed part of the narrow trail. Stepping out from his hiding place, the agent in charge, with the assistance of his bullhorn, announced: "We are United States Secret Service agents. Throw down your weapons and return to the bottom of the path, and you won't be hurt."

Caught totally by surprise, all six Samson operatives froze in their attempt to figure out what was happening. Realizing they had unwittingly walked into a trap, two of them began to scramble back toward the top. Two others opened fire in the general direction of the bullhorn, and the other two retreated down the path to the protection of the rock outcropping.

The two operatives trying to reach the top of the dome were fully exposed. From the protection of his rock, the lead Secret Service agent announced his second and final warning.

Watching the men continue their effort to reach the top, the lead agent motioned to one of the sharpshooters. Hearing the single shot and watching the other man fall, the second Samson operative froze in place, dropped his weapon, and raised his hands.

One of the Secret Service agents who had the rifle with the high-impact shells took aim on the jagged rock formation just above the outcropping and fired. The concussion dislodged a surprising amount of rock, which fell on top of the two crouching men, pinning them against the inner wall.

Witnessing what had just happened, the three remaining Samson operatives lowered themselves onto their stomachs and began inching their way toward the bottom. Hidden from view by the outer edge of the trail, they managed to make their way to the last turn in the path before it straightened out on the final stretch before reaching the floor of the cave.

As they slowly rounded the final turn, they were greeted by two Secret Service agents with rifles trained directly on them. Captured in short order, they were soon joined by their dusty and bruised colleagues who had been pulled out from under the fallen rock.

The trap had been sprung. One of the Samson operatives had been killed, and five had been captured.

Within fifteen minutes, Washington had received the Secret Service's report.

Pleased with their report, Secretary Ainsworth called Chairman Malone. "Roger, it'll be interesting to see what we can learn from the five captured Samson operatives. I'm going to have them transported to our special interrogation center at Quantico."

"I also have some good news to report myself," said Chairman Malone. "Morgan has just received a call from Jacques. Apparently, Mike sent Jacques a message asking that two of the bank's best attorneys be sent to Dallas. According to Morgan, Mike needs legal assistance to determine if the information he and

Perez smuggled out of Mexico is adequate to support charges of fraud, to define damages, and to determine that the oil companies have been dealing in bad faith."

"Roger, don't you think we should tell the President?" asked Secretary Ainsworth.

"Not yet. Who knows—when we understand the consequences of the Smith and Jones report, maybe there will be something else we will want to do. I think we can afford to wait. From the way things have been going, I'm not so certain who needs to be protected from whom."

Chapter 21

INDONESIA

Four days later, having dissuaded her father and Ted from sending her back to the United States, Cecelia was ready to resume her tour. For the first time since her kidnapping, she was forced to exercise a strong and conscious personal discipline. Balancing the demands of meeting provincial leaders and businessmen with her needs for sleep and a simplified diet introduced an entirely new dimension of personal behavior to her travels.

As she and Ted were finishing the last of their two-week China tour, they were making plans for their next trip to Indonesia and Malaysia. They expanded the length of their itinerary to include added time for rest and relaxation.

Ted was eager to talk about the next leg of their trip, and Cecelia was happy to indulge him as he gave her impromptu geography and history lessons. "After we take some time off to relax on some of the world's most spectacular beaches, you are going to find things in Southeast Asia quite different," said Ted. "Unlike the great landmass of China, Indonesia is an eight-province island nation that is rich in oil and many other natural resources. At last count, I think there were approximately a hundred and fifty million people, eighty percent of whom are Muslim. Geographically, it is a country divided by oceans, mountains, and dense jungles.

"For centuries, Indonesia has been under Dutch colonial rule, and more recently the country was occupied by the Japanese. After the war, following their withdrawal, national independence has become a vital issue of the native population. A forty-day period followed the Japanese withdrawal, before a small British expeditionary force of two thousand arrived to claim the Allied interests. During that six-week period, the Indonesians installed their own national government, the same government that had been organized and trained by the Japanese to be their national government.

"Indonesia's new national army, a Japanese-trained military unit originally developed to protect its postwar interests, was waiting to repel the two-thousand-man British expeditionary force. Defeated and forced to withdraw, what remained of that British force—troops conscripted from India and Australia—retreated to Darwin.

"Concerned about protecting its oil interests, the Dutch government quietly garrisoned a hundred and ten thousand of its own troops on the island nation. Until now, the Dutch have made no move to use the troops to take control. Their presence, however, leaves no doubt as to the Dutch government's ultimate intention of seizing both political and military control. They are only waiting to determine if such a move would receive support from the United Nations and the United States.

"The situation in Indonesia is a time bomb waiting to explode. Can you imagine the sensitivity of the problem the American government and the United Nations must be facing? On one hand, they are being asked to support the economic and political claims of historical allies. On the other, they are being asked to support a new popular government.

"Meeting with all these people is going to be an interesting experience. Who knows, maybe someone in the United States government will be interested in what you learn."

Postwar travel throughout the island nation of Indonesia was difficult at best. One day, Ted and Cecelia found themselves in a worn surplus military aircraft, flying over broad expanses of open sea. Because they were unpressurized, the noisy, drafty planes were forced to fly at lower, more turbulent altitudes. Despite their discomfort, neither of them wanted to ask questions about the experience of the pilot, the maintenance record of the plane, or the onboard communication and navigation equipment.

On other days, they traveled on old trains previously used to move troops and equipment during the war. The few surviving coal-burning, steam-driven locomotives had long since seen their best days. The tracks showed their age, wartime damage, and evidence of many repairs. Travel was slow and bumpy. The passenger cars, with their hard wooden bench seats, were dusty and ill-suited for long trips.

The preferred forms of transportation between cities and inland destinations were their local hosts' well-maintained Packards, Chryslers, Lincolns, and Buicks, all painted black. Pockmarked, corduroyed, and deeply rutted roads required a driver to proceed slowly, carefully avoiding the obstacles that would increase passenger discomfort or damage his boss's most prized possession.

Cecelia and Ted were forced to choose between the rolled-up window, which led to a hot and humid interior atmosphere, and the windblown, dusty condition when the car's windows were rolled down. Convoys of at least three cars were required to carry Cecelia's security detachment and to protect her car from possible land mines, snipers, or bandits, all of which could be waiting along their route.

Traveling by boat was the most enjoyable. Owned by local plantation, factory, and mine owners, the amazing assortment of oceangoing craft appeared to have escaped the attention of the

Japanese occupational forces. They varied from motorized junks and prewar pleasure craft to reconditioned navy patrol torpedo boats, all of which were able to move through the trade winds and open seas at surprising speed.

Chapter 22

THE FIRST ATTACK

As accustomed as she was to Asian cooking, Cecelia was totally unprepared for the highly seasoned procession of one unfamiliar dish after another. Frequently not knowing the source of the meat contained in one of these "new experiences," she was relieved when the meals contained only a combination of fish and fruit, vegetables, or rice.

Not wishing to appear unappreciative, she never refused any of the food, nor questioned sanitary practices or the source of the water. Her intestinal tract's growing reaction to this strange diet remained a well-kept secret. Ignoring her growing fatigue and the growing symptoms of her approaching illness, Cecelia always made a point of appearing to arrive fresh and prepared to talk to each of her hosts and their guests.

She listened, answered their questions, and asked questions of her own. Possessing a good memory, she made mental notes of each conversation, always associating them with some unusual visual observation that would help her remember what was said.

Cecelia had asked Ted to bring his thirty-six-millimeter Rolleiflex box camera and take pictures of all the different people with whom she conversed. Understanding the importance of matching the pictures with Cecelia's notes, Ted, in his polite way, would ask each subject for the proper spelling of their names, their addresses, and a few details about their background.

No matter the hour or her level of fatigue, Cecelia would transcribe her mental notes of each conversation into an indexed series of notebooks, one for each location, before she retired each night.

Word of Cecelia's interest in local problems was spreading, and Ted was receiving more requests for her visits from local businessmen who were concerned about preserving their wealth in the event of a Dutch takeover. As much as Ted was hoping Cecelia would complete her expanding tour, he was becoming concerned about her deteriorating health and loss of weight. Not certain how to deal with the growing dilemma, one morning he approached her and said, "Don't you think it's time to cut our trip short and return home?"

"Ted," she replied, "this is our only chance to see things from the bottom up. The bank is counting on me to submit a complete report. As long as we're here, and I can keep going, I want to take advantage of every opportunity to improve our understanding of what is really happening out here."

Ted frowned. "Cecelia, I don't want to alarm you, but we have been repeatedly warned about possible attacks. The success of one meeting after another has to be threatening those who want to recolonize Indonesia and take back their oil. Let's not forget, there are a large number of Dutch citizens, interned by the Japanese, who have been released and remain here in what they regard as their country. We've been out here long enough for them to have learned of our presence and make whatever preparations are needed to attack us."

"Listen, Ted, I know you're worried. But give me some time to think about it."

That night, they were guests of Lawrence Oh, one of Indonesia's few integrated timber- and finished-lumber sawmill owner-operators. When they arrived, Cecelia took notice of the high and thick perimeter walls and the guard towers that surrounded the company's headquarters and residential compound. It reminded her of a Hollywood set of an old Western frontier military fort.

Dinner was served in an elevated, open-air, Polynesian-style gazebo, through which warm tropical breezes slowly flowed. Ted and Cecelia were asked to sit to the left and the right of their host at a large, doughnut-shaped, highly polished redwood table.

They were joined by some of Lawrence Oh's closest friends: business owners, merchants, bankers, the local mayor, the regional military commander, and the area's labor leader. The selection of the guests, the elegance of the dinner, and the serving of such fine foods and wines had been carefully planned. It was all intended to leave no doubt as to the importance of Cecelia's visit. Absent from the meeting were any of the local gentry, representatives of the big oil companies, and those who favored recolonization by the Dutch.

The grounds were lit with kerosene torches. Their flickering light made this oasis in the middle of the tropical island seem like a quiet, peaceful resort. The dinner had been organized to proceed slowly, giving the guests ample opportunity to ask questions of Cecelia and Ted. A servant stood behind each of the guests, prepared to serve each of the specially prepared dishes, one course at a time. Empty wineglasses were immediately refilled, each dish from each course cleared away to make room for the next.

Cecelia was concentrating on a conversation with the man seated to her left, when suddenly, without warning, the tranquility of the evening was shattered by large explosions, the rattle of automatic weapons, and the glare of bright yellow-white flares fired into the dark sky.

Appearing calm but embarrassed, Lawrence said, "I'm certain that our security guards will bring things under control, but in the interim may I suggest that we retire to the safety of the nearby air raid bunker we used during the war? We will be quite safe there until all this is over."

Secure inside the well-protected bunker, Cecelia sat very still, ignoring the noise created by all the gunfire, exploding grenades, and flares outside the bunker. Some of the servants had thought to bring wine bottles and glasses. *How can it be?* Cecelia thought. *All these people are carrying on conversations as if nothing were happening outside. How can they remain so calm?*

Concerned with thoughts of their own safety and engaged in nervous conversation, the host and his other guests failed to notice the change in Cecelia as she sat huddled behind some ammunition crates, clearly in distress. Her arms were wrapped tightly around her, her head bowed, and she was silently crying.

Ted was the first to notice what had happened to Cecelia and was reminded of Mike's early descriptions of what he saw when he first entered Cecelia's hospital room following her kidnapping. Sitting down next to her, Ted put his arms around her, and whispered into her ear, "It will be okay, Cecelia. As soon as this shooting stops, I'll take you home. We've been out here way too long."

"Oh, Mike you've found me!" Cecelia murmured, staring absently into the distance. "I was so worried you wouldn't come."

Not quite certain what he should do, Ted continued to sit with his arm around her. He stayed there until the others had filed out of the bunker once the firing stopped. In a soft voice, he said, "The attack is over, Cecelia. Let me take you to your room; you will be quite safe there."

She didn't respond. Then, quite unexpectedly, she said, "Ted, I'm okay—don't you think we should join the others? We don't want to appear impolite."

Despite the unmistakable clarity of what she said, Ted could still see her fragile and strained appearance.

Seated back at the dinner table, Ted was anxious to deflect any questions that might be addressed to Cecelia. "That attack seemed to be over as soon as it started!" he said to the host. "Do you mind telling us what happened?"

"Living out here, between these wonderful forests and the river, one learns to be prepared for almost any eventuality," said Lawrence. "We still have to concern ourselves with the remnants of the former Dutch colonists, who resent our presence. For all intents and purposes, we have what you might call an undeclared civil war going on in this country.

"We are fortunate. The Dutch army can't move without the support of the outside world. Should they decide to proceed independently, our new national army is prepared to resist them at any cost. It's important the outside world understand that a very bloody war and destruction of all the oil facilities will be the result of the Netherlands' effort to recolonize our country."

Lawrence, always the consummate host, continued by saying, "Perhaps this has been a good thing; none of our people were hurt, and you have just witnessed a good example of what we hope you will explain to your friends back in America."

He paused for a moment to let the full significance of what he had just said sink in. "Miss Chang, now, if you will excuse the rude and unplanned interruption, I would like to finish telling you about my business and our hopes for our new country. In addition to its vast oil reserves, Indonesia is blessed with many other resources, a large and inexpensive labor force, and the will to develop both. My lumber company and the local businesses of some of my other guests are representative of thousands of small companies scattered throughout our island nation.

"Take my lumber operation for an example. Before the war, several generations of my family owned a logging lease that permitted us to harvest the different sources of high-quality hardwoods. We used hand-operated crosscut saws to fell the trees. With the aid of large axes, we cut off the branches before teams of oxen pulled the trees to the nearest river, where they were floated downstream to our collection points. Fastened together in large rafts, with the help of primitive oceangoing tugboats, the downed trees were transported to our millpond, the same one you can see right over there. Once we finished sorting the logs for variety and size, we organized them into separate queues for processing through our sawmills. The large logs were cut into bridge timber, structural posts, and beams; the smaller trees were cut into dimensioned lumber.

"Before the war, our business was regarded as a dirty, messy operation, an unglamorous business of marginal profitability. Correspondingly, it escaped the attention of the Dutch colonial government."

Pausing to make certain that all his guests' glasses had been refilled, Lawrence continued. "Once the war started, the Japanese needed more finished lumber. They shipped in modern equipment, which allowed us to increase the volume of our production and produce the standard-sized lumber needed for ship repair and residential and military compound construction. Now that the war is over, we have the equipment, the wood, the labor, and the technical expertise to supply the emerging demands of what is fast becoming a high-growth construction market throughout Indonesia. No longer would my company, in its revitalized form, be immune from colonial attention."

"Very interesting," said Cecelia. "Can you tell me about the most important challenges you must overcome before you can become a major supplier of wood products in this region?"

Without hesitating he said, "We have to know that we can operate independently of the Dutch colonial rule that threatens us. Until that threat is removed, we can't attract the financial resources or enter into the kind of long contracts required to take advantage of the emerging markets in Southeast Asia."

———

It wasn't until they were headed to their respective guest rooms in Lawrence's home that Ted said to Cecelia, "If you will excuse me, I want to talk to Mr. Oh for a while longer. I need to develop a better understanding of what that attack was all about. Tomorrow morning, when I file my report, I anticipate that I am going to be asked a lot of questions."

Back in her own quarters, despite the lateness of the hour, her fatigue, and her frayed nerves, Cecelia faithfully sat down at the small writing desk and began to document all that had happened: the names and comments of her host and each of his guests and her own observations and opinions. When she finally finished, she carefully placed her notebook in her heavy leather briefcase, locked it, and placed the chain that held the key around her neck.

Chapter 23

MEETING IN GENEVA

It was July 18, 1946. After speaking to Jacques in New York, Claudine had reached Mike in Dallas. She explained her fruitful conversations with David and Prince Habib before asking him to meet them in Switzerland. When Mike had suggested bringing along Juan Pablo, Claudine had enthusiastically agreed.

Joining Prince Habib and Sir David Marcus, Claudine, Mike, and Juan Pablo were ready to go to work at the luxurious and exclusive Beau Rivage hotel. Built in 1865, this ninety-three-suite hotel provided its distinguished guests with magnificent views of Lake Geneva and Mont Blanc.

Known for its distinctive architecture, luxurious atmosphere, and incomparable food and service, the Beau, as it was known, catered to the same clientele that could be found at the Winter Palace in Cairo, Claridge's in London, the Ritz in Paris, and the Plaza in New York. For the next four days, the hotel would be their home. The prince's staff had arranged for everything they would need.

The living room portion of the Imperial Suite had been converted into a conference room where the group could meet in total privacy. Meals were prepared in the hotel's special kitchen and were served in the privacy of the suite's spacious dining room. Overlooking the lake, the room could be used also for relaxation and casual conversation. For security, each of the adjacent bedroom suites could be entered only from the common living area.

As an additional precaution, the entire top floor had been reserved for their meeting. With the exception of the carefully screened service personnel and security guards, no one else was allowed on the floor.

Prince Habib and Sir David Marcus were standing in the middle the living room, enjoying the magnificent view of Lake Geneva, when Mike, Juan Pablo, and Claudine were escorted into the elegant suite.

After greeting Claudine, the prince turned toward the oil minister. "Welcome to Geneva. I don't know how to adequately express my respect for you and my appreciation of your work. It's hard to imagine how one man could bring about so much change in our industry. On behalf of my government and my friends in the Middle East, I would like to express our optimism regarding what we hope will be a productive visit."

Unaccustomed as he was to receiving such a fine compliment from a person of the prince's stature, Juan Pablo hesitated before answering. "Thank you for your kind remarks. I hope you realize that the people in my country think of themselves as only a very small part of the world's petroleum community. I regard the invitation to join you here in Geneva as a great honor. I am looking forward to our meeting."

Turning to his old friend and extending his hand, the prince said, "Mike, what a pleasure it is to see you again after all these years. For some reason that I don't totally comprehend, I've missed my straight-talking, tell-it-like-it-is old friend and study mate."

Shaking his hand, Mike said, "I've always valued those two short years we spent in Cambridge. As I remember, you and I were able to create what at least *we* believed to be some remarkable insight into a few of the cases we were asked to present. It's going to be interesting to see if we can be as constructive when the problems are far more complex and a bit more real."

The others, who were closely watching the initial encounter between these two powerful personalities, couldn't have been more pleased.

Well-rested and relaxed, they were all poised to start what promised to be three days of grueling work when the prince said, "Before we start working through the prepared agenda, I have another subject that I would like to discuss. No matter how quickly we are able to introduce the desired diversity, the major companies will still be in control of demand, distribution, and pricing of oil for a significant period of time. In the interim, before we are able to bring the new production on stream, retribution from the major oil companies could be a serious problem. Those of us who will be exposed to their wrath believe we may need to think about how we can protect ourselves. How would you feel if we spent some time talking about the Texas Railroad Commission?"

Mike's face lit up. "Congratulations! I see that you have been doing your homework!" he said, handing the prince a bound document. "Knowing this issue might come up, I thought we should be prepared. Here's a summary memorandum I had our people prepare."

The prince took the document and turned back to the group. "Perhaps it would be helpful if I explained the significance of the Texas Railroad Commission to the rest of you. Simply put, in the twenties, the larger American oil companies were using their control of delivery systems and refining facilities to manipulate production quotas and wellhead prices for their own self-interests.

"No longer willing to succumb to the financial tyranny of Big Oil, the independent producers organized themselves into a marketing organization known as the Texas Railroad Commission. Laws were passed allowing the Commission to negotiate price and production quotas on a collective bargaining basis. Having leveled the playing field, the oil producers were able to stabilize production and pricing. These laws are still in existence, and they have been tested and retested at every level of the American legal system."

"Once your people have had the opportunity to study this document," said Mike, "I would be happy to introduce you to the people who run the Commission and the lawyers who have handled their cases."

"As I see it, there isn't much difference between our emerging situation and what occurred in Texas," said Prince Habib. "In both instances you have a centralized processor and marketer of petroleum products, and then you have a fragmented population of independent oil producers."

"That's exactly right," said Juan Pablo. "It's a problem that we in Venezuela and our friends in Mexico have been concerned about for a long time. It has been suggested, when appropriate, that I should encourage conversation that will lead to the formation of a properly organized international coalition of oil-producing and oil-exporting countries. In Caracas, for working purposes, we refer to this proposed collective as Petroleum Exporting Countries, or PEC."

Facing the Venezuelan minister, the prince said, "Why don't we agree to establish a working committee? Juan, David, it is my recommendation that the three of us plan to cochair this committee. All in favor?"

Everyone at the table raised their hand.

"Well, that didn't take very long," said the prince. "Why don't we keep moving along?"

Reaching into his briefcase for a second time, Mike withdrew another thick file. "Perhaps this would be the appropriate time for us to discuss a different but related issue. From everything I have been learning, it seems that any long-term relationship with the oil-rich countries of the Middle East must be founded on mutual respect and understanding. This file contains the legal briefs and supporting data that describe, in detail, the two major oil companies' overcharging of refining and transport fees to the Venezuelan government.

"Why wouldn't it make sense for our new committee to use this information to assist emerging oil-rich nations in finding existing fraud or preventing similar practices from occurring in their countries? What better evidence do they need to realize that the major oil companies can't always be trusted?"

"May I see those files?" the prince asked. After taking a minute to read the summary conclusions, he said, "These files look exactly like we hoped they would. When you are forced to deal with companies that have such an exalted opinion of themselves, companies that act with such arrogance, you have no idea how one-sided negotiations on almost any subject can become. Knowing we have this information, and that we have Juan Pablo's assistance in showing us how to use it, will make an enormous contribution."

Turning to face Juan Pablo, the prince asked, "Are you certain that providing us with this information and helping us is something you want to do?"

"If it will help you balance the playing field for negotiations, I will be happy to assist you any way I can," said Juan Pablo. "Besides, I have written permission from my government to provide you with the copies I've just given you."

The prince was smiling, David was smiling, Claudine was smiling, and most important, Juan Pablo was smiling.

Without hesitating, Juan Pablo reached into his briefcase and withdrew another file. "The content contained in these files will tell you everything you need to know as you restructure your existing contracts with your production partner, Pan-Arabia Oil. The terms and conditions in this agreement, among other things, define the increasing of their royalty payments to fifty percent, as well as define the mechanics of how Venezuela is allowed to participate in twenty-five percent of the peripheral service profits. Should Venezuela decide to accept its share of the profits in the form of petroleum production, they will, with the exception of Mexico, control the first commercially viable supply of oil to be produced in Latin America outside the control of major oil companies. Independent American oil companies are already lining up to bid on this production."

Pausing to absorb what he had just heard, the prince said, "What wonderful suggestions! I feel safe in saying that if the same constructive atmosphere I'm seeing here today continues to prevail, you might be surprised how quickly things could change."

Resuming control of the meeting, Mike said, "The time has come for us to complete what we came here to do. Let's concentrate on solving the remaining problems so we can start organizing the prototype project the prince has suggested."

Chapter 24

THE SECOND ATTACK

To reach Indonesia's principal military base, local authorities responsible for Cecelia and Ted's security had strongly suggested they travel on a specially reconstructed military supply train. Boarding the train, the two weary travelers had difficulty understanding what made this train so special. The hard wooden seats looked no different from what they had seen on other military troop trains. The splintered floors clearly revealed their age and history of hard use. The windows were locked shut, and the only sources of air were the open doors at the front and rear of the car.

As they waited for the last of the weapons and their military escort to be loaded into the first and third cars of the three-car train, Cecelia and Ted looked around at what would be their traveling facility for the next eight hours. "Ted," said Cecelia, "remind me why anyone thinks that riding on this train is our best alternative for passing through the mountains and heavy jungle. I must be missing something."

Cecelia was having a difficult time enduring the hard seats and the hot, humid, dust-laden air while the slow-moving train made its way up the mountainous jungle terrain separating one side of the island from the other.

Lost in studying her notes from previous meetings, Cecelia was startled by the sound of two thunderous explosions, one in front and one behind the train. She felt the car brake to a sudden stop. Almost immediately, the head guard stationed in the rear car entered and motioned for them to lie down on the floor, under the heavy wooden seats and against the inner wall of the passenger car. In his best English he tried to explain: "The walls of this car, they are made of hardened steel, and the windows are bulletproof."

Wedged in the cramped quarters, unable to see anything, Ted and Cecelia could only surmise what must have been happening from the sounds they heard outside. At first they could hear the yelling of what must have been a large group of bandits attacking the train from the left side. Judging by the pinging sound of bullets bouncing off the metal sides and the windows, they assumed their attackers were only armed with light weapons. Next, they heard the automatic fire of weapons that must have been positioned from behind the sliding doors of the front and rear cars as well as those that were located on top of the cars behind a circular wall of sandbags. If the situation hadn't been so serious, Ted would have remarked that it felt like they were in the middle of an Old West train robbery.

"As long as you stay down on the floor, you will be quite safe," the guard said. "We should have no problem stopping them from reaching the train. They are not too many and they are only armed with small weapons, nothing that should be able to penetrate the car. Once the rescue train that's ahead of us backs up, we should be able to change trains and proceed."

The sound of a different weapon and the shattering of the bulletproof glass signaled that some kind of heavier weapon's fire was being concentrated on their car. Realizing there was nothing to do until the rescue train arrived, Ted positioned himself on top of Cecelia to protect her from any ricocheting bullets that might enter the car through the windows. Lying there with his arms wrapped around her, Ted began to reflect. *I don't know what scares me the most: Is it the sound of the bullets shattering the windows and rattling around inside our car, or the effect all this must be having on Cecelia? How much can she take? How long are we going to have to remain on this rough, splintery, dirty floor? How will we know when the other train arrives?*

The sound of a whistle was their signal that it was time to move. Almost immediately, the guard motioned for them to crawl forward to the car door and climb down the stairs on the side of the train opposite the attackers. Using the cars to shield them, the two bankers worked their way forward. Thirty yards separated the two trains. Picking up Cecelia, Ted wrapped his arms around her and made a dash for the protective cover of the next train.

Arriving at what must previously have been an important Japanese military reservation, they were greeted by K. Kai Wan, a general in the Indonesian regional army. He was dressed in a pressed, tailored uniform. A folded blue-and-white polka-dotted silk scarf was carefully arranged around General Wan's neck, separating his green military uniform from his thick, heavily pomaded, jet-black hair. His combat boots were shined to a mirror-like finish. To complete the effect, he wore a red beret, carefully placed at a jaunty angle. Cecelia was having difficulty deciding whether he was an actor from central casting or the real deal.

Speaking English with a British accent, he formally greeted his guests.

General Wan's personally conducted tour required the better part of the day. They visited the vast array of underground bunkers used to store armored vehicles, troop carriers, artillery pieces, and row after row of cases filled with ammunition, all left behind by the Japanese army. Troop barracks, mess facilities, and the officers' quarters and club were located on the right side of the parade grounds. A fully equipped machine shop and aircraft hangars were located to the left. As she watched planes land and take off, Cecelia concluded that an airstrip must be located on the far side, beyond the compound.

Ted, no stranger to military reservations, said, "Cecelia, judged by any standard the scale of this outpost is enormous. It's a modern, well-designed facility, untouched by the ravages of war. It must have been designed by the Japanese to supply their outlying command centers, and if necessary, defend the island from an Allied invasion. If we knew the extent of these command posts we could make a pretty good guess at the true strength of the Indonesian military capability. It will be interesting to see what General Wan shares with us."

They were midway through dinner when the general turned to Cecelia and asked, "Would it be expecting too much for you to inform Washington what kind of a battle the Dutch would face if they decide to initiate military action? Out here, we hope that when the Dutch, the Communists, or anyone else understands our true military capability and the depth of our resolve to protect our country, they will leave us alone."

In response, Ted said, "Tell me, General, is this your only base? Why couldn't an advancing hostile force just skip past you here and proceed with the attack elsewhere, on some other island?"

Smiling, General Wan walked to the rear wall, which was covered with a large curtain. Pulling it back, he revealed a wall-sized topographic map of Indonesia, showing the entire island nation in minute detail. From where she was sitting, Cecelia could see many colored markers. Watching his guests study the map, the general said, "You will note the location and the different colored marks. Each of them denotes the nature and location of another of our bases.

"Miss Chang, I am going to give you letter-sized copies of this highly classified map. We can only hope they will make interesting reading back in Washington and act as a deterrent to those who would attack us."

Chapter 25

A ROTH FAMILY REUNION

Jacques was becoming impatient. Left in New York, he was receiving regular reports from Claudine and Cecelia. Although the information was sketchy, he was able to surmise both of them were making substantial progress and were safe.

Reports of the two attacks against Cecelia were alarming, but not as concerning as Ted's subtle attempts to downplay growing problems with her health. *I hope Mike returns from Geneva in time to greet her when she returns; he'll know what to do.* He was having a difficult time waiting for the meetings in Geneva to conclude so he could meet Claudine in Paris. He'd asked her to travel there once her business was done so they could consult with Jacques's father on the Sentinels' developing plan.

Annoyed by the ringing of his telephone, without thinking he picked up the receiver and said, "Yeah, what do you want?"

A polite but firm voice answered, "Excuse me, Mr. Roth, this is Agent Brown of the Secret Service calling. We were wondering if you would allow the service to arrange your upcoming trip to Paris? We need to coordinate your travel plans with MI5 and Paris's Sûreté while you and your wife are in Europe."

Claudine and Jacques had arranged to communicate by telegram to avoid the risk of having their telephone conversations intercepted. With the exchange of two messages, they planned to meet in Paris.

As promised, Jacques was waiting on the platform of Gare St. Lazare when Claudine's train from Geneva arrived.

Jacques was not the only person standing on the platform that day. Members of the Sûreté, dressed to resemble baggage handlers and family members waiting to greet their relatives, were positioned all along the platform.

Not certain from which car Claudine would be disembarking, Jacques was standing midway before the stationary train when he saw her step down, two cars to his left. A nod of his head was all that was required for the security force to move in and form a protective curtain around each of them.

The excitement of seeing Claudine emerge from the train drove any thought of Samson from Jacques's mind. The newlyweds half-walked, half-ran toward each other.

Ignoring the curious crowd, their protective guard, a cloud of escaping steam, and the noise and commotion of the departing train on the other side of the platform, Claudine and Jacques were lost in each other's arms. Wrapped together, engaged in a long passionate kiss, and enjoying the physical sense of being together, they were oblivious to what was going on around them.

Finally, as the intensity of their mood began to fade, they turned and, in the protection of their plainclothes police escort, proceeded to walk along the platform toward the depot and the waiting Roth family limousine.

The long black car with opaque windows immediately pulled away from the curb, proceeded two blocks, turned right into a covered parking lot, and emerged from the other side as part of a three-car caravan of identical limousines.

An hour later, the three cars passed through the gates of the Roths' country estate. The two guards closed the heavy wrought-iron gates and reassumed their positions in front of the facing gatehouses. Twenty minutes later, a nondescript car carrying the couple's luggage passed through the gate.

That evening, as they waited for Claudine and Madame Roth, Jacques and his father were standing in front of the big fireplace, in the soft light of a mellow fire. They were enjoying a glass of champagne. The conversation was light and casual, until Pierre Roth brought up the subject of his son's safety.

"One of the drivers thought he spotted a car following you," he said. "He called in to report it. When you passed through that last little village earlier today, the local police were waiting to intercept the car he described. It would appear you and Claudine were their targets of interest. It may be that Samson has European teams assigned to capture you."

At that moment, the ladies walked through the large double doors leading into the study. "No more of that serious talk, Pierre," scolded his wife. "Claudine and I have decided you stuffy old men are going to pay attention and talk to us this evening, right, Claudine?" Elaine flashed her most conspiratorial wink at her daughter-in-law.

Once the butler had refilled their glasses a second time, Pierre proposed a toast. "Until the recent ABA meeting in New York, the last time I saw you two was the summer of 1940," he said. "Even then your mother and I could see how attracted you were to each other. The next thing we know, five years later, we receive a letter from Sun Valley telling us you are married, and now, here you are. Please accept our belated congratulations! And I assume you won't mind filling us in on some of the blanks!"

Jacques's parents were eager to become better acquainted with their daughter-in-law. Despite the busy schedule of business events planned for each day, they faithfully observed daily rituals: an early morning walk, breakfast on the veranda, the evening cocktail hour, dinner, and an after-dinner cognac in front of the gentle flames in the big fireplace in the library. Each evening when Claudine and Elaine entered the library, they would find Pierre and Jacques engaged in deep conversation. Each time, Madame Roth would say, "What could be they be discussing that's more interesting than talking to us?"

One night just before they fell asleep, Elaine asked her husband, "What has happened to the free-spirited soccer player who left our home in 1935? I hardly recognize this exciting, serious, and committed leader we call our son! Could Claudine's influence account for so much change?"

Toward the end of the week, Claudine and Jacques were having a private conversation with Pierre. He was talking. "There is no doubt in my mind that developing a reliable supply of affordable oil has to be one of France's and Europe's highest priorities. A significant amount of American aid is being used to purchase oil from the Oil Club companies at very high prices, well above published market rates. These artificially high prices are absorbing money that could be put to much better use in rebuilding Europe's industrial capacity.

"Don't misunderstand what I am saying," Pierre continued. "It's not that we don't appreciate the aid and the supply of oil; our problem is one of growing resentment. We don't understand why the American government is allowing this kind of gouging to take place. The British and American oil companies are the only game in town, and it's becoming obvious that they move together, with full support of their governments and certain large Wall Street firms.

"There are some of us who are questioning whether we wish to become involved. Proper interfacing between the American and European industrial and financial communities could become a very serious problem!

"That said, if you are expecting strong financial support from the European investment community, you must face the reality that their decision will not only be based on their perception of the quality of your plan, but also on how committed you are to becoming involved."

"Poppi—may I call you Poppi?" Claudine asked. "It's important that Jacques and my efforts be viewed as the work of independent people committed to an agenda that serves the public interest, not the political and economic self-interests of either the American or European governments. Why else would Jacques have turned down a cabinet appointment from the President?"

"What!" cried Pierre. "Jacques, you never mentioned anything about a cabinet position! What a great honor! You must have had a very good reason for turning down that offer."

"If Claudine and I have any hope of helping to stitch economic cooperation between the United States and Europe together," said Jacques, "it's important that we be perceived as independent problem solvers, committed to the task at hand, not intent on furthering the agendas of one government at the expense of the other."

After pausing to think, Pierre continued. "If you step back and look at what you are really attempting, you might think about how it appears from the European point of view. Almost everyone you will meet will see your proposal as the first big effort that requires a consortium of European investors to participate with the United States. If things go well, the consummation of your oil fund could create an important precedent for things to come. Failure could delay all intercontinental cooperative programs for a long time. That is a risk many of us in Europe will hesitate to take.

"The financial leaders here in Europe are concerned about effective leadership and representation within the U.S. government and in the financial community. Fortunately or unfortunately, you two are the only ones they know who have a proven track record, and you are the only people they feel they can trust. It's important that you understand their concerns and be prepared to listen to their suggestions.

"I might add, if you two are expecting me and the bank to provide our complete support, I, too, will need to know your thoughts on this crucial issue."

Jacques and Claudine both started to speak, but Pierre put up his hand. "Maybe you should hear me out before you reply," he said. "You and Jacques may not realize it, but the work you two have already accomplished is widely recognized and respected in the European business community. There doesn't seem to be anyone else who commands so much respect. You'd be surprised by how many people are familiar with your previous achievements, particularly your proactive roles in solving so many major problems with such a broad and diverse number of people."

Now it was Jacques's turn to talk. "Father, Claudine and I have come back to Europe to pursue our legacies of leadership and banking responsibilities, but for us to be effective we can't be viewed as servants to the European financial community, responsible for the implementation of its national economic and political agendas.

"Our friend Sir David Marcus is a perfect example. He felt he needed to resign his position with English Oil and learn to operate from a neutral position before he had any chance of earning the trust and respect of Middle Eastern governments."

"Jacques," said his father, "no one is suggesting that you need to work for any particular bank or government. Your heritage, your future ownership of the Roth and Demaureux banks, and your knowledge of the business communities on both sides of the Atlantic already make you a legitimate choice. While we want you to be available, there are those of us who also believe that your effectiveness will, among other things, depend upon on how well you maintain your independence and objectivity. Put yourselves in our position. When you ask us to consider making such a large commitment, why shouldn't we expect the same from you?"

For the remainder of the newlyweds' visit, Pierre continued to invite his friends to the chateau to speak with his son and daughter-in-law. Each meeting was held in the privacy of Pierre's personal library.

Jacques had never quite understood how the chemistry between men of respect really worked. Like birds flying in formation, each of his father's guests—future leaders, bankers, industrialists, and government officials—seemed to be communicating on the same frequency and appeared to sincerely respect the thoughts and comments of everyone else in the room. It was in this carefully staged atmosphere that Claudine and Jacques found themselves meeting with Pierre and many of the brightest minds in Europe.

As the participants left the meetings, they were careful not to show any emotion or reveal anything about their reactions to what they had just heard. It was clear they had a lot to think about before they made a commitment.

Within forty-eight hours after each meeting, each of Pierre's invited guests would call Pierre to thank him for being invited to meetings of such importance and express their pleasure in meeting his charming daughter-in-law and son. They would also invariably say, one way or another, "But that is not the real reason for my call. I want to discuss the content of the meeting."

After listening to Jacques and Claudine describe their plan, these men seemed quite sure that it would make an important contribution to the economic future of their countries. But they had concerns; they knew that challenging the major oil companies, mobilizing the American government and the world's financial community would be an enormous undertaking. They wondered how realistic it was to believe a small group of admittedly talented, well-connected people can perform such a massive and complicated task.

"What happens if they fail?" the callers asked, explicitly or diplomatically. "How can we protect ourselves? Equally important, what happens if they succeed? Who can we depend upon to provide the required leadership and find solutions to the myriad problems that are bound to appear?"

These powerful men understood that, to provide the Sentinels with the requested support, they would have to contribute a significant amount of their financial resources. They would be involved in a major banking transaction; moreover, they would be making a strategic decision. To the man, in their several ways, the callers told Henri, "We're going to need some time." He knew that Jacques and Claudine would have to schedule that time to explain their ideas in depth, to with the support they needed.

Chapter 26

ESCAPE FROM PARIS

After a pleasant and productive week at the chateau, Jacques and Claudine knew it was time for them to leave the sanctuary of the Roth home. Their plan was to fly back to Geneva for a short visit, which would allow Jacques some time to exchange ideas with Claudine's father. All the necessary security precautions were still in effect. The same three-limousine caravan was waiting to transport them to the airport and the waiting Demaureux plane.

The caravan was passing through one of the many small villages that dotted their path en route to Paris's Orly airport when their path was blocked by what appeared to be a broken-down truck. Its cargo of live chickens was scattered all over the road. There was no room to pass.

Seated in the rear car of the caravan, Jacques and Claudine watched with concern as the two leading cars slowed to a stop. Worried about the safety of the chickens, they failed to notice the large old bus that emerged from a side street and blocked their rear path of retreat.

Realizing the danger of their predicament, the driver of the lead limousine wasted no time. He accelerated his heavy vehicle directly into the stalled truck, hitting it hard enough to push it aside and create a pathway for the other two limousines. The second limousine drove through the mass of chickens, scattering them in all directions.

Without any hesitation, the driver of the third car accelerated through the narrow opening and continued at top speed to cover the remaining distance to Orly airport and the safety of the Roths' private hangar. Alerted to the problem, the crew of the Demaureux plane had the engines warmed up and ready to go. Once the car braked to a stop, Jacques and Claudine quickly moved from the limousine to the plane, their baggage was loaded, and the door was closed. Almost immediately, the plane taxied out of the hangar and down the runway and took off without further incident.

Settled comfortably in their seats, Claudine and Jacques finally had a chance to take a deep breath and silently reflect on the series of events that had just so rapidly occurred.

Finally, Jacques said, "Claudine, correct me if you disagree, but I believe we were just ambushed by Samson operatives. Other than trying to either kill or capture us, what purpose could they have had?"

"That is a question to which I hope I never know the answer," said Claudine as she peered out the window. "Wait—what's going on, Jacques? I thought we were flying to Geneva . . . but this plane is headed due south."

"Who said anything about Geneva?" said Jacques, smiling.

Becoming annoyed, Claudine asked, "If this plane isn't going to Geneva, would it be too much for you to explain where we are going? I was planning to visit my father! This isn't funny!"

"Relax. I talked to Henri—"

"You talked to my father, without telling me? What's going on?"

"Two days ago," said Jacques. "I was concerned about the predictable nature of our using the Demaureux bank plane to fly from Paris to Geneva, so I called Henri to discuss possible alternatives. After he reminded me that both your home in Geneva and your chalet in Chamonix would be difficult to protect, he suggested we meet at a more protected and less predictable location.

"He called your old friend, Lady Cumberledge, who from what he led me to understand is also a friend of his. After he explained his concern, she invited the three of us to be her guests at La Garoupe, and to enjoy a nice leisurely vacation on the French Riviera. He believes that even if our location is detected we can be properly protected at La Garoupe. It's been a while since you were there, and we thought you might enjoy seeing your old friends under more pleasant circumstances. Pardon me for not telling you, but Henri and I were hoping to surprise you."

Claudine's expression had softened at the news. "And to think I was hoping this was a romantic interlude that would take us back to the land of the midnight swim! I'm going to miss getting naked, diving off that rock, and later making passionate love to you on the hearth in front of that old fireplace in the chalet. Really, Jacques," Claudine teased, "you would pass up all that just to avoid a couple of murderous Samson operatives?"

―――

"What do you mean the bank plane didn't land in Geneva!" Fred Clarke, the managing partner of Samson America, screamed into the telephone.

Trying his best to answer in a calm manner, the Samson operative responded, "At least not initially. When the plane finally arrived, Mr. and Mrs. Roth were no longer on board."

"Did you question the pilots? Are the Demaureux pilots still at the hangar? Did they tell you where they stopped? Did you get a look at the logs?"

Two hours later, a thoroughly angered Fred Clarke received a call from his European counterpart. "My people tell me that the Sûreté had their people waiting near the Demaureux hangar when our agents approached the pilots. Almost as quickly as one of our operatives began to question them, the officers appeared out of nowhere and arrested our two men."

Sensing his frustration, Clarke asked, "They were waiting for us? Obviously this means Mr. Demaureux, his daughter, and Jacques know of our presence and are taking precautions of their own. What do you think we should do?"

"Ten of our operatives have either been killed or captured. Maybe it's time we step back and take a fresh look at our assignment. It's becoming apparent that we aren't just being asked to go after the Sentinels; we are being forced to challenge the British, French, and American security agencies as well. I think the time has come for us to reevaluate our assignment!"

———

As she and Jacques continued their journey, Claudine began to recall the days in 1944 when Denise and her mother, Lady Cumberledge, the owners and operators of La Garoupe Estate, provided her with much-needed sanctuary from the German agents who were pursuing her. *Where better to hide a tree than in a forest? Who would have thought to look for Claudine at Lady Cumberledge's estate on the French Riviera, which after the start of the war had been commandeered as a high-profile German officers' retreat?* Claudine was pleased that this visit would give her the chance to personally thank Lady Cumberledge, her daughter Denise, and all their staff, who at great risk to themselves helped the new French maid remain safely hidden in the midst of all those German officers.

Henri and the two ladies were waiting at the gate when Jacques and Claudine arrived at La Garoupe. In typical European fashion everyone exchanged hugs and kisses on both cheeks. Without appearing obvious, Claudine watched the exchange between her father and Lady Cumberledge. It seemed Henri held her a little longer and tighter than a friend would find necessary. He kissed her slowly, softly, and gently on both cheeks.

"Dear friends," began Lady Cumberledge, "first, I insist that everyone call me Margarite. And second, let's assume that whoever may be chasing you won't be a problem, at least not tonight. Who knows when we will have another opportunity to relax and enjoy the many special places here in Nice?"

Chapter 27

LA GAROUPE

The next morning, Jacques was awakened by the smell of hot coffee and warm croissants. "Wake up, lazybones, it's a beautiful day!" he heard Claudine say. "Father is talking about wanting to have brunch with the new Mr. and Mrs. Jacques Roth."

It was Sunday, the servants' day off. Henri had taken advantage of the situation and was busily working in Lady Cumberledge's kitchen when Claudine and Jacques arrived. Wiping his hands on the tea towel wrapped around his waist, he hurried to greet them. It was obvious that he was excited. Before anybody could say anything, he said, "Come into the kitchen! I'm preparing my specialty, crêpes Henri."

The kitchen looked as if a cyclone had hit it. Flour dusted the counters, the stove, and the floor. Mixing bowls were scattered everywhere, and several frying pans were set on the stove. Even the refrigerator door had been left open.

Hearing the noise and conversation, Margarite entered the kitchen. Pausing to survey the situation, she said, "Henri, perhaps you should allow Denise and me to finish preparing breakfast? I thought I noticed a bottle of champagne in the refrigerator; the staff usually leaves a pitcher of freshly squeezed orange juice in there as well. Why don't the three of you go out on the terrace? It's a beautiful morning and I will bring you your morning cocktail—a Chez Garoupe mimosa."

Henri didn't need a second invitation.

Seated at the glass-topped table on the terrace overlooking the azure Mediterranean and the jagged, cypress-covered coastline on the opposite side of the bay, Jacques was having difficulty remembering why they had to seek the sanctuary of La Garoupe and the hospitality of the Cumberledges. He was already contemplating a second mimosa when Denise and her mother appeared holding two steaming platters. "Crêpes Henri, slightly modified by Chef Margarite, are about to be served."

The light, thin pancakes were filled with a mixture of bacon crumbles, chopped green onions, and diced Gruyere cheese, and the coffee was La Garoupe's special blend of freshly ground French roast. Seated around the sunlit table, looking out over the Mediterranean and enjoying crêpes, Henri and the others were engrossed in what they all knew was a special experience.

It was Henri who broke the spell. "Jacques, did you really turn down the President's offer to join his cabinet? I've been receiving calls from Morgan, Roger, Pete, and your father, all of whom have heard about your plan to try to break the grip of the Oil Club. Do you think you can actually raise the fifteen billion dollars?"

The questions were coming so fast that Jacques was having a difficult time deciding which one to answer first. "Let's start with the money," he said. "Unfortunately we were given the fifteen-billion-dollar figure and we have to meet it. We wish the number was smaller, but that's what is required to fund the development of fifteen million barrels per day of new production."

"That is a lot of money to have to raise all at one time," said Henri sympathetically.

"Actually, we are not planning to organize the money in a

single raise," said Jacques. "We're planning to raise it in two stages. The first stage, which we call our prototype phase, calls for one billion dollars. If all goes well, we'll try to raise the remaining fourteen billion. In breaking the process into two parts we are hoping the successful implementation of the prototype phase will legitimize and make the second phase less difficult."

"I don't think I've ever heard of a billion-dollar trial balloon," said Henri. "You people certainly like to think big. Whose idea is this, anyway?"

"It was Prince Habib's suggestion," answered Claudine. "He believes a billion-dollar prototype provides enough money to fund one million barrels of daily capacity, or approximately twenty percent of the world's current capacity. At this level, he believes a working model will be large enough to convince all the different stakeholders that the serious problems have been solved, yet small enough to be more easily funded."

"I understand your logic, but even at the one-billion-dollar level, I'm not clear on how you plan to raise so much money . . ."

"Our plan calls for us to raise two hundred million from an assortment of independent oil companies and private equity investors. We are hoping the Demaureux, Roth, Stone, Hong Kong, and American West banks will consider contributing the remaining eight hundred million of debt. The two hundred million of investment equity will be used to locate, develop, and determine the productivity of the new reserves. Once the revenue-generating capacity of an oil field has been clearly established, the eight hundred million dollars of debt will be used to pay for the costs of installing all the refining facilities and delivery operations required to distribute the new oil to the ultimate consumer."

"And where are you thinking you will find all this oil?" asked Henri.

"The prince has committed some of his proven but undeveloped oil reserves held in trust by some of the oil-rich countries on the perimeter of the Persian peninsula."

"Jacques," said Henri, "I know you like the prince. Mike respects him; Claudine has always spoken highly of him. And now that I think about it, it's only been a couple of weeks since I last met with him. Unquestionably, he is emerging as the region's oil leader. But even so, there is a lot at risk if anything goes wrong."

Although her father's comment was directed at Jacques, Claudine decided to answer. "Ordinarily, I might agree with you, but someone needs to begin believing in someone. Besides, until we can determine the presence of the oil and approve the operative contracts, we are under no obligation to fund anything. The burden will be on us to perform."

"Jacques, you and Claudine, as always, make a very compelling argument. I guess I understand the billion-dollar prototype issue, but the remaining fourteen billion is still one hell of a lot of money to fund under any circumstances. Knowing the reach of Big Oil, and its ability to limit U.S. investment, I have to believe that raising that additional money represents your biggest problem."

Chapter 28

THE ADMIRAL

Each morning during breakfast, Denise and Claudine made their daily list of places to go and things to see. After breakfast, Lady Margarite always had some new art gallery or an artist's studio to see or an old friend she wanted to introduce to Henri. The four of them would scatter like birds, always agreeing to meet back at La Garoupe to enjoy their late afternoon ritual of sipping a cocktail as they watched the sun set behind the hills of Cap d'Antibes.

Left to his own devices, Jacques took advantage of the peaceful morning hours and the warm sun to sit on the veranda and read, sketch, and think through the Sentinels' assignment.

He had always wanted to learn how to sail. It took two days for him to make the rounds of the local yacht clubs in search of a suitable small sailboat he could buy or rent. On the third day, he found the right boat: sixteen feet long, rigged with a jib and a mainsail, and small enough for one man to operate. After a shakedown lesson, during which the owner helped him sail the boat around the point separating the Cap d'Antibes Yacht Club from the Bay of Garoupe, Jacques was ready to embark on his new venture.

Each morning, Jacques would set sail, always taking care to remain well inside the protected bay, away from anchored boats, the docks and jetties of the other seaside homes, and the swimmers near the beach.

Word began to spread that Jacques Roth, France's national soccer team captain and heir to a French banking empire, was learning how to sail. On the occasion that he would pass within earshot of one of the boats anchored in the bay, people standing on the decks would wave and shout encouragements. As he became more proficient, Jacques would maneuver his boat close enough to answer back. It wasn't long before he was being asked to raft up and join his new friends for a cool drink and some pleasant conversation.

The British and French aristocrats who summered along the Riviera quickly became engaged in trying to tell Jacques's stories. It was becoming a contest to see who could tell the best or latest story. Jacques-watching became a regular event. His new admirers were beginning to refer to him as "the Admiral."

Sometimes, in the afternoons, Denise and Claudine would arrive home to find Jacques's boat missing. Unconcerned, they would pour themselves a glass of wine and wander down to the end of the jetty. With the aid of high-powered binoculars, they would search for the Admiral. As long as they could see his boat tied up somewhere in the harbor, they didn't worry. *He'll come home when the wine runs out and he doesn't have any more stories to tell*, Claudine would think.

Jacques soon became bored by limiting his sailing to the confines of the protected bay. One day when there was very little breeze and no clouds in the sky, he began to maneuver his craft toward the better wind that lay beyond the mouth of the bay. Always mindful of the increased danger of sailing in the open sea, Jacques limited his route to tacking back and forth in front of the bay, in clear view of the beach, the chateau, and all his new friends.

Having made a few uneventful passes back and forth, he thought, *Oh, what the hell, why don't I sail around the point to the yacht club at Cap d'Antibes? At least I can have lunch and a cold beer and meet some new people.*

He made it without incident, and lunch at the yacht club was glorious. With the aid of several beers and a new audience for his old stories, Jacques was in his element. The time flew by, and before he realized it, the sun was beginning to set. He had barely cleared the outer buoys of the marina when he felt the wind begin to pick up and saw the dark clouds forming over the hills to the west.

The wind was becoming stronger; the seas were rising and the sky was becoming darker. Watching the coastline, Jacques realized that despite having lengthened his westward tacks, he wasn't getting any closer to the shore. The wind was taking him further out to sea. He decided his best bet was to try and tack north and west against the wind in order to make it back to the safety of the harbor at Antibes.

The growing intensity of the wind and the further rising of the sea forced Jacques to focus on the seaworthiness of his small craft. His first thought was to drop some sail. Unable to work his way forward to release the jib, he untied the mainsail line. With considerable effort he succeeded in pulling the sail down the mast and wrapping the descending canvas around the boom. His job completed, he firmly lashed the boom to separate cleats on opposite sides of the boat's cockpit.

Exhausted from the effort, Jacques looked up to see the coastline rapidly growing smaller. The effect of the jib was no match for the force of the wind. No matter what he tried, he was being pushed further out to sea. Returning to shore was no longer an option. He had no choice but to let the wind propel his boat further away from the shore.

Despite his inexperience Jacques realized he needed to make sure the boat didn't capsize. Using the jib and the rudder to keep the bow of the small boat pointed into the wind became his most important objective.

He was so focused on the task at hand that he failed to notice the effect the increasing wind was having on the jib. The sound of a loud crack, like the report of a rifle, signaled the tearing of the jib. The wind had split the smaller, triangular sail in half; both parts were flapping wildly in the wind.

Drifting around in what had become a very heavy sea, with no effective sail, Jacques realized it was only a matter of time before one of the big waves would break over the side of the boat and fill the cockpit with water.

He was too busy thinking to be scared. Looking around, he saw two life preservers, the canvas bag in which his sails had been stored, and an extra line stored in the forward bilge. He put on one of the preservers and stowed the other in the stern. Ignoring the fading light and the lowering temperature, Jacques tied one end of the rope onto the handles of the canvas bag, dropped it over the stern, and began to feed out the line. The canvas bag soon became a bucket that acted like a sea anchor, which would keep the bow of the sailboat headed into the wind and waves.

It was almost dark by the time Jacques finished cutting the right number of holes in the bottom of the canvas bag and determining the proper distance for his improvised sea anchor to float behind the boat. Thoroughly soaked, exhausted, and chilled, he removed his survival bag from under the stern deck. In it were his lunch, a canteen filled with drinking water, a pocketknife, a compass, and a map of the southern coast of France. He put the compass and the pocketknife in each of the front pockets of his dungarees. Sitting down in the bottom of the cockpit, out of the wind, Jacques took a small sip from the canteen while he took stock of his meager inventory. Then he sliced off small pieces of the salami, cheese, and baguette he had packed, and settled down to enjoy his makeshift meal and survey his situation.

I can use the remaining life preserver as a mattress and a piece of the jib for a blanket. The sea-anchor solution appears to be working. Tomorrow, with the aid of my compass and the mainsail, I will start sailing back toward France.

The sudden arrival of a heavy rainsquall interrupted his reverie. Instinctively, he knew the solution to one of his biggest problems had just presented itself. Scrambling to cut the remaining porting of the sail off the jib line, he fashioned the sailcloth into a shallow bathtub-type arrangement that could be attached to both sides of the cockpit to collect the rainwater and drain the captured water into his survival bag.

Jacques, old boy, you have food, you have water, and a relatively sheltered place to sleep. Why don't you try to rest and see what tomorrow brings?

The rhythmic movement of the boat helped Jacques fall asleep. It must have been about two o'clock in the morning when he was awakened by a new and violent movement. Thinking his sea-anchor line might have broken, he rose up from the floor of the cockpit and started to inspect the problem.

Jacques never knew what hit him. During the night, one of the lines securing the boom had come loose from its cleat. Without warning, the heavy boom, covered as it was with a rain-soaked sail, struck and knocked him unconscious. Jacques lay in the bottom of the boat, blood oozing from a deep gash on the right side of his head.

After her first pass with the binoculars in the late afternoon, Claudine failed to spot Jacques's boat. When she couldn't spot him after her second, more thorough inspection, she could feel the tension of worry begin to build within her. While Denise went up to the house to start making phone calls, Claudine—the thought of Samson never far from her mind—began her third search. This time she concentrated on the uninhabited coastline as well as the beach, the boats, and the jetties. When her third inspection failed to produce results, Claudine knew something was very wrong.

Would an inexperienced sailor like Jacques be able to handle the mistral that had brought the change in the weather? *Maybe he's put ashore someplace where we can't see him. Has Samson finally caught up to him?*

Claudine began to make her way toward the chateau when she spotted Denise running down the jetty toward her. "He's been at the Cap d'Antibes Yacht Club; he left about an hour ago. He has to be in his boat out there someplace! Come on, we can take the car and follow the coast road. From up on the bluffs, we should be able to spot him."

Denise had braked her car to a stop at each of the bluff's several vistas overlooking the sea. They failed to see anything that remotely resembled Jacques's sailboat by the time they arrived at the yacht club. Denise used its phone to call the local coast watch.

"Don't worry, madam!" said the person she reached. "We'll start the search as soon as it's calm. According to our calculations, the combination of the winds and the currents would have taken Jacques in a southwesterly direction in a line with Algiers in North Africa. By the time this thing blows itself out, he could be three or four hundred kilometers out into the center of the Mediterranean. If he's out there, we'll find him."

The headline that greeted Henri the next morning after he walked down the drive to the front gate to collect the paper read, "Jacques Roth, Heir to France's Largest Financial Empire, Feared Lost at Sea." It was the same headline Jacques's father, in his Paris home, saw on the opened paper that had been placed on the table in his breakfast room. And, after hearing their morning security brief at the White House, Chairman Malone, Secretary Ainsworth, Senators Hess, Armstrong, and Lucas, and the President all became concerned.

Several days passed. The French Navy's search failed to reveal anything. No ransom demands had been made. No wreckage from Jacques's boat had been sighted. The world was ominously silent. There were no rumors on the street, no police reports, no sightings, nothing. There had to be some explanation; someone as prominent as Jacques Roth didn't just disappear.

The French navy was ordered back to sea. Once again in Geneva, members of the Sûreté interviewed the captured Samson operatives. Other than reporting rumors that Samson had canceled its contract with its American employer, the two operatives convinced their captors that they knew nothing of Jacques's disappearance.

The search was expanded to the Spanish border to the west and the Italian border to the east. Pierre Roth placed an announcement in *Le Monde* that he was offering a reward of 100,000 francs for any information that led to his son's safe recovery.

The next morning, articles announcing the reward and featuring recent pictures of Jacques appeared wherever reputable French newspapers were sold in every city in France, Italy, and Spain.

In Washington, Roger Malone said, "Well, that really does it. I guess it's time for me to call in Jack Hardy."

Chapter 29

CECELIA RETURNS HOME

Mike's return trip from Geneva to San Francisco had been long and exhausting. Three days and two nights of changing time zones, varying meal patterns, disembarking from planes, trying to sleep in airports, standing in long lines, and passing through customs would tire out almost anybody. Any effort to sleep on the last leg of his trip from St. Louis to San Francisco had been made impossible by the crying of more than one small child. The pressure in the cabin from the high altitude was causing the young children a great deal of ear pain.

To make matters worse, he had to come home to an empty apartment. He knew Cecelia was doing a lot of good for the Sentinels' cause in Indonesia, but he still worried about her daily. One morning on his way into the office Mike, half asleep, walked past a newsstand. Jacques's picture stared out at him. *What's he done this time?* Mike thought as he reached into his pocket for some change. But when he read the headline and the first part of the article, the realization of what had happened to his friend was too much for him.

Feeling light-headed and as though his knees were going to buckle, he slowly moved over to a nearby bench, sat down, and carefully reread the article. There had to be some rational explanation. *Jacques would have enough sense to realize you can't sail a small boat in a mistral. He's from France, for Christ's sake—he knows about those sorts of things! There has to be some other explanation. I need to talk to Cecelia. Maybe she knows something.*

As the time for her departure approached, Ted noticed a growing sense of fatigue enveloping Cecelia. He had also heard her complaining of a strange tingling in her fingers and toes. As they stood on the tarmac in front of the waiting plane, he said, "Wouldn't you prefer to let us put your briefcase with the rest of your baggage in the luggage compartment? You should use the flight home to get some rest."

Standing at the bottom of the stairway leading up to the U.S. government plane with the blue and white markings, she said, "I need to do some work on the flight home. I need to keep it with me."

In what appeared an almost frantic motion, Cecelia reached out and grabbed the heavy case, clutched it against her chest, and before anybody could say or do anything, retreated up the stairwell and disappeared into the plane.

Strapped into her seat, the one next to the fold-up table that swung up from the side of the plane, she had already opened the case and was extracting her notebooks when a pretty stewardess asked if she would like a cup of tea before takeoff.

Surprised by the woman's presence, Cecelia looked up in what would later be described as a deer-in-the-headlights stare. After taking a moment to reorient herself, she said, "Thank you, that would be very nice."

Pausing only to accept more cups of tea or partake in the light fare of air travel, Cecelia focused the last of her energy on her work. Having put her notebooks in chronological order, she began to condense each one into her version of a descriptive summary. Once she finished this phase of the work, she began to apply her conclusions to a sequential logic chart, in much the same way as she had seen Jacques do so many times before.

Hour after hour, working at a feverish pace, she continued the process until she closed the last notebook and made the last marks on her charted outline. Only then did she allow herself the luxury of a glass of wine.

Reporting to the chief pilot, the stewardess said, "I don't know what she's doing, but whatever it is, it must be very important. It's certainly producing a marked change in her physical appearance. I've only seen that look once in my life; it was when I was hunting with my brother and he had trapped some kind of a mountain cat in a cage. I will never forget the look in its eyes—the same look I see in her eyes. When you have a moment, maybe you should come back in the cabin and see for yourself. I'm not certain of what we should be doing."

Knowing that they would be landing shortly in Hawaii, the chief pilot made his way to the rear of the plane. "Good morning, Miss Chang. I hope you have enjoyed your flight. We will be landing in Honolulu in a few minutes to refuel and change crews. I was wondering if there is anything we can do for you during our short layover?"

Confused by the look in her eyes and her failure to respond, he reached forward in an effort to relieve her of the effort of holding what appeared to be a very heavy briefcase. Recoiling, Cecelia made an effort to clutch the briefcase even more tightly to her chest. At the same time she emitted a strange hissing sound.

Motioning for the stewardess to follow him forward, the pilot said, "I'll call ground control and request they arrange for a doctor to be standing by when we land. Maybe he'll be able to advise us about what should be done. In the mean time, I suggest that, other than serving her food and drink, we plan on leaving her alone. Maybe she'll fall asleep and the added rest will cure whatever it is that is bothering her."

Once the plane landed in Hawaii, Cecelia resisted the suggestion that she disembark with the rest of the crew. Insisting that she had to work, she remained on the plane. Withdrawing a fresh notebook from her briefcase, she began to compose the first of what would eventually become three separate reports.

Apprised of Cecelia's situation, the new cabin attendant, trying to think what might distract her only passenger, purchased several newspapers in the airport before boarding the plane. *Maybe reading these will help get her mind off whatever seems to be bothering her.*

Several hours after takeoff, physically and mentally exhausted, Cecelia put her last report in her briefcase and took one last sip of tea before she noticed the newspapers lying in the adjacent seat. It took a moment for her overloaded mind to comprehend what she was reading. The article reporting Jacques's disappearance was prominently displayed on the front pages.

―――

The jolt of the plane's wheels hitting the runway of San Francisco International Airport failed to awaken Cecelia. When the fresh air from the open cabin door failed to revive her, an anxious stewardess walked back to where she was sitting. When Cecelia didn't respond to her soft words, she reached forward for her wrist to check her pulse. It was weak, but she was definitely alive.

Thoroughly trained to deal with crises, the stewardess pushed the emergency button before reaching for the oxygen bottle stored nearby. After turning on the oxygen and placing the mask over Cecelia's face, she loosened her collar, unbuttoned her waistband, pulled up the armrests between the seats, and laid her down across the three seats. She placed a pillow under her head and covered her with one of the blankets stored in an overhead compartment. Satisfied she had done everything she could do, she turned and proceeded to the front of the plane in search of help.

Mike, who had been standing at the bottom of the stairs, sensed something was wrong. He climbed the stairs, entered the cabin, and walked through the deserted plane to find Cecelia lying across the seats. Kneeling down so he could hold her in his arms, he whispered in her ear. "It's Mike, I'm here to take care of you. You're safe in San Francisco; as soon as we can, we will get you to a hospital where they can take better care of you."

Despite everything that had happened, she still had a tight grip on the handle of her heavy leather briefcase. Mike tried to loosen her grip, but he was startled by the hissing sound she made as she clutched the case to her chest.

When the ambulance crew entered the plane with a narrow gurney, Mike—hoping to avoid any further agitation—instructed them to lay the briefcase on top of her before suggesting they take her to the Peralta hospital, the same hospital in Oakland where she was taken after her kidnapping. "They're familiar with her case," he said. "The doctors there will know what to do!"

Riding in the back of the ambulance, Mike anxiously held Cecelia's hand and worried about how much damage had been done. Having been separated for weeks by vast oceans, totally absorbed in solving entirely different sets of problems, Mike was not entirely unprepared for what had happened. Although he hadn't wanted to think about this possibility, in his heart he suspected it could happen. *Any sign of recognition, a squeeze of the hand or a few words, would be a very encouraging sign*, he thought.

As soon as she awoke on the morning of the fourth day, Cecelia was aware she was approaching the abyss of emotional trauma. Instinctively, she knew she could be in real trouble. *The strain of my trip and the shock of Jacques's disappearance must be overloading my circuits. This feeling reminds me of how I felt just before I entered that trance-like state during my kidnapping. I must be way out there on the thin ice of emotional safety.*

For the next three days, Cecelia slept, only waking for brief intervals for bathroom breaks, to drink large glasses of water in an attempt to cure what seemed like unquenchable thirst, and—strangely enough—to devour peanut butter and jelly sandwiches.

With the attacks and all her worry about Jacques, Cecelia knew three days of rest hadn't provided her with enough time to recuperate. *The minute I begin to worry, I can feel myself moving out toward the thin ice. I need more time.*

In Cecelia's presence, Mike didn't have the luxury of his own feelings. He was completely exhausted and depressed over the Jacques situation. Despite his effort to hide his concern about his friend, Cecelia could sense his depression. *I can't remember ever seeing him appear as anything less than the warrior in the center of the ring, trying to corner his opponent*, she thought. *His new sense of helplessness is scaring me. Are things worse than they appear?*

THE SENTINELS: CRUDE DECEPTION 179

Monitoring her situation, the medical staff was becoming convinced she might make better progress in the familiar setting of her own apartment. Partly to cheer her up and partly because there wasn't much else they could do to help her, early one morning they announced she was free to leave the hospital.

For the next four days, Cecelia and Mike only left their apartment to do the necessary shopping at the small neighborhood markets, buy newspapers, and go for walks. In a strange way they were hoping the phone wouldn't ring. A ringing phone was likely to bring bad news.

Two days passed before they allowed themselves to talk about their work. Mike seemed anxious to discuss the implications of what he and Juan Pablo had discovered in Venezuela. "Cecelia, forget the financial damages—do you realize how our proof of fraud is going to affect the future of the major oil companies? The day is rapidly coming when they will not be able to get away with operating beyond the letter of the law. Suspicious suppliers, customers, operating partners, and government regulatory agencies are going to be checking everything they do.

"You have no idea how much of an impression that information made on our meetings in Geneva. Finally, oil-producing countries have the excuse they need to look beyond the Oil Club. If there was ever a time when Big Oil's arrogant attitudes can be challenged and new alternatives introduced, this is it. No longer will these oil-rich governments, even on a begrudging basis, be willing to trust them. Talk about creating a new environment . . . I think that our day may have finally arrived."

"Mike," said Cecelia, "for completely different reasons, what you are describing is similar to what I was exposed to on my trip to Indonesia. The future political status of Indonesia is going to be decided by how the attitudes of the major oil companies are managed. Believe it or not, the presence of a competing independent oil consortium can be used to separate local governance issues from historic resource claims and future petroleum-development aspirations.

"As you can imagine, I had a lot of time on the flights back from Hong Kong to study and organize my notes. I really need to talk to someone in the State Department about what I learned in Indonesia. Do you think Roger Malone could arrange a meeting?"

Pausing to make certain Cecelia was finished, Mike said, "I don't see why not. Before we have our Sentinel planning session, I'm going to meet with Roger and our other government friends. That would be a good opportunity to provide them with a copy of your summary analysis. After they understand the relevance of your report, I wouldn't be surprised if they pass it along. And it should only be a question of time before they contact you to present the rest of your report."

Chapter 30

ADRIFT

The mistral had finally blown itself out. Jacques's craft was bobbing around in the quiet, its boom swinging slowly in the gently rolling sea. The sun had been out for several hours and there was practically no breeze.

When Jacques began to regain consciousness, his first sensation was that of feeling parched, gagging from thirst, with a terrible pain on the right side of his head. Instinctively, he grabbed the free line of the swinging boom and resecured it to the starboard cleat.

Looking around, all he could see was water in every direction. Jacques had no idea where he was, or how he had gotten there. He was confused by the pain in his head and the sensation of warmth as blood continued to ooze from the open wound.

No amount of searching revealed anything he could use to clean the wound or apply as a bandage. It occurred to him that his underwear was the only thing he could use.

Taking off his pants, normally something he would do without thinking, had become a difficult chore. Any effort to lower his head was immediately met by terrible pain, light-headedness, and an oncoming sense of unconsciousness. By sitting up he was able to push his pants and underwear down to his thighs. By raising his knees he succeeded in pushing the garments below his knees, and by standing up and putting one foot on the cuff of his pants, he succeeded in pulling them off, one leg at a time.

Using the knife he found in one of his dungaree pockets, he cut his boxer shorts into a series of long strips. Next, he dipped one of the remaining oddly shaped pieces into the saltwater and began to gently clean his wound as best he could. The briny water stung like crazy. Folding over another strip of underwear, he made a small pad-like bandage that would at least protect the wound from the sun. Selecting two of the longer strips, he tied them around his head to hold the bandage in place.

When he was finished, he placed the remaining pieces in his rear pockets to be saved for another day. Instinctively, he reached for his canteen and took several slugs of water before realizing that the remaining supply of fresh water would become his most precious possession.

As confused as he was, Jacques nevertheless began taking inventory. He had found a compass in his other dungaree front pocket. Next to a canteen he found a map of southern France, wrapped in sealskin, and a stick of salami, a brick of cheese, and part of a baguette, all wrapped in wax paper. Pulling up the line secured to the stern cleat, he found the large canvas bag with holes cut in its bottom. *I have no idea who I am or where I am, but I do have food, water, a compass, a map, one good sail, and a makeshift sea anchor.*

He presumed from studying the map that he must be in the Mediterranean and that by sailing north, sooner or later he should run into some part of the French, Italian, or Spanish coastline. Using what little strength he had, he raised the mainsail. With the aid of his compass, he began to sail north, tacking against the prevailing offshore northern breezes. Using his watch, he timed his tacks to port, always trying to limit each tack to ten minutes.

From the readings on his compass, he was able to determine how many points off North he was forced to sail. When ten minutes had expired, he tacked to starboard, being careful to set his course exactly the same number of degrees on the opposite side of North and limit his progress to another ten minutes. *I may not know where I'm going*, he thought, *but at least I know I'm sailing there in a straight line.*

On the morning of the third day, with his meager supply of water running low and no rain in sight, Jacques began to worry about how many more days it would take to reach the French coastline.

What Jacques had no way of knowing was that while his tacking was taking him north, the currents were pushing him westward. The combination of the two succeeded in moving his boat well away from the designated search area.

Chapter 31

THE CONFRONTATION

It was eleven o'clock at night in New York City. The phone on the nightstand next to Jack Hardy's bed began to ring. Such a late-night at-home call could only signal serious trouble for the chairman and president of Titus Oil.

"Hardy here," he grumbled, half asleep. "Excuse me, who did you say is calling?" All of a sudden he was wide awake. "What? The FBI has arrested Sam Clarke? How on earth could they have known that?"

Hardy could feel the blood drain from his face as he listened to his lawyer give him the details of the arrest of Samson America's managing partner and about the taped phone conversations the FBI had found. *If the government can make the connection between Samson and me, the Oil Club could be in a lot of trouble!* thought Hardy.

"Are those tapes admissible as evidence in a court of law?" he said. After a few seconds, he asked, "As far as you know, have there been any other arrests or warrants issued?"

After a sleepless night, Hardy showered, shaved, dressed, and went to work with a sense of foreboding. He always kept three laundered and pressed shirts in the bottom left-hand drawer of his desk. Prone to perspire when he was under stress, he would dry himself off and change shirts between meetings. At ten o'clock that morning, when his secretary told him Roger Malone was waiting, Hardy had already changed his shirt once.

"He knows he doesn't have an appointment, Mr. Hardy, but he was wondering if you would see him anyway. He wouldn't tell me the purpose of his visit."

As Roger Malone walked through the open door of Hardy's office a moment later, the Titus Oil chairman rose to greet him.

"Good morning, Roger, what brings you to New York?" Jack asked cheerfully, trying his best to conceal his anxiety as he extended his hand toward his old friend in anticipation of the customary handshake.

Ignoring his gesture, Roger placed a copy of the *Paris Herald Tribune*, the edition that described Jacques Roth's mysterious disappearance, on Jack Hardy's wide desktop. Jacques's picture and the headline lay face-up.

"Jack, this is not a social call. I am here to talk about Jacques Roth, the Samson organization, and its association with Titus and the other major oil companies."

Watching Jack react to his opening statement, Roger knew his verbal bullet had found its mark. To prevent Hardy from regaining his composure, Roger continued, "Before you react, let me tell you about the evidence we have regarding your secret meeting with the other major oil company executives and your employment of the Samson organization. We have a recording of your conversation with Fred Clarke regarding his assignment. Under normal circumstances, I wouldn't be the member of the government calling on you. If this didn't involve Jacques Roth, I would have been pleased to leave the pursuit of this case to the appropriate authorities."

Looking straight into Hardy's eyes, Roger said, "Jack, this time you and your friends have gone too far. Do you think the government is going to tolerate your employing Samson or anyone else to conduct paramilitary operations here or in Europe? That day is over. Unless we can come to a quick understanding regarding the unharmed release of Jacques Roth, you and your oil buddies will be subjected to some very interesting consequences."

"Roger," said Hardy, clearly shaken, "I don't want to appear disrespectful, but do you really think you can come marching in here, tell me your suspicions about Samson, and try to convince me that we can be proven guilty of all those charges? Do you expect Titus Oil and the other oil companies to change our strategic course because you have a recording of one conversation?"

"Don't screw around," said Roger. "I don't have time to play games. Do you really think I would be here if all we had was a recording of one of your telephone conversations? How do you know that we don't have other tapes of conversations between Clarke and your friends at English Oil? Or tapes between you and them? How do you know that Clarke hasn't already told us about his relationship with you and his other employers? Don't forget, we have the sworn confessions of Samson operatives—those are the ones who weren't killed.

"But that's not the point. I am here to offer you a choice. Either you agree to sign this affidavit I'm about to hand you, immediately cancel all your arrangements with Samson, and produce Roth within the next twenty-four hours, or you can expect to face the full investigative energies of the Justice Department, the Department of Commerce, the FBI, and the IRS. And, I'm sure that I don't have to remind you that your commercial banking friends will have to receive the approval of the Federal Reserve before they can expect to access the funds they will need to finance the development of new oil fields. This is *not* the time for you to be fucking around!"

"Roger, you still don't understand!" said Hardy. "Threaten us any way you wish, but before you decide to take action, it might be best if you understood our position. If we are successful, we will have gained control of ninety percent of the world's oil supply. If we fail, we can slow down production of our current oil fields, reducing the supply of available petroleum and driving up the price of oil. The value of our existing oil reserves will become incalculable. It's a win-win situation. Knowing this, do you really believe your threats are going to deter us?"

"Jack, your reputation for being a tough, hard-driving force in the oil industry is not in question," said the chairman. "If I didn't acknowledge your leadership, I wouldn't be here. It's the Jacques Roth situation that concerns me. Sign this affidavit, and I'm out of here. Once you produce the French banking empire's scion, alive and unharmed, you and your pals can do whatever you think best when it comes to the oil industry."

Roger watched as his adversary digested what he had just said. "Roger, for the sake of argument, what happens if I sign your affidavit and we can't produce Jacques Roth because we don't have him?"

Reaching for the document, Roger said, "Let me add a postscript!"

After returning to his Washington office, Roger placed three phone calls.

The first was to Secretary Ainsworth. "Henry, Jack signed our document. I think you folks at the Treasury and I may have heard the last of Samson, at least for a little while. If they have Jacques, they should release him in the next twenty-four hours."

He then made another call: "Mr. President, things went as we hoped. Hardy has signed the affidavit. I think we have seen the last of the Oil Club's attempts to blackmail our government."

The final call was to Henri Demaureux at La Garoupe. "Henri, the affidavit has been signed. For all intents and purposes, I think you can consider Samson neutralized. They should no longer represent a threat to you or your daughter, and they should release Jacques within the next twenty-four hours. I do think, however, it is entirely possible that Samson doesn't have Jacques. In that case, we'll have to look for another explanation."

Chapter 32

EL SUERTUDO

On the seventh day of Jacques's disappearance, a crewman on a Catalonian fishing boat spotted a small craft with its mainsail flapping about in the breeze. Unaccustomed to seeing small sailboats in the fishing lanes off the Mediterranean coast of Spain, the crewman motioned for the captain to navigate toward what appeared to be an abandoned craft. As the commercial fishing boat drew closer, the two men could see the boat's sole occupant lying unconscious in the bottom of the small cockpit.

The motionless body did not show any signs of recognition as the fishing boat approached. After two blasts on the air horn, there was still no movement. Pulling alongside the sailboat, the captain climbed down and secured the smaller boat to his own. He inspected the body and felt a slight pulse. "He's alive, but just barely. His lips are parched, his tongue is swollen, and he has burns over most of his exposed body."

The captain and one of his crew succeeded in rolling the unconscious man onto what was left of the jib and carefully lifted him onto the larger boat. After carrying him to a small room that served as the captain's cabin, they gently lowered him onto a bed. After instructing the crewman to soak a clean cloth in a pan of fresh water, the captain squeezed the wet cloth and slowly dripped water into the man's mouth. Once he saw the man lick his lips, the captain went above and gave the crew orders to finish what they were doing. He was preparing to return to port.

The man carried no identification. An inspection of the boat yielded no clues as to his identity. Not certain what to do, the captain thought, *If he's still alive when we get him to my home, perhaps my wife and daughter will know how to take care of him.*

As the captain navigated toward the coast, he looked back at the sea behind them. They'd left Jacques's battered sailboat bobbing, abandoned, on the water.

Torreblanca was a small coastal Catalonian fishing village, well off the track of tourists or commercial vendors, with the exception of the regular visits of Parisian fish buyers. The people of Torreblanca had long adhered to a Catalonian custom of preserving their independence from the rest of the world.

Located on the eastern coast of Spain, midway between Valencia and Barcelona, near the mouth of the Ebro River, the small village had survived for centuries by harvesting the unusual and bountiful species of fish that were attracted by the nutrient-rich waters that drained from the watersheds of the Pyrenees.

It took all four crewmen to lift up the sail and carry the unconscious man up the narrow side street that led from the dock to the captain's home. As predicted, the captain's wife and daughter knew exactly what to do. They washed off the tall, dehydrated, sun-charred man. They changed his bandage, cut his hair, and gave him a shave before putting him in bed. Water was slowly dripped into his mouth until he would swallow involuntarily.

"Getting enough fluids back into him must come first," said

the captain's wife. "Next, we will treat his burns with the juice of the aloe plant. We'll worry about nourishment after he wakes up."

For the next two days they repeated the process of giving him water every half hour. On the third day, when Jacques regained consciousness, he was all alone in a dark and strange room. His yell of terror brought the wife and her daughter running.

"Where am I?" Jacques shouted in English and then in French. "What has happened to me?" Understanding neither language, all the woman could do was respond in her gentle Castilian tongue. Unable to understand the words, he could sense the kindliness in her voice. He looked around and saw that he wasn't captive; the door was open, he was comfortable, and the woman was smiling. A pretty young girl entered the room carrying a bowl of soup, a big wooden spoon, and a large napkin.

Sitting down on the bed next to him, she laid the napkin on his chest, filled the spoon with the clear broth, and tasted it for warmth before slowly pouring it into his mouth. Patiently, she continued feeding him and talking to him in the same strange language, in that soft, lyrical voice. On the fifth day, Jacques was able to get out of bed on his own and make his way into the bathroom. He had barely enough strength to return. He remained in bed and slept as best he could between his regular intakes of water and food.

Finally, by the end of the week, he was able to get out of bed, walk around the house, and sit in the chair on the small balcony that looked out over the Mediterranean. It was when he was looking out over the sea that he experienced his first flash of memory. The view had brought back a vision from another time and another place.

He learned the name of the pretty daughter was Gloria. She

began to take him for short walks around the fishing village. As they ventured about, Jacques would see familiar sites and his visual memory would briefly reopen, only to close again as soon as he tried to analyze what he was seeing. *At least the flashes are coming more frequently*, he thought.

Now ready for stronger nourishment, Jacques would join his new family at the dinner table, enjoy the food they put on his plate, particularly the fish, and quietly listen to the strange-sounding conversation. His strength was returning, and he was taking longer walks.

By the start of the third week, Jacques was beginning to understand some of what he was hearing and started to speak a few words of the strange language. He was gaining weight, and the wound on his head had healed. One night over dinner, the captain decided that Jacques should go out on the fishing boat and begin to earn his keep. The crew, always needing an extra hand on deck, would be pleased to teach him the different tasks.

Jacques's strength was returning; he was gaining weight and becoming tanned like the rest of fishermen. His six-feet-three stature and blue eyes clearly differentiated him from the others.

For reasons no one seemed able to explain, both the size of the catch and the quality of the fish on the captain's boat seemed to be improving. Members of the other crews and the buyers in the market could see that there *was* something special and mysterious about the man they now called El Suertudo, "the lucky one."

Each afternoon, Parisian fish buyers would be waiting to inspect and bid on each fisherman's daily catch. Interested but not qualified to participate in the age-old haggling routine, Jacques would stand aside and watch the process unfold, casually talking to one of the fish buyer's helpers.

Late one afternoon, after the market had closed, he was flattered when one of his new companions asked him if he could take his picture.

Chapter 33

A MEETING WITH ROGER

Mike had arrived in Washington the night before his scheduled meeting with Reserve Chairman Malone and a few key senators. Distracted by his continuing thoughts of Jacques, who had now been missing for several weeks, Mike had to force himself to prepare for the meeting. *If only Jacques were here, he would know what to do! I never expected to be the one responsible for convincing these men of the necessity of issuing our proposed oil development bonds.*

Mike was greeted warmly upon his arrival at Roger Malone's private office the following morning.

"Mike, I understand what an important and sensitive subject we are going to be discussing today. It occurred to me, however, that it might be a good idea if we talked about Jacques before we join the others."

"I agree," said Mike, waiting for the chairman to continue.

"I know you understand that the five gentlemen waiting in the next room are some of your greatest admirers in Washington, and that they don't need to be convinced of the merits of your plan. They are, however, concerned about a couple of subjects. The first, and by far the most important, concerns your resolve and that of the others about proceeding with your plan in the event that Jacques fails to reappear.

"Second, if we are going to pass the necessary legislation, they need to ask you the same tough questions they are expecting to have to answer themselves. It's important that you assist them with the answers as best as you can. While we understand it is critical that you develop public support at the grassroots level, passage of the enabling bill will still require a full-court press at the congressional level."

"I understand, Roger. Before we start, is there any new news on Jacques?"

"Yes, two things. First, I met for a second time with Jack Hardy yesterday. As an addendum to our agreement, we have agreed to withhold our attack on Samson and the oil companies until we can determine what happened to Jacques. I'm not quite certain why I believe Hardy, but he has convinced me that there has to be some other explanation for Jacques's disappearance; we just don't know what it is. I've known Jack for a long time and believe he is capable of doing almost anything, but he is not a liar! All I can say is, God help them if we learn that they are responsible for Jacques's disappearance and have deliberately misled us."

"You said there was something else?"

"Two days ago it was reported that what was left of a small wooden sailboat was found near the eastern coast of Spain. It could be nothing, but until we have checked it out, we can't know for sure that it wasn't Jacques's."

"How could he have been in that area?" said Mike. "That's more than two hundred and fifty miles from where the French navy has been searching!"

"As I said, we don't know. But in the meantime, I have asked the authorities not to contact either Pierre or Claudine. There's no point in raising their hopes until we know for certain that the wreckage was indeed Jacques's boat."

"But if he'd made it to shore alive, he would have contacted us by now," said Mike.

"We've thought the same thing. But it's possible that he can't. He could be lying hurt in some local hospital or any number of other places. Claudine told us that he left his wallet at La Garoupe. Without any identification, no one would be able to determine who he is."

———

An hour later, Mike, Roger, and five of Roger's government colleagues were sitting around the chairman's elegantly furnished office.

When Roger signaled it was time for Mike to begin, he said, "Perhaps it might suffice if I briefly recap some of the more important things that have occurred since we last met?"

"This should be interesting," Senator Lucas of California murmured sarcastically.

Ignoring him, Mike explained the need to develop a plan of their own to slow down the quest of the major oil companies to perpetuate their control over the world's oil supply. "The heart of our plan calls for our producing a separate source of financing, one that eliminates the dependency on the balance sheets of the Oil Club. The only source of money capable of creating a viable alternative is the international private investment market."

"Come on, Mike, are you serious?" said Senator Hess of Pennsylvania. "How do you know that there's sufficient capacity, much less the motivated cooperation you will need to fund fifteen billion dollars?"

"Sir, we've done our homework," said Mike. "We believe, contingent upon our receiving the assistance we are seeking from the federal government, that it will be difficult, but not impossible. We think we can make it work!"

"Just exactly what are you asking us to consider?" asked Senator Armstrong of Indiana, looking very suspicious.

"Two things: the formation of a new government agency, authorized to issue international oil development bonds, and the support of those bonds with the full faith and credit of the United States government, once they can be secured by the revenues of the proven production of the subject oil fields."

Senator Lucas was the first to respond. "Mike, you understand that the formation of a government agency and providing those kinds of guarantees will require an act of Congress, right? Even if the White House is prepared to support your plan, you are talking about challenging the well-entrenched Washington oil lobby. Obtaining consent from both houses of Congress could be a very tall order."

Mike nodded. "Understanding that we would need public support, at the grassroots level, we knew we had to expose the vulnerable underbelly of the oil lobby."

"So that was the real motive behind Walt Matthews's crusade against the foreign profits tax provision?" Senator Lucas asked.

"The modification of the tax code represented a trial balloon," said Mike. "It was Walt's contention that by appealing directly to the American people, we would force Congress to publicly choose between supporting the vested interests of the oil lobby or the best interests of their informed and angered constituencies."

"You and your friends have certainly developed an interesting technique for serving notice on the Oil Club," said Senator Lucas. "You may have caught them by surprise the first time, but they will be prepared and waiting for you this time."

At this point, Chairman Malone broke in. "Mike, why don't you lead us through the details of what you have in mind?"

After listening to Mike's presentation, Senator Hess asked, "If we are not prepared to put up the money, why should we consider putting up our guarantees? What's the difference?"

"There are differences, Senator. One, the government doesn't have to fund fifteen billion dollars, and two, the transactions can be structured in such a manner that the exposure becomes quantifiable. The related cost of the guarantees can be included in the cost of capital charged to the borrower. Put another way, the borrower pays for the risk associated with his borrowing."

"Roger," said Senator Armstrong, "this young man knows what he's talking about. Currently, my committee is considering a similar approach to help finance the exploding postwar demand for housing. I don't know why, for collateral purposes, we can't conceptually consider revenue-generative oil fields as the equivalent to interest-bearing notes secured by properly constituted home mortgages."

"I have a different problem," Chairman Malone said. "I believe I must introduce an additional stipulation. To prevent the diluting of the plan below acceptable levels, the Fed will require all fifteen billion dollars be raised in the form of enforceable letters of credit. Mike, to me, that sounds like a very big order."

Senator Lucas spoke up. "While I am reasonably certain that what I want to talk about is implicit in your plan, I just want to make sure. Am I correct in assuming the terms and conditions of the offering will permit the funds to be used by all qualified applicants, be they major or independent oil companies? Unfortunately, it means you will have to raise all the funds required to support the total development costs for the next three to five years, not just what is needed by the independents. While banks, insurance companies, and investment bankers can be as discriminating as they wish, the federal government does not enjoy the same privilege."

"Senator, let me assure you that is the case," Mike replied. "As much as we would have preferred to construct our plan to help only the non-major oil companies and limit the amount of money we would be required to raise, we realized early on that our plan had to be nondiscriminatory if we were to ask for the cooperation of the federal government."

Senator Lucas pushed Mike further. "Your deal, as you describe it, is technical and complicated. Why should we go to all this trouble and accept all these risks when the oil companies are prepared to provide the needed capital?"

Looking the senator directly in the eye, Mike said, "Because that is the cost of preventing seven oil companies from controlling an unacceptable amount of the world's oil production."

Chapter 34

THE PRESIDENT

Cecelia sat quietly in the sun-filled dining room of her apartment, opening her mail and enjoying her first cup of coffee. Mike had left the day before for his meeting in Washington. Her attention was immediately drawn to an envelope with the engraved emblem of the United States President. *Why would the President be sending me a letter? Is this a fundraiser?*

Almost afraid to open the letter, she poured herself a second cup of coffee and adjusted her position to take full advantage of the light shining through the nearby window. When she opened it, she saw that the content was clearly not campaign-type correspondence. *My God, it's a handwritten letter from the President.*

Straining her eyes to read the President's difficult-to-decipher handwriting, she carefully studied his invitation. Having a hard time believing the President would invite her to the White House to discuss matters in Indonesia, she reread the note three times.

Traveling to Washington, Cecelia wished she had received the letter earlier; she could have simply come to the capital with Mike.

Making her way to the White House and presenting her credentials at the gate was a new experience for the mighty warrior from Hong Kong. *How can it be that I can travel around the world, talk to heads of state, powerful bankers, and prominent investors, and not experience any particular discomfort, yet here I am, headed to the Oval Office, feeling like a little girl attending her first day of school!*

As she was escorted to the President's office, she felt her sense of intimidation intensify. Standing and waiting to greet her were the Secretary of State, the Chairman of the Federal Reserve, the Chairman of the Joint Chiefs of Staff, the President, and his Chief of Staff.

Flashing his legendary smile, the President said, "Welcome to the Oval Office, Miss Chang. I'm familiar with your many accomplishments, and I've been looking forward to meeting you for a long time."

Not certain how to respond, Cecelia gave a half-curtsy, half-bow, said thank you, and waited for the great man to continue.

Motioning toward an open seat, the President said, "Why don't you sit down, Miss Chang? Roger has been filling us in on your recent tour of the Orient, and he believes that you can help us better understand the situation out there. He has also been telling me you have some very interesting ideas of what can be done to solve our dilemma in Indonesia."

Sensing the President's sincere interest, Cecelia immediately revised the speech she'd planned on giving. Surprising even herself, she went right to the heart of the matter.

"Mr. President, at first glance, the United States may be faced with a difficult problem. The Dutch and the British, now that the war is over, believe they are entitled to their historical petroleum interests. In that matter, I am not aware of any material disagreement. What *is* in dispute is the issue as to whether they are entitled to reimpose their colonial rule over the island nation. From what I have been able to learn, they are basing their claim on the need to control the government as a necessary prerequisite to protecting their oil interests."

Pausing to allow her words to sink in, she listened as the President said, "Well, that pretty well sums up what we have been led to believe. I understand you believe there may be an alternative course of action that won't require us to deny the emergence of Indonesia's newly formed national government?"

"Yes, sir," said Cecelia, "I believe it's important that we question the British and Dutch assumptions. First, I am assured that the new Indonesian government is prepared to recognize the British and Dutch claims over their existing developed oil interests. About that, there is no debate. It is the issue of developing suspected but unproven reserves that is causing the larger problem."

Pausing to catch her breath, Cecelia continued. "As long as it is believed that the development of those new reserves can only be accomplished by a coalition of the major British and American oil companies, there isn't much that can be done. If you change that assumption, then the picture becomes quite different."

"Miss Chang, I'm not certain I understand what you mean by 'changing the assumption,'" said the President. "What are you implying? Who else can develop those quantities of oil?"

"Before I answer your question, I would like to say that the issue your government is facing in Indonesia is symptomatic of a larger problem that is about to emerge in Southeast Asia, the Middle East, and North Africa, where new large reserves of oil are believed to exist. Unless America is prepared to deny its recognition of emerging self-determined governments, it needs to pay very careful attention to the developing situation in Indonesia. It would appear that the United States and the rest of the free world are faced with a simple choice. We must learn how to separate local resource issues from local governance issues or face the possibility that we will be forced to support local military dictatorships and foreign colonial rule, heavily influenced by the dictates of the seven major oil companies. If we don't get it straight in Indonesia, what are we going to do when the same problem emerges in all these other places?"

"Miss Chang, I couldn't agree more with your assessment," said the President, impressed. "I wait with great anticipation to hear your solution!"

"Mr. President, my friends and I are convinced these oil-rich nations need to have some other choice than to submit to the demands of the major oil companies. Let us suppose, for the sake of conversation, that Indonesia had other interested and qualified parties willing to bid competitively for the right to develop its untapped petroleum reserves. Should that become the case, the independent Indonesian government would no longer be dependent on the British and the Dutch."

Having made her point, Cecelia sat back in her chair and waited for the response.

Each of the men in the room was thinking to himself. The protracted silence that permeated the room only added to the tension. Finally, the President focused his attention on his Secretary of State and asked, "Is she right?"

"What she says makes sense," the secretary replied. "It's just that we have never been able to give any consideration to the existence of a competitive petroleum development source. Perhaps Miss Chang would like to explain why she believes her suggestion represents a realistic alternative."

"Mr. President, my friends and I have been developing a plan that will encourage qualified independent oil companies to become competitive bidders for all these new oil concessions. As we speak, my friends and I are engaged in the process of creating a billion-dollar prototype of what we hope will become a fifteen-billion-dollar international oil development fund. Once that fund is in place, sovereign oil nations or consortiums of independent oil companies will have access to the magnitude of capital they require to develop new oil fields."

"Now I understand what Roger has been telling me," said the President. "Do the rest of you agree with Miss Chang's suggestion that by helping her to create this fund, we will be, among other things, providing the United States with a new set of options for dealing with this problem of self-determination she has so eloquently described?"

The Secretary of State said, "I'm impressed enough by Miss Chang's suggestion that I would like to recommend that we not only delay any consideration of Britain's and Holland's requests for support but also consider sending the British Prime Minister a letter clearly stating our opposition to any attempt on their part or the part of the Dutch to superimpose their colonial governmental rule over Indonesia."

Finally the Chief of Staff spoke up. "Mr. President, we have reliable information reporting that the Dutch have moved a hundred and ten thousand of their own troops into Indonesia. It's important that we remove any possibility that the Dutch and the British will move unilaterally. I respectfully suggest you consider allowing me to move some of our ships into the area and schedule some naval training exercises."

After nodding his assent, the President said, "Miss Chang, as we used to say in the army, 'One hand washes the other.' Now, with regard to this oil fund of yours, Roger tells me that you want our government to form a new agency and issue fifteen billion dollars of U.S.-guaranteed bonds. Am I to surmise it is the presence of this new fund that will provide the financing needed by independent oil developers to bid competitively against the big British and Dutch oil companies?"

"Yes," said Cecelia. "That's correct."

Glancing at his advisors, the President interpreted their smiles as encouragement to proceed. "Roger, it might be a good idea if you would keep me fully informed about the progress of the oil development fund," he said. "This is something that needs to happen. And, while you're at it, I suggest you and Henry begin to investigate different options we might use should Miss Chang require our assistance."

He turned to Cecelia. "Miss Chang, I think it would be appropriate for you to tell your friends that your request for new legislation will have the full support of the White House. Good luck—you're going to need it!"

Chapter 35

FINAL PLANNING

At last the time arrived for the Sentinels' final planning meeting. Although he hadn't been actively involved in any of the Sentinels' activities since he retired to manage the Sentinels' winery, Tony Garibaldi, one of the original six, had kept in close contact. The five-thousand-acre premium wine operation represented one of the investments the Sentinels had made to prevent the proceeds of their German bond sales from being detected. It was Mike who suggested they kill two birds with the same stone, as he and Cecelia flew back to San Francisco from Washington. "If we ask Tony to host our next meeting at his ranch in California," he said, "we could receive his winery status report and at the same time figure out how we are going to raise all the money."

"Let's make certain we select a time when Ian Meyer can be there," Cecelia added. "Not only do we need him to take notes, but it will be difficult enough to meet without Jacques. Despite the fact that he has been forced to reduce his involvement to that of our scrivener, I still consider Ian as one of the original six. With his presence, at least five of us will be there."

"My dear," said Mike, "at last count I think we will be more than five. I'm assuming we will want to invite Juan Pablo and Sir David . . ."

Mike's phone conversation with Tony was much more than a talk between two old friends. "Of course, Mike," said Tony. "I would be pleased to invite all six of you to the ranch. It just won't be the same without Jacques, though."

"Speaking of Jacques," said Mike, "his absence is something I need to discuss with you. I'm going to need your help. You and I understand, better than the others, how Jacques would want us to proceed. Claudine is a trouper, but she is going to need to rely on us for support. While I am certain we can count on her to complete the European part of the equation, I think she would be relieved to know we are going to lead the charge."

Mike's next call was to the Secret Service. The agent in charge said, "You don't have to tell me about the ranch; I was there last time, when those Samson operatives shot up the place and almost killed Tony Garibaldi. Give us a few days to prepare, and this time we'll make certain nobody who shouldn't be there will even get close!"

During the day preceding their meeting, the Sentinels and their guests began arriving in ones and twos. Always the proud vintner and consummate host, Tony was present to greet his old friends, colleagues, fellow investors, and new guests.

He made certain each arrival was properly situated in the guest quarters and told each person that he would conduct a tour of the ranch and the surrounding vineyards as soon as everyone was assembled. Two years had passed since the Sentinels had last visited, and five years had passed since they had put together the five thousand acres required to support an emerging national market for premium wine.

"First we will tour the vineyards," Tony explained to each guest. "After three years, we have planted more than fifteen hundred acres. I think you will be impressed by the different microclimates, the diversity of the grapes, and the vigorous growth of the vineyards. Plan to be ready by eight o'clock in the morning. The tour will take most of the day, and it will work its way up the Napa Valley, cross through the Alexander Valley, and drive south through Sonoma's Russian River Valley. Then we'll pass through the Carneros region on our way back to ranch headquarters. Hopefully, we'll return in time to tour our winery, the bottling operations, and the warehouse where we store and age our bottled wine inventory."

To complete the tour, Tony's staff had organized a dinner that would take place in the limestone caves where the wines were stored and aged. Each course had been selected to complement the wines that would be served.

―――

As impressive as Tony's progress was, Jacques's absence was never far from anyone's mind.

The next night, after a long day of touring the sprawling vineyards, the Sentinels and their guests were all seated around a wide table placed inside the mouth of the limestone caves, allowing guests a magnificent view of the vineyards of the Napa Valley and, in the background, the rolling green hills spotted by the majestic oak trees that populated the region.

Mike tapped his glass and waited until he had everyone's

attention. "Before we start, Tony has something he would like to say."

A teary-eyed Claudine stood up, champagne flute in hand, and said, "It's time to break the silence about our dear friend. Jacques, I lift this glass in a toast to you. Each of us misses you very much in our own way and is concerned about embarking on our new mission without your guidance and assistance. Wherever you are, we hope you are safe. Please hurry back to us. We know if you were here you would be telling us to proceed. Jacques, we hear you, and we know what we have to do!"

The next morning, after Tony's staff had cleared away the breakfast dishes, the group was enjoying a second round of coffee. Addressing Tony and Ian, Mike said, "How nice it is to have you join us. Given Jacques's absence, having all the remaining Sentinels and our new guests gathered here makes things seem a little less forbidding.

"Now that we have finished organizing the prototype fund," Mike continued, "the time has come for us to focus on raising the balance of the money. For the last few weeks, each of us has been busy studying the problems we must solve if we are to raise the fifteen billion dollars required to meet the Federal Reserve's minimum stipulation. I think this would be an appropriate time for each of you to give a brief report of your activities toward achieving this objective."

One by one, each of the Sentinels and their guests described their progress. Following their analysis of what they had learned, they provided Mike with their best guess regarding their estimated range of funds raised. Mike scratched figures on the blackboard as they spoke:

Cecelia	Asia	1.5 – 2 billion
Mike	USA	6.0 – 8.0
Jacques/Claudine	W. Europe	1.5 – 2.5
David	Great Britain	0.5 – 1.5
Juan Pablo	Latin America	0.5 – 1.0
Total		**$10.0 – 15.0 billion**

After reviewing his work, Mike continued, "If my math is right, it appears that we only expect to raise between ten and fifteen billion dollars. Even if we achieve our most optimistic forecasts, we'll barely achieve our minimum stipulation. At the low end of the range, five billion dollars is a lot to make up. In other words, we'd have to have a lot of luck on our side to achieve our goal. It also means we have to raise the maximum limits. Should any of us fail, the shortfall could place us well beyond the get-lucky range."

Tired and frustrated by the result of their presentations, the Sentinels looked to Mike for encouragement. It was Claudine who asked, "What are we going to do if all we can raise is ten billion dollars?"

"I think we need to be careful about putting too much credence in these numbers," Tony responded. "Perhaps we should look at our problem from a different angle. So far, all we have talked about are the quantitative issues. What about the qualitative issues? Do we know how motivated these investors may become once they focus on the potential threat of the seven oil companies? Although I regret not being able to actively join you in the raising of the money, I would like to volunteer our communications system, here at the ranch. I don't see any reason why each of you can't utilize the same private network we use to communicate with all our brokers and institutional customers."

Standing up, Mike said, "Tony, thank you for your words

of encouragement and the use of your system. I would like to add something to what you just said. We need to consider the trust factors that the information gleaned from Señor Perez's files revealed. We also should consider the influence of U.S. guarantees. I think we may have underestimated the persuasiveness of our own argument. We've even been assured we have the support of the White House.

"If any of you have had the opportunity to study David's investment-center map, I have to believe you share my amazement how broad and diverse the potential sources of economic interest are. There is no way to gauge the effect of these qualitative arguments or the attractiveness of our offering terms until we begin to meet with the investment managers."

"The American people haven't yet spoken," said Cecelia. "Once we've created and passed the necessary legislation, the will of Americans might play a more influential role. Imagine how the big banks might react when faced with the possibility of being excluded from one of this country's most important financings. Maybe the strength of the Oil Club's position is not as commanding as they would like us to believe."

Ian Meyer, who had been sitting quietly and listening to all the talk of numbers, finally said, "I'm not certain I understand all the numbers, or what they mean. All I know is that we are talking about a very complex and large transaction. I don't think I need to remind you, it was only five years ago that we conjured up the idea of forging a hundred million dollars of the Germans' gold certificates. If a hundred million seemed like a big number then, can you imagine how people are going to react to the suggestion that we need to raise fifteen billion dollars? Before we overreact to the big number, why don't we concentrate on completing the funding of the one-billion-dollar prototype? I know we're done organizing that exercise, but once we complete it, maybe we will have a better feel for the remaining fourteen billion."

Chapter 36

A LINE IN THE SAND

Following the passage of the bill that eliminated the foreign profits tax, rumors were beginning to circulate. A second bill authorizing the formation of a government agency to issue oil development bonds was making its way through Congress. While the first bill was viewed as an anti-oil tax issue, the second bill was regarded as a direct threat to the Oil Club's desire to perpetuate its majority control of the world's oil supply. The battle lines were being drawn.

The executive management of the seven major oil companies understood that if the law were to pass, the presence of an alternative source of development financing could upset their desire to organize an economic blockade. They had no alternative but to utilize their highly organized oil lobby in Congress to oppose the pending legislation.

A line in the sand was about to be drawn. Congressmen were going to have to choose. Would they back their sources of financial campaign support, or were they going to protect the interests of their voting constituencies?

Proponents of the new bill would argue that its genius came in providing the funding needed to ensure the orderly and competitive development of reliable and adequate supplies of least-cost oil.

Opponents of the bill contended that the same result could be achieved without the public's involvement.

The bill's effects weren't limited to Congress and the oil companies. The Oil Club's banking partners were attempting to support the needs of their biggest clients, and the Sentinels were preparing to take their case to the people.

The battle had become big news. Walt Matthews was reporting on it regularly in the *Times* and in thirty-two syndicated newspapers. Time was scheduled for the bill's sponsors to hold press conferences and make guest appearances on radio talk shows. They made themselves available for interviews by the financial press, citizen activist groups, and the reporters of the leading magazines.

The policies of both political parties were being reshaped. The democratic process of the United States was being fully tested. Control of the world's oil supply was at stake.

Walter was no longer having trouble generating funding for new surveys. The polls were beginning to reveal favorable ratings for the government's ingenuity in solving important problems. The public's interest was growing in what was rapidly becoming an important national issue.

The members of both houses of Congress were going home on weekends. They were talking to the local political bosses, they were holding town meetings, and they were reading and answering their mail.

The issue was also rousing the people. Voting records of their congressional representatives were being studied. Independent views were being aggregated into a single, loud voice of public opinion, all amplified by the reporting of each new opinion poll.

It wasn't long before the elected representatives had a clear understanding of the sentiment of their voters. Hiding in the shadows was no longer an option; they were going to have to make a choice.

Oil Club lobbyists were working overtime. Private meetings were being scheduled, questions were being asked. Campaign donors were making veiled threats of future abandonment. The rank and file of both political parties was attempting to exert its maximum influence.

Walt Matthews saw an opportunity to appeal to an even larger national audience. Knowing that certain key congressmen were caught between the unreported backroom pressure of the Washington lobbyists and the well-reported interests of their local constituencies, he wasn't willing to settle for limiting his energies to writing his syndicated column. He was using his influence with the working press to encourage them to poll and report more complete accounts of local voter interests and preferences.

News of the battle began to spread. The results of local polls were being picked up by news agencies and were reported across the country. Public interest was growing. What had started out as a state-by-state issue was rapidly turning into a national issue that pitted the public's needs against the agendas of those with vested interests. David and Goliath cartoons appeared in the editorial sections of the local newspapers, the *New Yorker*, *Life*, *Time*, and the *Saturday Evening Post*.

The mounting public hue and cry was not only making it more difficult for the Oil Club's Washington lobby to maintain control over the congressional vote, but it was also negatively influencing the public's trust of the seven major oil companies.

Unexpectedly, the voters were beginning to raise a second issue. Why should they purchase gasoline from companies they didn't trust? When the more consumer-oriented members of the different boards of directors began to realize that the problem wouldn't go away, they were forced to consider the possible consequences of what was happening at the service stations. At an increasing number of board meetings, directors were saying, "Losing a key vote in Congress is one thing, but antagonizing the public consumer is quite another matter. Is this a risk we should be taking?"

In the House, straw votes were becoming more frequent. The early results, while still favoring denial, demonstrated that an increasing number of middle-of-the-roaders were beginning to favor passage. Then a strange thing began to happen. One by one, some of the congressmen who had traditionally supported the Oil Club began to switch their votes. When asked to explain their change of heart, they would say, "Oh, I don't think I've changed. It's always been my position to support the interests of the voters I represent."

The Oil Club's reaction to the negative news was equally surprising. There were few threats of retribution. In some quarters there were vague reports that certain major oil executives appeared to be relieved. "After all," said one, "by not publicly opposing the proposed legislation, we can still privately use our influence over the American banks to prevent the independents from getting their financing, without risking the possibility of further antagonizing our customer."

The momentum for passage was building. Each day's poll revealed steady progress toward the needed 228 votes. When the straw count for passage exceeded 235, people stopped counting. By the time the bill reached the floor, it was approved by acclamation and sent on to the Senate for approval.

Chapter 37

A REUNION

Pierre Roth's secretary knocked gently on the door of his private office before entering. "Excuse me, Mr. Roth," she said, "there is a man waiting outside who would like to see you. He says it's extremely important. Apparently it has something to do with Jacques. He gave me a copy of your reward poster and this photograph to show you."

I hope this isn't someone's idea of a very cruel joke, Pierre thought. *After all this time, how is it possible that someone would show up with a photograph of Jacques?*

Almost afraid to look at the picture, Pierre reached for the photograph. The man in the picture seemed taller and gaunter than he remembered Jacques being. He was deeply tanned, wore a beard, had long unkempt hair, and wasn't wearing shoes. But as Pierre studied the picture, he realized, *If I took away the beard and the long hair, the person was definitely Jacques. The blank look on his face confuses me, but I would recognize my son under any conditions.*

Walking over to the window of his office, Pierre used the

natural light to help him study the picture more carefully. Finally, he turned to the man, whom the secretary had just ushered in, and asked, "Is Jacques alive? Can I see him?"

"I don't know about a man named Jacques," the man said. "We know him as El Suertudo—'the lucky one.' The man in this picture is very much alive. Promise to pay me my reward, sign this letter, and I'll take you to him."

The small specialty fish market in Torreblanca comprised eight separate booths. For as long as anybody could remember, the same eight fishing families had been selling their daily catch to the same Parisian fish buyers. Today, only seven of the booths were occupied; the eighth was conspicuously vacant. Asking around the market, the man with the reward poster failed to learn anything except that the captain's boat had not returned to its berth in the harbor. The slip was still empty. All he was able to learn was that the captain must have run into trouble. Without radios, no one in the market had any way of knowing what might have happened.

Pierre stood watching the fishermen clean up their stalls and the fish buyers load their daily purchases into their trucks. The market day was coming to a close, and he was beginning to think his hope had been in vain. Deeply disappointed, he was turning to leave when he heard shouting behind him.

Pierre watched as a man, presumably the captain, busily made his way forward through what was left of the crowd. Following behind him were his four crewmen, who each carried stacks of fish-laden wicker baskets, their faces hidden behind their precious cargo. Watching them carefully, Pierre focused his attention on the tallest of the men. Even from the back, he recognized his son.

Rushing forward, he grabbed the tall, gaunt fisherman just as he was turning away from the table where he'd set down his burden. Wrapping his bewildered son in the mightiest of hugs, Pierre said, "Jacques, thank God, it's really you! You are alive!"

Surprised and confused, Jacques failed to respond.

Unprepared for Jacques's reaction, Pierre pulled back to inspect the man he knew to be his son. Detecting what he thought was an initial sign of recognition, followed by an otherwise blank stare, he said, "Jacques, it's me, your father. I don't know why you don't recognize me, but I've come to take you home!"

At that point Pierre noticed the freshly healed scar on Jacques's head, and he moved closer to inspect what must have been a recent wound.

Needing Jacques to return to the boat for more of the day's catch, the captain became annoyed by the delay. He approached Pierre and said, "Excuse me, Señor, perhaps I can be of some assistance?"

In his poor but passable Spanish, Pierre attempted to explain. "Captain, please excuse the intrusion. My name is Pierre Roth, and this man is my son, Jacques. He has been missing for many weeks, and we presumed he was dead. Do you have any idea why he doesn't recognize his own father?"

When the phone rang at the chateau, Claudine immediately recognized her father-in-law's voice. "Claudine, we have found Jacques! He's alive! He's physically all right, but he is suffering from some sort of post-shock amnesia. We have him in a hospital here in Barcelona. Except for very brief moments when I see something flash in his eyes, he doesn't seem to recognize me. I'm not even certain if the moments really occur or it's just my wishful thinking.

"The doctors are suggesting that I arrange to have Jacques transported to Paris, where he can receive more expert treatment. It would be best if you could meet us there; maybe the sight of you will jog his memory."

Grateful that she'd returned from California in time to get the news, Claudine was out the door and on the road within minutes.

Twenty-four hours later, when Claudine walked into Jacques's new hospital room in Paris, she found Jacques lying on his side, his back toward her. He was sleeping peacefully. His head had been shaved, and there were red and blue dye marks painted on his skull along both sides of the jagged fresh scar. Intravenous tubes extended from each of his arms. Wires connecting small adhesive patches on his head and body to strange-looking monitors were all over the place. It was obvious they were recording much more than his vital signs.

Pierre was sitting in a chair next to the bed, holding one of Jacques's hands and staring anxiously at his sleeping son. Seeing Claudine enter the room, Pierre put his index finger up to his lips, signaling the need for silence. Without hesitation, she took off her coat, shed her shoes, and carefully climbed into Jacques's hospital bed. Putting her arms around him, she held him while he slept and hoped to be there when he awoke.

Jacques would never know whether it was the warmth of her arms around him, the sound of her quiet weeping, or the feeling of her tears rolling down his back that awoke him—but whatever it was, it caused his mind to flash open. At that moment he recognized his father, and he knew that his wife was in his bed. Afraid to move, think, or speak, he was worried that whatever he was experiencing would vanish. He was content to lie there and enjoy his moment of lucidity, hoping that it would last for more than a second.

As soon as he heard the door open and the nurse enter his room and begin checking his monitors, he could sense his memory begin to fade. Seeing Claudine, the nurse said, "Oh, Mrs. Roth, we are so glad you are here. Not only are we hopeful that seeing you will help Jacques make some progress, but we need your approval before we can operate."

Sensing Claudine's alarm, she continued. "This is a good thing, not a bad thing. From the tests we have been running, we suspect that some scar tissue or a small crushed segment of his skull is pressing on his brain. The doctors believe that by reducing the pressure they might be able to help him to recover his memory. I should caution you, however, that in other cases of this type we have found the recovery process to be very slow. It just takes time and patience."

Chapter 38

THE LONG ARM OF BIG OIL

Mike kept putting off his tour of the banks. He was bothered by his intuition telling him that he was in for some very difficult sledding, but he was even more concerned about Cecelia returning to Hong Kong and China to raise funds so soon after her recent illness. What if the strain was too great? Even the knowledge that her father and Ted Lee would be accompanying her didn't relieve his fears. *They certainly know her well enough to be able to spot any early signs of change*, he told himself. *I have to comfort myself by believing that they will know what to do.*

Realizing he should start in familiar West Coast territory, Mike's first call was to his old friend Pete Ferrari.

"Mike," said Pete, "although American West National Bank would be one of the last banks to hear such news, some friends of mine have told me the big banks are being pressured by Big Oil to limit their commitments to your oil fund to the minimum end of their investment range. Apparently, the pressure being applied is so great, if it weren't for their concerns over possible restraint of trade lawsuits, many of them wouldn't subscribe, even at their minimum levels. Based on some calculations I've made,

I concluded it might not be a good idea for you to anticipate an aggregate commitment of more than two billion."

"Should your observation prove accurate," said Mike, "it means we will be two to four billion dollars below our American quota. It will put even more pressure on our offshore sources."

"The unfortunate part of all this," said Pete, "is that the bond issue contains a number of qualities that make it very attractive. Under normal circumstances your problem would be one of over-subscription, not under-subscription. All we can do is try."

"Who knows, maybe something will happen to encourage some of these money center banks to abandon their minimums."

"I wouldn't get too discouraged, Mike. There are a couple of factors that might be working in your favor. It's important for you to remember that these other big banks are realists; as loyal as they may be to their Big Oil clients, they still have to worry about their bottom line. They understand that their profitability depends upon their continued support from a much broader customer base than just the oil community. If there is one thing you and your friends understand, it's how to apply elbow grease and play hardball. If the larger bankers become convinced that you are putting a significant amount of money together, there's no telling how they might react."

Mike's requests to meet with the bank presidents in the principal cities in the west and southwest parts of the United States were immediately accepted, and meetings were promptly scheduled.

The first few seemed to go well. The questions were direct and on point. The Oil Club issue was rarely raised. It was only after he kept hearing, "Of course, our staff needs to review your proposal before I can submit it to my loan committee for formal approval," that he began to question what was really happening. *Am I winning the battle and losing the war?* he asked himself. *Since when does participation in a U.S. government–guaranteed loan program require anything more than a rubber-stamp approval by a board of directors?*

After two strenuous weeks traveling from town to town, Mike was becoming very concerned. He hadn't heard back from any of the banks. He was tired, he was depressed, and he was lonely. He was worried about Cecelia and he couldn't stop thinking about why he wasn't getting any response from the banks. Finally, his curiosity compelled him to call his father.

Morgan Stone was glad he called. "If I had known how to reach you, Mike, I would have called you. You've been moving so fast, no one seems to know where you are. We're running into a problem. It isn't your presentations or even the quality of the investments that is causing the delay in response. It's the pressure the Oil Club is exerting on their banks. If I hadn't seen for myself what they are doing, I wouldn't have believed it. The banks are all talking among themselves and they will be providing you with one aggregated answer, one that protects them from acting on an independent basis.

"Based on what I've been hearing, I think you and your friends may have to further adjust your success ratio downward. At this point, even the potential for two billion dollars seems unlikely."

"Dad, what do you suggest I do?"

"First of all," said Morgan, "don't take any of this personally. Second, switch your focus to community banks and plan to cover as much local ground as you can. I think you might be pleasantly surprised by the reception you receive. Don't underestimate the importance of grassroots America; they control an enormous amount of our country's capital. The aggregate amount of their commitments could add up to a lot of money."

Chapter 39

RETURN TO ASIA

The closer her plane got to Hong Kong, the more excited Cecelia became. *I'm doing exactly what I was asked to do—returning with a proposal that is responsive to most of the issues we discussed on my previous trip. If there's any doubt, I will be able to refer to our prototype. What an advantage—there's nothing more convincing than to be able to talk about an actual working model.*

Tai-Pan had been following the progress of his daughter's work ever since she left Hong Kong. No matter how hard he tried to picture her as an acclaimed international banker trying to solve some very big problems, he could only see her as the little girl, sitting on his lap, asking one question after another. As complicated as her mission might appear, he knew the escalation of the Communist revolution was going to make her job much more difficult. *How am I going to tell my daughter that all her work could rapidly become one big academic exercise? No matter what, I have to warn her. I just hope my comments will not have a detrimental effect on her physical and mental well-being.*

The three bankers—Ted Lee, Bob Arnold, and Ray Tolles—rose to meet Cecelia and Tai-Pan when they arrived at Mai Li's teahouse. Once their greetings were complete and the tea was served, Ted came right to the point. "The progress of the Communist revolution is accelerating much more quickly than we imagined. There are many who believe it is only a matter of months before Communist forces drive Chiang Kai-shek's army off the mainland to the island of Taiwan. Unfortunately, the Chinese Nationalist government still has an appreciable amount of its funds trapped in Nanking. They could have a very serious problem."

"Thank you for the warning," said Cecelia. "I hope I have come sufficiently prepared. Hopefully, we'll be able to alleviate at least part of their problem. As you recall, when I was last here I took very careful notes. Your comments were well received by our people, and most of your concerns should be reflected in the proposal I have brought with me."

After pausing to reach into her briefcase, she withdrew a copy of her brief. "In anticipation of our meeting, I prepared a synopsis of our plan. Perhaps we could save time if I summarized its principal features and then answered any preliminary questions you may have. As soon as I have the opportunity, I will ask my father's secretarial staff to produce more copies."

After listening to Cecelia's brief synopsis, Ray Tolles spoke. "Well, Miss Chang, it appears you have come well prepared. When we suggested that you find a way to obtain American guarantees and remove the fractious nature of oil development from consideration, we never really believed you'd be able to devise and deliver such an effective instrument. Given the dire nature of our circumstances, we had braced ourselves to consider an alternate solution, not nearly as attractive as the one you have presented."

"Indeed, you are to be congratulated," chimed in Bob Arnold. "You had no way of knowing, though, that recent developments in our civil war have materially reduced our time frame. Pending our review of the documentation, how quickly could you complete a transaction?"

"I have all the necessary documentation I need to complete the transaction while we are here. Once the gold has been deposited in your banks in Hong Kong or Taipei and you have issued letters of credit, we are prepared to proceed with our end of the documentation."

"Why don't you tell us how you were able to complete the organization of the prototype fund in what appeared a very short period of time?" asked Arnold.

Cecelia explained that after ten independent oil companies and ten private equity firms committed ten million dollars apiece toward the equity side of the fund, the remaining 800 million was invested in 200-million-dollar increments by banking consortiums led by the America West, Stone City, Roth, and Demaureux banks.

"Not that I am questioning their judgment," said Ray, "but would you mind telling me how they were able to make such fast, early-on decisions?"

"Well, I don't know how fast they made their decisions," said Cecelia. "Informally, each of the companies involved had a substantial amount of time to become familiar with what we were attempting. The bottom line is, they wanted to be in on the ground floor of a financing program that in their opinion has significant long-term potential."

Bob asked the next question. "If all that is true, then why haven't many of the other money-center banks asked to be included?"

"Maybe I should answer that question," suggested Ted. "Today, in the United States, it appears there are two separate coalitions of banks developing. The group led by Morgan Stone is committed to the idea of expanding and diversifying the oil industry. The opposing group of money-center banks appears intent on restricting oil development financing to the seven major oil companies that compose what we call the Oil Club."

"Are you serious?" Ray asked. "You're telling us all those fine and reputable banks are committed to the idea of perpetuating the control of ninety percent of the oil supply? Don't they realize what a dangerous strategy that could become?"

Chapter 40

RECUPERATION

Within twenty-four hours of being admitted to the private hospital in Paris, Jacques underwent surgery to relieve the pressure on his brain. What was supposed to have been a two-hour surgery ended up requiring more than four hours. The damage was much more extensive than originally anticipated.

For his recovery period he was moved into a corner room where he was greeted each morning by the blossoming green trees and colorful flowers in the garden that was visible through the open windows. The gentle breeze circulating through his room brought with it the delicate scents of the roses blooming just below his window. A second bed had been moved into the room for Claudine. She breakfasted with him, read him the morning paper, and talked to him about previous experiences that he might remember. Every day, more than once, she would say encouragingly to him, "Your recovery is like so many other challenges we have had to face—as long as we are together, my love, that is all that counts."

In the afternoons they would take a walk in one of the city's verdant parks, which often included stopping at one of the many restaurants Jacques had frequented in the past. The maître d' always seemed to recognize him and engage him in friendly small talk. Claudine would carefully watch for any signs of recognition in Jacques's eyes or facial expressions.

Jacques was beginning to talk. At first his comments were limited to what he remembered about his life in Spain and his work on the fishing boat, frequently retelling Claudine many of the same stories. Then one day as they passed by a large pond that was filled by water gushing from a cliff high above it, he asked her if she had ever dived off high rocks into water. Instantly, Claudine knew Jacques had made a connection with their past.

Later that night, having closed the door to the hospital room and propped a chair up against the doorknob, she slowly took off her clothes, watching Jacques watch her. As she climbed into his bed, she felt his arms reach out to embrace her. They were communicating again, at last, as husband and wife.

For the next few days, watching the growing frequency of his lucidity excited the doctors, the nurses, and the staff.

One afternoon they were walking in the Bois when he said, "Isn't that the Pavilion d'Armenonville? Didn't I hear that Queenie and George sold their gelato shop in Nice and bought this place? Why don't we go in and see if they are there? Maybe we can say hello."

Claudine was encouraged. Jacques had remembered their old friends. "That's a wonderful idea!" she said.

Entering the restaurant, Jacques walked up to the maître d' and said, "Good afternoon, George! How is Queenie? It's been a long time since I last saw you. Weren't we all in Nice?"

Fascinated, Claudine said to herself, *Why don't I relax and see how far this goes before his mind shuts down?*

Excited about seeing their old friends, George called Queenie in from the kitchen. Unaware of Jacques's situation, George insisted that they all sit at his private table, order a good bottle of wine, and have a late lunch. When the waiter suggested a Pouilly-Fuissé, Jacques said, "No thank you, I would prefer the Bordeaux; it goes best with the steak tartare I'm planning to order."

Fascinated by what she was seeing, Claudine watched as Jacques handed the waiter the menu before turning to resume his conversation with Queenie. Almost immediately, she could see the change in Jacques's eyes; one minute it appeared as if he were collecting his thoughts, and the next minute his mind went blank.

Noticing the shift, George and Queenie immediately looked to Claudine for an explanation.

During the course of the next week, Jacques continued to experience intermittent flashes of memory. Claudine, after reporting these events to Jacques's doctors, was assured his behavior was normal. The doctors advised her, "Mrs. Roth, when he tries too hard, he may be overloading his circuits, causing everything to go blank. We think this is a good thing. The more he remembers, the stronger his nerves will become. Now that we have removed the physical pressure, we think the increased activity is helping to stimulate and restore his memory.

"The time for you to take him home is rapidly approaching. We think if you can keep him in a tranquil environment and expose him to as many things he will recognize as possible, his recovery could proceed more rapidly. The positive stimulus of recognizing something or someone will exercise his brain and benefit him immensely."

Chapter 41

NATALIE THE BRAIN

Sir David Marcus's flight into Heathrow from the United States landed long behind schedule. Despite the lateness of the hour and his fatigue, the first call he placed was to the backstage area of the St. James Theatre. He was hoping to catch Natalie before she left. He couldn't wait to share the results of the Sentinels' meeting with her.

"Wait a minute," said the stagehand who answered the phone. "I think she's just leaving, but maybe I can catch her."

Entering Claridge's, all David could see of Natalie through the crowd was her New York Yankees baseball cap. *I don't know what pleases me more: the sight of her sitting over there at our regular table or knowing how excited she seemed about accepting my last-minute invitation.*

It was all he could do to keep from wrapping his arms around her and kissing her as soon as he got to the table. Instead, he sedately put a hand on each of her shoulders, bent over, and gave her a long, gentle kiss on her right cheek. "I'm so excited to see you, Natalie. I have so many things I want to share with you!"

"Then why don't you sit down and buy a girl a drink?"

He watched as she reached down and pulled out a copy of the evening newspaper from her purse. "Listen to what the *London Times* has to say about you and Prince Habib."

OIL INDUSTRY TO DIVERSIFY

Geneva, Switzerland

In a press conference held today at the Hotel Beau Rivage, Prince Habib of the House of Saud announced that with the assistance of his personal oil consultant, Sir David Marcus, he has completed the arrangements for the development of a new oil field which is expected, upon completion, to produce approximately one million barrels per day, or about 20 percent of the world's oil production.

According to the prince, the plans call for the development of several of the high-quality, shallow oil reserves that are known to exist in previously untapped areas in the oil-rich countries bordering the Persian Gulf. The project calls for the construction of state-of-the-art refining facilities and the installation of the pipelines and port facilities required to transport the finished product to markets in Europe and the United States.

When asked to identify the operating oil company, the prince stated, "The concessionaire will be determined by a competitive bidding process which will include both major and independent oil companies. Arrangements are being made to fund the estimated billion-dollar cost from private sources of independent capital."

When reached for comment, Jack Hardy, president of Titus Oil, responded, "Developing a million barrels of daily capacity is one thing; developing the other fourteen million barrels of additional oil required to supply the world's growing demand is quite another issue."

"Well, hot shot, how does it feel to be identified as an acknowledged opponent of the Oil Club? Congratulations, my friend! It sounds as if you are becoming recognized as a real troublemaker!"

"Thanks, I think!" said David. "I must admit that in this situation, we are talking about a far more complicated transaction than anything I have ever attempted before. This is the first time I've been involved in a multiple-party transaction, scattered all over the globe, that involves so much money. I can't even imagine what the consequences might be if anything goes wrong."

Reaching forward and placing her hand over his, she said, "David, I have learned from my experiences in organizing a new play that when you look at all the separate elements at the same time, it's very easy to fall into the trap of worrying about everything bad that can happen. It's a lot easier if you concentrate on one element at a time. When you solve it, you move on to the next element, and before long, you realize you are able to see light at the end of the tunnel."

"What happens when you include up to as many as five independent oil companies in developing a new oil lease, versus working with just one?" David asked. "Haven't we just raised the risk by a factor of five?"

"Well, that's one way to look at the problem," said Natalie, "but I think you might consider a different approach. I've just finished reading a book where the author talks about evaluating risk in the context of economic diversification. He describes what you should do to analyze the risk of being linearly dependent on only one alternative. He then suggests that you compare that situation with being exposed to a small, diversified, and more manageable set of linked operators. He concluded that it's important to compare the two situations before determining which represents the greater risk.

"I was particularly impressed with his conclusion: he suggested that before reaching a final solution, you try to determine how difficult it would be to replace a major failed link in the chain or one of the smaller ones. He also suggested considering whether the performing parties have the capacity to replace the failed party."

David was surprised by Natalie's grasp of the issues at hand and her ability to apply what she was reading. Could she be an asset to the Sentinels in general—and himself in particular?

"I'm impressed!" said David. "It's been a long time since I've heard anyone reply in such an intelligent way."

"There you go again. Don't you think it's possible for me to use the same aptitude I rely on to memorize the script, music, and choreography of a new play to learn about business and the oil industry? Don't forget, your old friend still wants to be appreciated for her wit and intelligence as much as for her beauty and talent!"

Without realizing it, David and Natalie had become good friends, and they now relied on each other for companionship and support. David would relate the news to Natalie and she would comment.

Occasionally she would ask when he was going to have a free night or Sunday afternoon. "We've been introducing some new twists into our play, and I'm anxious to have the benefit of your input," she would say.

Sometimes they would meet on Tuesdays for a long lunch, and if he was in town, they never missed a late Thursday-night dinner. This particular Thursday night, they were sitting at the far end of the bar in Shanty Malone's, an old Irish pub, enjoying their second cognac, when David started talking about the changes in the play, which he'd made time to see the previous week. "Natalie, I was naturally more focused on your performance than the rest of the play. I made a few notes. If you're interested, I would enjoy discussing them with you."

Regular patrons of Shanty Malone's, who by now were used to the duke and the famous actress frequenting the bar, watched discreetly from their tables as David shared his observations with Natalie. She listened intently to his words, frequently smiling and nodding.

After David had finished sharing his notes and had ordered their third cognac, he brought up a sensitive subject he had been waiting all evening to discuss.

"Natalie, I've been given the assignment of calling on the leading bankers and investment houses here in the British Isles and the Commonwealth countries of Canada, Australia, and New Zealand to raise money for the new oil development bonds. To do things properly, I need to personally meet with each prospect. For something as new and different as this is, it's important that someone with my background and experience identify and discuss other problems and issues they may be trying to solve. The Sentinels and I have all concluded the key to raising so much money from such a varied group of investment managers will depend upon their perception that their help is needed to solve both their problems as well as ours.

"In all my years of financial engineering, I've never been faced with problems of this complexity. Not only will a trip of this kind require several weeks and traveling halfway around the world, but the research and preparation will require as much time as the trip itself. Under normal circumstances, it's exactly the kind of thing I would look forward to doing."

"*Would* enjoy?" said Natalie. "What's holding you back?"

"For the first time in my life, I'm not looking forward to making the trip alone. It's not just the idea of not seeing you, and it's not the idea of having to do all the research myself. I've thought a lot about it, and my real problem is not being able to discuss my work with you. Life just seems so much more complete when I can share it with you."

"Well, have you ever considered inviting your Thursday night dinner companion to join you?"

"What are you suggesting?"

"What I am suggesting, David, is that you take me along as your research assistant. Surely, by now, I have convinced you that there are a multitude of subjects that I can help you brush up on in preparation for your meetings. Even you mentioned how impressed you have been with my work and my questions."

"Natalie, I'm talking about leaving within the next two weeks and being gone for more than a month. What about your theater contract? I know it doesn't expire in time for you to accompany me."

"Don't worry about my contract, David. I'm sure with two weeks' notice the producers will be happy to let me go. Now that the success of the show has been established, just think about all the money they will be saving if they can replace me with a younger, less expensive actress. As a matter of fact, there's an excellent understudy who has been patiently waiting in the wings. She has tons of talent. All she needs is an opportunity."

"Are you sure this is something you want to do?" asked David.

"My offer stands, providing it's on a strictly professional basis. I don't want to risk our friendship by trying to turn it into a romance. If you would like me to come along with that understanding, I'll talk to the producer tomorrow. My bags will be packed and I can be ready to go in two weeks."

The smile written that spread across David's face testified that his secret wish has just been granted. "Strictly professional?" he asked.

"Strictly professional, that's the deal."

Chapter 42

CHAIRMAN WANG

For security purposes, Cecelia's meeting with Chairman C.K. Wang of the Chinese National Bank was to be held in Taipei. Accompanied by Ted Lee and her father, Cecelia could feel the tension the minute she entered the great hall where the meeting was scheduled to take place. The chairman and several of his advisors were waiting. *You'd better brace yourself,* she thought. *This is not going to be as relaxed and personal as was your previous meeting.*

For the first thirty minutes, Cecelia was kept busy answering Chairman Wang's questions about the different parties who would be involved in the Sentinels' prototype and why they had agreed so quickly to participate in such a complicated and novel concept.

After carefully listening to Cecelia's answers, the chairman said, "Someday, China will become one of the world's biggest consumers of oil. It's important that we learn to think of China as a sleeping dragon. As our country learns to utilize its vast and inexpensive pool of rural labor, it will become a major global manufacturer-supplier. People will move from the country into the cities. Our cities will grow, and more industrial plants will appear. Mark my words, the availability of a reliable supply of affordable oil will become one of China's most important concerns."

As Chairman Wang continued to speak, Cecelia was impressed by his curious mind, his ability to absorb information, and his willingness to ask questions. She had been concentrating on his remarks when he suddenly said, "Well, Miss Chang, I understand you have brought us an interesting proposal. Would you be so kind as to tell us about it?"

"Mr. Chairman, much of what I have to say involves technical financing issues, all of which are contained in the synopsis that I have prepared. We believe this new form of interest-bearing bond, supported by proven oil production and the full faith and credit of the United States government, contains most of the important suggestions made by the people I visited on my last trip. I believe investment in these bonds will provide the investor with the ability to transfer its wealth offshore, earn an attractive rate of interest, and continue to service its loyal customers." She went on to explain the mechanics of the transaction.

Ted was watching Chairman Wang's face as Cecelia described her proposal. He showed little if any emotion as he concentrated on her words.

Cecelia had expected to be questioned by the chairman when she finished her presentation. When he made no effort, she became confused by his silence. Unsure of how to react, she stood quietly, her head slightly bent, focusing her gaze on a small spot on the Oriental rug she had first noticed when she entered the room.

Finally, after what seemed like an interminable length of time, the chairman looked at his advisors and then turned his gaze toward her. "As you may know, Miss Chang, the families we represent have already placed much of their gold bullion on deposit in banks safely beyond the threat of Mao Tse-tung and his forces. I have been informed that you are about to receive their authorization to convert one billion dollars into your interest-bearing bonds. In addition, the Nationalist government would like to commit one-half billion dollars of its reserves that are safely deposited in Hong Kong and Taipei.

"Unfortunately, a great deal of our wealth remains in the vaults of our bank in Nanking. Under normal circumstances, I would commit another half billion dollars of our nation's capital toward the purchase of your bonds. For some time, the Generalissimo has been developing a highly secret plan for the removal of the national treasury. Since we need time to complete the transfer of those funds, it would be helpful if you could grant us an option to purchase the additional half billion dollars of your bonds, subject only to its delivery in Hong Kong."

Cecelia couldn't resist the urge to glance down at her notes. She had written the Asian quota: one and a half to two billion dollars.

"Chairman Wang," Ted said, "we understand and appreciate your concern, but under the terms of our agreement, there is no way we can provide you or anyone else with an enforceable commitment until the corresponding amount of funds has been placed on deposit and we are in possession of letters of credit in corresponding amounts."

Noticing the chairman's look of alarm, Ted continued. "Mr. Chairman, it may be possible for the Bank of Hong Kong and two of its American correspondent banks to commit their own reserves toward the purchase of the last half billion. Should that become an option, the bonds would remain the property of our banks until you exercise your option. If that is agreeable, Miss Chang and I need to make a few confirmation phone calls."

"Mr. Ferrari, Miss Chang is calling from Taiwan," said Pete Ferrari's secretary. "She says there is some urgency to her call."

"Good morning, Cecelia!" said Pete when he picked up the phone. "What's happening?"

He listened intently as she spoke. Finally, he said, "Half a billion is a lot of money. We need to discuss it with Morgan, who, by the way, is livid over the attitude of the money-center banks. Under pressure from their Oil Club clients, they are limiting their investment to less than two billion dollars, or less than twenty-five percent of what they might normally commit.

"Morgan is concerned the increased shortfall could prove catastrophic. I've never seen him so mad or so determined to complete anything. He said something like, 'What's the banking industry thinking about? Have they all lost their minds—letting Big Oil push them around? Do they really believe they can survive on Big Oil's patronage alone? What about all the other industries they serve? When they wake up, it'll be too late!'

"But you know how Morgan is," Pete continued. "He can be very persuasive. Subsequent to that discussion, he called me to talk about our anticipating some sort of contingency plan that could require our added support. In any event, we have agreed in principle to providing up to a half a billion dollars of our own support. You understand that this kind of commitment requires our banks to invest their own funds, right? While we are comfortable with the investment, we were hoping that those funds would represent the last dollars to be committed, not the first dollars."

"I'm not sure how things in China are going to resolve themselves," said Cecelia, "but whatever the outcome, this gesture will go a long way toward creating goodwill from a country that is really struggling."

"Cecelia, give me a few minutes to explain the situation to Morgan. I'm sure he will agree that it warrants our support. But, under the circumstances, I need to obtain his approval before authorizing you to proceed."

Morgan picked up the call to his private line on the second ring.

"Two billion dollars from the Chinese?" he said. "What an incredible demonstration of support. When I think of all the things Cecelia has been able to accomplish, I guess I shouldn't be surprised."

"Morgan, there is a problem with the last half billion," said Pete.

When Ferrari finished explaining, Morgan said, "Under the circumstances, I don't see how we can say no. Why don't you inform Cecelia that we would be pleased to grant the chairman his option? At the same time, I would remind her that should the Chinese succeed in producing the last half billion dollars, they would free up our capital to cover any other last-minute contingency."

"By the way," said Pete, "I should explain that there are some other extenuating circumstances that make this decision a little less difficult to make. This might be a good time for me to pass along Mike's most recent progress report. He seems obsessed with the possibility that his inability to produce more than two billion dollars could destroy the Sentinels' plan. While intellectually he understands it wasn't his fault, he is taking the reduced raise very personally. So he shifted direction and started calling on community banks."

"Glad to hear that!" said Morgan, laughing. "I'm the one who pushed him in that direction."

"He's working his heart out," said Pete. "Every day he's in a different city calling on as many as three banks per day. He is learning that community banks are not only anxious to create relationships with American West, Stone City, the Bank of Hong Kong, and Dean Securities but also have surprising amounts of surplus deposits that need to be invested in secure, higher-yielding bonds. The commitments are small, but they're adding up. Believe me, he's leaving no stone unturned—no pun intended."

Chapter 43

A SEA OF CAMPFIRES

Mike Stone was finding that the presidents of the regional banks across the United States were as eager to meet with him as he was to meet them. During the Second World War, their banks had become ever-increasing depositories for the savings of hard-working people, local manufacturers, and retail service companies. Despite the rapid growth of their deposit base, federal bank lending regulations prohibited the community banks from making some of the larger loans to their commercial customers.

One by one, Mike met the proud owners of these community banks. It didn't take long before he began to realize how myopic the New York banker's view of the United States had become. These bank presidents didn't sit behind some grand mahogany desk on the thirty-fifth floor of a skyscraper. They sat in a more modest office on the first floor, immediately accessible to the public and the loan officers, who needed them to provide quick answers.

These regional bankers were leaders in their communities, members of the Rotary Club, supporters of the local chamber of commerce, contributors to area art museums, and donors to worthy charities. If there was a college located in their town, they often served on the board of trustees, helped the colleges with fund-raising, and offered summer jobs to some of the more qualified students.

The bank presidents and their senior officers were always prepared to ask questions in response to the memo Mike sent in advance of their meeting. Mike couldn't help but think, *These decision-makers believe in character lending, and I'll bet they think their word and their handshake are better than any contract.*

Mike had never seen anything like it. It was not uncommon for the bank president to call in his key vice presidents and, while Mike was sitting there, ask them to start adding up the bank's surplus cash reserves. He was amazed by the magnitude of the liquidity controlled by these banks, as well as their ability to make decisions. They gave him straight answers and their tentative commitment before he left each meeting.

Some of these bank presidents even suggested which banker he should visit next, and before he left their bank, they were already busy calling to arrange introductions and the scheduling of his next appointment.

Returning to his hotel room each evening, no matter the level of his fatigue, Mike would make detailed notes of everything that had happened that day. When he took time to review his notes, he was impressed by how different the community banking system was from the big city money-center banking system he had been raised in. As he traveled, he would often think, *Someday, the polarization that separates the two different banking networks will have to collapse. When executive management learns how desirable it will be to match the loan demand of one system with the deposits of the other, my notes could serve as the database for forming a national network of banks.*

Every two or three days, he would call Morgan and Pete to provide them with a progress report and all the other observations he was making. "Dad, when you look at the world of community banks and all the local enterprises they serve, you get an entirely different perspective. From New York, the economy may appear to comprise a huge bonfire of banks and big companies. But from here, it looks like an endless sea of individual campfires."

Chapter 44

NORTH AFRICAN OIL

Although Jacques had not recovered sufficiently to accompany Claudine, his mental processes were improving. To help him utilize his mind, she would show him her notes and solicit his advice. She would focus their discussion on whatever he remembered about the person she was visiting and ask him for his help in preparing for the meeting.

The doctors had instructed her to keep notes on his progress and pay particular attention to his degree of comprehension and the length of his attention span. Watching him struggle wasn't always easy. Deliberately, she would limit her questions to the easy ones, the ones that in the past would not have been sufficiently complicated. Learning to hide her disappointment, she concentrated on complimenting him on the astuteness of his answers.

Each day, little by little, he would ask more questions and she would watch as the length of his period of interest improved. Some days his progress was imperceptible, but other days he would surprise her.

Claudine's first fund-raising meeting was to take place in the offices of Cecil Arnof, chairman of France's second-largest bank—and the Roth Bank's principal French competitor. Entering the chairman's office, Claudine immediately felt at ease when she saw the smile of the dear friend of both her family and Jacques's. Cecil had been a guest in both their parents' homes on many an occasion. Monsieur Arnof and his young protégé, Benjamin Dupree, both greeted her in their warmest and most charming manner.

"Claudine! What a pleasure it is to see you once again," said Cecil. "You have no idea how valuable that gold bond program you developed during the war has been for the bank and so many of its customers. What an excellent piece of work!"

"Why, thank you, Monsieur Arnof!" said Claudine. "It's wonderful to see you as well."

"Pierre tells me you two are considering moving back to Europe and are committed to helping us rebuild our economy," said Cecil. "What good news! Your understanding of the personalities and the sensitive issues on both sides of the Atlantic could prove very valuable. Like the rest of us, you are going to quickly realize there are more problems to solve than there are people to solve them."

"Thank you for your kind remarks," said Claudine. "Jacques and I deliberately scheduled our first meeting with you. Knowing Ben's penchant for doing his homework and asking the tough questions, we are hoping that you will be able to assist us in developing a greater appreciation for the key issues we will be asked to respond to on the rest of our tour."

"Not to worry! Knowing you were coming, Ben has been working overtime to not disappoint you. Ben, if you please?"

"Mrs. Roth," said the young man, "I have prepared four questions that reflect our highest-priority concerns. First and foremost, we are concerned about becoming increasingly dependent on the seven major oil companies. Not only are we suspicious of some of their practices and motives, we are also reluctant to become more dependent on them in light of some of the national political interests they appear to represent."

"Perhaps the best way for me to answer your concern," said Claudine, "is to say that my friends and I are committed to the idea of encouraging the development of oil on an international basis, independent of any political and economic agendas, in whatever manner is necessary to satisfy emerging global needs with a reliable supply of affordable oil. We have every reason to believe that once the Oil Club's economic barricade has been eliminated, consortiums of independent oil companies will come forward and provide competitive bidding on the development of new oil concessions.

"Once you have had the opportunity to examine the fine print of what unfortunately has become a very large document, you will discover that, beyond seeking the approval of the U.S. government to pass needed legislation, the administration of our plan will be provided by representatives of the investors."

"I've been studying your prototype," said Ben, "and I noticed the equity portion of the funding was provided by the Sentinels and your inner circle of investor friends. Are you expecting future applicants needing equity support to work with the same group of investors?"

"Good question!" said Claudine. "No, that was a special situation designed to facilitate the first deal. Unless our help becomes necessary, we prefer that applicants create their own equity sources. I hope that our investment won't be misconstrued as anything other than a one-time measure born of expediency."

"Very good! Does the fact that new Saudi reserves were used to organize the prototype indicate that future funds must be limited to Saudi or Persian Gulf reserves? Is there anything in the energy fund agreements preventing qualified French oil companies from bidding on proven reserves in our protectorates in North Africa? Properly developed, they could very well represent the solution to France's growing appetite for oil and provide an important source of wealth we need to reconstruct our postwar economy."

"Once again," said Claudine, "we wanted to take advantage of our relationship with Prince Habib and the House of Saud. Because Saudi Arabia is the region's leading oil producer, we believed its involvement would not only make it easier to complete our mission but also might provide us with the best possible endorsement for our bond fund. Beyond that, there is no significance to Saudi involvement. Quite the opposite. I remind you that our goal is to encourage the production, on a worldwide basis, of a reliable supply of least-cost oil."

"Does your answer mean," said Ben, "that subject to meeting the stated feasibility qualifications of the funds, there are no restrictions, political or otherwise, that will prevent us from using proceeds from the energy fund to finance the development of North African oil?"

"Subject only to satisfying the requirement for competitive, arm's-length bidding procedures, that is exactly what it means."

The chairman turned so he could watch Claudine's reaction to the fourth and last question. "Once a new oil field becomes proven, how committed are you and your husband to assisting our French clients with their applications to the energy fund? And afterward, will you be available to assist them with post-approval problems, should they occur?"

"Ben, the real issue you are raising is one of our continued involvement and availability. No one understands the personalities, the terms and conditions, and the small print involved in this transaction better than we do. The moral bargain we are prepared to strike calls for us to remain personally involved until the fund is fully vested and distributed. The entire process could take as long as three to five years. Beyond that time, we believe the administration of the fund should shift to its managers and the management of the subject oil companies. All that notwithstanding, we hope that our decision to return to Europe will be regarded as part of our commitment to assist with the long-term interfacing between the United States and Europe on this and other situations that may arise."

Chairman Arnof concluded the meeting by turning to Ben and saying, "Are you satisfied with Claudine's answers?"

"Mrs. Roth's answers have exceeded any expectations I may have had," said Ben. "I am prepared to recommend her investment proposal."

Cecil said, "Claudine, I congratulate you; it appears you have satisfied both our quantitative and qualitative requirements. That's the good news. I am worried about what the size of our commitment may be. It will take some time for us to determine the extent of our discretionary funds and those of our cooperating fund managers. We will have to also resolve what percentage of those funds can be used to fund a single investment. Whatever that calculation turns out to be, I will recommend we make a maximum contribution.

"On a more personal note, Claudine, I would like to express my gratitude for what you are attempting to do. Let me reassure you there are those of us who understand and appreciate the strategic importance. I am certain that I speak for others when I say we will try to be as helpful as our circumstances allow. Please convey my best wishes to Jacques and assure him that until he can rejoin you, the presentation of your program is in good hands."

Chapter 45

ASLEEP AT THE SWITCH

Sir David Marcus was only too familiar with the history of the oil industry in England, including its ties to the British government and its collective devotion to perpetuating the monopolistic practices of its established producers. Since 1905, this consortium of oil companies and the government had remained the center of Great Britain's centuries-old policy of economic liberalism. During his tenure at English Oil, the company had demanded he support what he considered to be an outmoded system. The conflicts involved in enforcing economic liberalism and remaining empathetic to emerging conditions in the Middle Eastern oil market were the biggest factors in his resignation.

Sir Desmond Muirhead, chairman of the London Bank of Commerce, out of respect for his long-standing friendship with David, had agreed to his request for a meeting. The discussion proceeded smoothly until Sir Desmond said, "Beyond our bank and the Roths', I think you are wasting your time calling on any established banks in London. You might, however, want to talk to the Bank of Scotland and the Commonwealth banks of Canada and Australia. They have two things in common: they have vast energy deposits in one form or another, and they have their own problems with the British oil industry and with Britain's political system.

"Before you talk to them, however, you might want to determine whether the proceeds from your bond fund can be used for the development of alternate forms of energy. In addition to oil, these countries possess enormous deposits of coal, natural gas, and hydroelectric power. Rather than refer to your program as an oil development fund, you might want to call it the 'energy development' fund. From a bankers' point of view, assuming that all critical credit criteria can be satisfied, I don't see why oil reserves need to be the only thing underwriting the fund. Why can't any proven form of energy be used for collateral purposes?"

"Sir Desmond," said David, "if we were to pursue your line of thought and broaden our definition of developable energy, what effect might it have on our fund?"

"Knowing you might ask the question, I made a little chart." Sir Desmond pushed an open notebook toward David. "The inclusion of Scottish coal could make a big difference. The same might be true for eastern Canada's hydroelectric power industry. The coal deposits and oil sands in Alberta are some of the biggest in the world. Finally, the coal mining industry, in addition to being one of Australia's largest industries, represents one of the world's largest and most accessible sources of high-energy coal. When you add all that potential together, you could be talking about a substantial amount of developable energy. The added interest could very well make the difference in funding your fourteen-billion-dollar goal."

After pouring them both another cup of tea, Sir Desmond continued. "Ever since you called, I've been thinking about your plan. How do we know that if the big oil companies succeed in their quest to control so much of the world's supply of oil, they won't use their collective power in much the same way the German industrialists planned to when they brought Hitler and his National Socialist party to power? We could once again find ourselves asleep at the switch, with a well-organized group executing the early stages of a plan which, left unopposed, could result in their virtually controlling the world's oil supply. That is a risk we don't want to take. Even now, when you consider how much financial capital, management expertise, technology, transportation, processing capacity, and retail distribution these seven companies already control, it might be too late. If you and your friends don't organize the capital you need within the next ninety days, you could jeopardize the momentum you need to make this deal happen."

Two days later, sitting in the privacy of their special compartment on the train as they were returning from Glasgow to London, David and Natalie were excited. "Natalie, do you realize what we have accomplished? If the chairman of the Scottish banks is able to persuade Sir Desmond to join him, we could have our first commitment. Two hundred million dollars would represent one hell of an endorsement from war-weary British banks. Not a bad way to start before we leave for Canada!"

The change in the sound of the engines told David and Natalie their plane was leveling off for their long flight over the Atlantic to Montreal. David wanted to take advantage of the uninterrupted time to review with Natalie the energy issues they'd be asked to discuss in their upcoming meetings in Montreal, Toronto, Calgary, and Vancouver.

"Natalie, Let's go over that one more time. I want to be certain I understand the key issues concerning the energy business in Quebec."

When they got to Montreal, they found the bankers there had also done their homework. Their friends in Scotland, Europe, and the Middle East had carefully briefed them on David's background and experience in the oil industry, and on the growing trust and respect he appeared to be earning with sovereign political leaders in the Middle East.

From Scotland came one report urging the Montreal bankers not to be fooled by Miss Natalie Cummins. She was indeed the same woman who had starred in many a London musical, but she was all business during the meetings. She took careful notes, answered questions about details and background, and was not shy about asking her own questions.

Natalie, very conscious of her new role, had paid detailed attention to how she dressed for the meetings. The cut of her suit was conservative, the collar of her blouse high, and she wore very little makeup and jewelry. Although it was unintended, her conventional garb made her appear even more mysterious and intriguingly attractive.

The curious bankers were determined to learn whether she was a legitimate student of the energy industry. Although polite, their first questions were always directed to her. Initially, the answers required only a general knowledge of the business. Gradually, the complexity of the questions grew, and the answers, correspondingly, became more detailed.

David was amused by the process. It was apparent that most

of them had never been face-to-face with a woman as beautiful and charming as the celebrated Natalie, much less one so intelligent and well-informed. Once the bankers had been convinced that she knew what she was talking about, they directed the more strategic questions toward David.

As they proceeded from meeting to meeting, it became apparent to David and Natalie that the jungle drums had been beating. Each group of bankers looked forward to meeting the smart and irrepressible Natalie. Not ready to believe what they had been told, they still insisted upon directing their first questions toward her.

It's almost like a game, David thought as he watched the process. *Is it possible that they are more interested in trying to trip up Natalie than they are in completing their due diligence with me?*

Convinced that Natalie was as reported, the bankers would then focus their questions on David. Typically, they wanted to be heard: "Sir David, it's important that you understand our position." Their projections for the growth of energy needs in eastern Canada and the northeast part of the United States assured them that demand would dramatically increase. The good news was that they have abundant sources of energy. The bad news was that they lacked the capital to develop them. And as one banker put it, "Big Oil and the British and American governments understand our predicament and are waiting like vultures to be asked to enter our market. For a lot of reasons, that is something we would like to avoid."

———

On the second leg of their flight to Calgary, Natalie and David were on a plane enjoying a surprisingly good lunch and an even better bottle of wine, when Natalie said, "I wasn't expecting the airplane fare to be so good. A girl could get used to this kind of travel. Don't you think that second glass of wine tasted better than the first?"

David responded, "That will be enough of that—we only have so much time to prepare for our next set of meetings. If the Calgary bankers are a reflection of all I have heard about the pioneering spirit of the Alberta frontier, we could be in for quite a night."

The Calgary bankers, having heard from their Montreal banking cousins, were looking forward to meeting David and his attractive assistant. Waiting for their guests to arrive, Calgary's four principal bankers were seated in the lobby of the Calgary Hotel. Dressed in pressed gabardine slacks, highly polished cowboy boots, and Western shirts with the little pearl buttons, the banking executives made quite a contrast to their formally dressed counterparts in Montreal.

The plane carrying Natalie and David was delayed by weather. By the time they arrived at the hotel, the bankers had consumed more than their accustomed share of drinks. The trouble started almost as soon as the introductions were being made. The youngest of the four bankers said, "Ma'am, how is it that a beautiful woman such as yourself comes all this way to talk to a bunch of stuffy old bankers?"

Before she could respond, David interceded. "Natalie has worked very hard studying your local energy industry and she arrives well prepared to ask and answer questions. I hope you're prepared to respect her professional skills, because she's ready for you."

Fortunately, one of the older gentlemen interrupted. "Miss Cummins, you are in the heart of cattle country. From what I understand, the restaurant in this hotel serves a very fine steak. How would you like to join us for dinner?"

Over dinner, the mood of the conversation quickly changed. It wasn't until coffee was served that the congenial conversation switched to business. Natalie could tell by the growing complexity of their questions that she was being tested. Taking her time to answer each one in a thoughtful manner, it didn't take long before she could sense they were impressed by her answers. She was beginning to win the respect of all the bankers, except the younger man who had made the impertinent comment. At just the wrong moment he said, "Ma'am, would you mind telling us how a woman of your beauty and stage experience can expect to be regarded as a credible expert on the oil industry?"

Thoroughly irritated, Natalie thought, *Oh, what the hell, we will only come this way once.*

"Young man, if you don't mind, perhaps you wouldn't mind if I asked you a couple of questions of my own?"

The three other bankers, embarrassed by their colleague's behavior, remained silent.

David sat back in his chair, smiling. *This is going to be interesting!*

Still focused on being called a young man, the subject of Natalie's ire was distracted and failed to hear the first part of her question. "Excuse me, ma'am, do you mind repeating the question?" he said.

"If everything I have read about the unusual abundance of natural resources in Alberta is true, how are you planning to fund the costs of all this anticipated development?"

Neither Natalie nor anyone else sitting at the table felt sorry for the man as he struggled to answer her question.

"Well, *young man*," said Natalie, relieving him after he'd stuttered out an unconvincing answer, "perhaps you can answer my second question. How high does the price of oil have to rise before the production of bitumen becomes a commercially viable enterprise and satisfies collateral requirements for lending purposes?"

Attempting to answer her question, he said, "I was reading a report the other day on this particular subject. If I correctly recall, I think they felt that the price of oil would have to approach fourteen dollars a barrel."

"You *think,* they felt? Is that the kind of preparation you do before attempting to determine the feasibility of the amount and timing of financing required by your customers who want to participate in the growing demand for energy production?"

The next morning, there were only three bankers sitting in the large boardroom waiting to meet their guests from England.

David and Natalie ended their Canadian tour in British Columbia, where the situation was entirely different from what they'd observed in Alberta. The future of this western province was bright and immediate. It had been blessed with large reservoirs of easily extractable oil. To make things even more exciting, pipelines had been built during World War II to transport the oil from British Columbia to the United States.

David and Natalie found the local bankers to be a sophisticated, cosmopolitan, and highly informed audience. Like their counterparts in the rest of Canada, they were faced with an abundance of opportunity and a scarcity of capital. As a result, they listened eagerly and politely to the promise offered by the International Energy Development Fund.

Chapter 46

NO STONE UNTURNED

A tired yet happy Claudine was returning to Chamonix. Traveling along the highway she had taken so many times in the past, her mind was only half on her driving. She couldn't wait to tell Jacques all the details of her meeting.

"Jacques, you won't believe what happened!" she said as soon as she burst through the front door of the chalet. "I'll bet we spent less than half the time talking about the investment economics of the bond program. Once Cecil and Ben understood the objectives of the fund, they began to talk about their own problems. There is no doubt, in my mind, that the successful implementation of our plan will help them resolve a number of these problems. When you suggested the best way to sell our program is to frame it in the context of solving their problems, you were absolutely correct."

Claudine was so excited to tell Jacques everything she had learned that she had forgotten to pay attention to his ability to absorb what she was saying. Stopping to catch her breath, she was surprised when he asked, "Did they give you any indication what their investment range might be?"

Not expecting the question, Claudine asked, "Jacques, how much of my carrying on were you able to understand?"

"Everything you said seemed perfectly clear; why do you ask?"

Claudine and Jacques had settled into a comfortable routine at the chalet. Each morning, she would try to have breakfast prepared when he returned from his early morning walk into the village to retrieve all the local newspapers. Discussing their content and meaning was another part of his rehabilitation program.

Later in the day, she would accompany him back into the village while he concentrated on purchasing each of the items he had written on his daily shopping list. One of her favorite games was to ask him, "Where are you taking me to lunch today?" Watching him sort out the different restaurants, their menus, and when they had last been there represented another way she could measure his progress.

As much as Claudine liked shopping and dining with Jacques, it was the intimate atmosphere of preparing dinners and the more serious conversations afterward that she enjoyed the most. Confident that Jacques was rapidly recovering, she began to discuss the complexities of her meetings. After repeating the intellectually challenging conversations word for word, she would also give him her notes.

"Jacques, what does it all mean? Sometimes, I think they are speaking in some kind of code I'm expected to understand. The financial reserves of war-shattered banks can't be all that great. Two and a half billion dollars is an enormous goal. What are we going to do if all our commitments fail to produce the minimum we need? What kind of a backup plan can we develop?"

"Rather than worry about a backup plan," said Jacques, "I think we should concentrate on identifying every investment source we can and commit ourselves to calling on each one. At the end of the day we will have either met our goal or know we have left no stone unturned.

"One of the things I can do in your absence is to establish a prospect list. Don't forget: someday I should be able to travel and help you by dividing up the work of calling on half of these prospects."

Claudine's next visit was to The Hague to speak with the Queen of the Netherlands, an old friend of the family's and a longtime client of the Demaureux Bank. Claudine was scheduled to present her case to Victor Duits, the Queen's personal financial advisor and Holland's new representative in the emerging European community.

"Victor is an interesting man and a devoted historian, Claudine," Jacques said as he helped his wife prepare for her trip. "Before the war, he and the Queen shared a similar conviction regarding the investment of the country's surplus funds. They believed the United States was the most politically and economically stable country in the world, and they have always been comfortable investing in America's government bonds.

"It's important to remember that once they become convinced the bond issue will be supported by the full faith and credit of the United States, Victor will concentrate on learning how investing in our bond fund will generate increased yields."

While Claudine was at The Hague meeting with Victor and the Queen, Jacques began to worry about her next meeting, which was with the Berlin National Bank. They had been informed that John von Heusen, an old nemesis of Jacques's, would be attending. Before John had been appointed executive vice president of the bank, he had worked for one of New York City's biggest banks. It was one of the money-center banks that had been particularly outspoken in its support of the Oil Club's plan to control the future development of oil.

If it weren't for our need to turn over every rock, Jacques thought as he sat in the empty chalet, *this is a meeting I would have preferred her to skip*. In New York, von Heusen had been very vocal in his opposition to the energy fund idea. Even worse, on at least one occasion in the past, the differences in his and Jacques's opinions and their strong personalities created such an acrimonious atmosphere the deal they were working on failed to close. Jacques knew that this meeting could turn out to be very different from the positive meetings Claudine had enjoyed with the other bankers.

In Berlin, a week later, Claudine sat in the expansive conference room of the Berlin National Bank. The meeting had started badly, just as Jacques had warned her it might. Almost before the introductory pleasantries had been completed, the bank's chairman said, "As you know, Mrs. Roth, there are many of us in Europe who don't share America's concerns about monopolistic practices. As a matter of fact, we prefer the greater sense of control and economic stability they appear to introduce. Knowing our feelings, perhaps you might wish to explain why it's in our best interests to join you in your quest to oppose the major oil companies?"

Flashing her most engaging smile, Claudine launched into her reply. "The short answer to your question is that we are not opposed to the efforts of the individual major oil companies to compete for new oil concessions; it's their collective plan to control ninety percent of the future production that concerns us. The concentration of so much power in such a small number of hands could create a new and very threatening form of economic colonialism."

Despite the frowns of the men in the room, including that of John von Heusen, Claudine forged ahead. "We have just finished fighting a war of which the imperial pursuit of oil was one of the major contributing causes. We are of the belief that economic colonialism can produce the same concentration of power that Hitler and the Japanese were attempting to achieve during the last war. These efforts on the part of the Oil Club, left uncontrolled, could result in a collection of power we will all regret. There are those of us who believe something needs to be done while there is still time.

"As a net importer of oil," Claudine continued, "you may wish to consider what is required, long term, to ensure an adequate and reliable supply of affordable oil. Do you really want to be dependent on an oligopolistic oil industry capable of establishing its own production quotas and managing prices?"

Speaking up for the first time, von Heusen said, "If you listen to our banking friends in New York who represent many of the major oil companies as clients, they want to restrict new oil field financing to the members of the Oil Club. Unless Claudine and her friends can generate the support they are seeking from the unaligned financial community, that could very well become the case." Claudine was shocked he hadn't immediately contradicted her. In fact, she realized his face had softened, and that his tone was almost supportive.

"On the other hand," von Heusen continued, "I'm not so sure the big banks' position is as firm as they would have you believe. I've sat in meetings where these bankers discussed privately, among themselves, their feelings about the pressure Big Oil is applying on them. They are very resentful. If they were to become convinced that your efforts to replace their funding capacity could succeed, you might be surprised by what they do."

"Claudine, I think you have made your point," the chairman said. "You and von Heusen appear to agree on the strategic purpose of your plan. I will be interested in what John has to say once he becomes familiar with the fine print. May I suggest that we take a break and reconvene when we have completed our homework?"

Claudine couldn't remember when she had been more excited about returning home. From the way he was talking during their nightly phone calls, she could sense that Jacques was extremely concerned about the outcome of the Berlin meeting. She knew he'd be especially relieved to hear of von Heusen's change of heart. He also seemed to be making progress in his recovery; each day he was venturing farther on his daily walks, and his mental health and physical condition seemed to be rapidly improving.

Maybe the day is coming when he can accompany me on trips, she thought as her car sped toward Chamonix. *If it turns out he can handle the pressure of traveling with me, it shouldn't be too much longer before we can begin to divide up the load.*

It doesn't seem fair that he has to rely on my descriptions of how our plan is being so well received. He needs to understand, if it weren't for the respect all these bankers have for him, none of this would be possible.

Chapter 47

MESSAGE FROM CECELIA

After four cities, twelve meetings, and six days in Canada, Natalie and David, exhausted, boarded the flight that would eventually take them from Seattle to Sydney. With plenty of time to rest and collect their thoughts, it was only natural for them to speculate on the results of their meetings.

"Did you notice a difference between our meetings in Vancouver and Calgary?" David asked Natalie. "Do you realize no one asked you any questions in Vancouver? You don't suppose that they were being more formal and polite because they were concerned about incurring your wrath? Or maybe they've learned you're a serious student and don't want you to ask them any difficult questions. It will be interesting to see what happens in Australia."

Natalie nodded in agreement. "David," she said, "since I have no experience, I'm not sure that I should be asking this question, but didn't you find it strange that all of the bankers promised to give our proposal serious and prompt consideration, but no one has given us a direct answer?"

"If I had to guess," said David, "I wouldn't be surprised to learn they are all talking to each other and that they won't have an answer for us until we have completed our tour. Bankers are a strange lot. Rarely do they move on their own; they are more comfortable moving together. I have often thought that by being a part of a 'standard' investment they feel more comfortable if anything goes wrong."

"Does that mean if something goes wrong in one meeting it could undo all the good we have accomplished in all the other meetings?"

"You've met all these bankers," said David. "How many of them are prepared to stand up and argue for what they believe? I have always been convinced they are looking for reasons not to do something, rather than the other way around."

"Well if that is the case, maybe we should begin to prepare for our next meeting," Natalie said. "Let me tell you just a little bit about the land down under."

A message was waiting for David and Natalie when they checked in at Sydney's Victorian-Excelsior Hotel:

David,

Imperative we talk. There are problems developing in Indonesia between the Dutch colonists, the major oil companies, and the country's new independent government. Your experience and familiarity with the British and Dutch oil companies may be needed. Call me as soon as possible.

—Cecelia

Dead tired, Natalie was debating whether to unpack or climb into bed for some much-needed rest when she heard a knock on her hotel door.

"Don't bother to unpack," David said as he came through the door. "I've just finished talking with Cecelia, and our presence is needed in Jakarta. The Dutch are threatening to take over the government with the 110,000 troops they have garrisoned in Indonesia. They're desperate to protect their oil interests, and Cecelia thinks things could get very ugly soon."

An envelope with the White House seal clasped in David's hand caught Natalie's attention. She had David read her the short note: *"Sir David, I would appreciate any assistance you can provide Cecelia with her most delicate task in Indonesia."*

An interesting contingent was waiting to greet Natalie and David at the U.S. government's private terminal when the American military plane landed in Jakarta. Cecelia and Ted, accompanied by representatives of the new Indonesian government, the regional executives of the British and Dutch oil companies, and officials of the prewar Dutch colonial government, were congregated at the end of the red carpet.

They had all been looking forward to David's arrival; the negotiations between parties had failed to reach any positive outcome. For days, the group had been unable to satisfy the Dutch demand for its historical oil interest, and the Dutch were still refusing to recognize Indonesia's independence. And the stakes were high. A breakdown in negotiations could signal the release of the Dutch troops and the outbreak of a bloody, costly war.

Each of the parties hoped that Sir David Marcus, with all his

Middle Eastern oil experience, would find a way to break their logjam.

For the next two days, there was rigorous debate. It was during the third day that they had a breakthrough. Quite unexpectedly, David asked, "Let me get this straight, is it the Dutch position that you are claiming ownership of *all* petroleum resources in Indonesia, developed and yet-to-be-developed?" Armed with copies of contracts and recently renegotiated operating agreements, David proceeded to demonstrate a clear precedent for separating the two classes of petroleum resources.

Speaking directly to the Dutch representatives, he asked, "So, if your position is that you claim only the ownership of the oil reserves you have developed, then I think the world is prepared to recognize your claim and make whatever arrangements are necessary to protect your interests.

"If, on the other hand, you are claiming an interest in the yet-to-be-developed reserves that may exist in Indonesia, then the world will perceive your actions as nothing more than economic imperialism. In that case, all will agree that you must be stopped."

Caught without an answer, the lead negotiator for the Dutch oil company said, "Prior to my talking with my people, would it be appropriate if I asked what your solution would be if we were to recognize the difference you are suggesting?"

All eyes turned toward David. Afterward, they would all agree that watching David respond to the question was like observing a great hunter measuring his prey for the final shot.

"If your people are willing to limit their claims to your historical assets," he said, fixing his gaze on the flustered Dutch negotiator, "I'm quite certain suitable arrangements can be made to protect your interests and at the same time preserve the sovereignty of Indonesia's new government. Provided that you can be satisfied with protecting your historical petroleum interests, the rest of the world would be interested in learning what other objectives you hope to achieve by demanding recolonization of Indonesia. Unless there is some other problem we have failed to understand, we would consider any effort your government and its garrison of troops might make to restore your political control over Indonesia as an act military imperialism. Do you really believe the United States and the United Nations can be persuaded to support that type of action?"

Not to be boxed in so easily, the Dutch lead negotiator asked, "How can the world expect British and Dutch oil companies to explore and develop any new reserves that may exist without political and military control?"

"Who said anything about granting Dutch or British oil companies the exclusive right to develop new reserves?" David shot back. "We're talking about you protecting your *historical* interests, as I just explained."

The Dutch negotiator was now thoroughly agitated. "If not us, who else? Who has the resources needed to develop new fields and bring the product to market? Nice try, Sir David! Maybe it's *you* who should be talking to your people. Perhaps the time has come for us to teach you some of the simple truths of our industry. You may not appreciate our position, but unless you are willing to recognize new Dutch colonial rule, not another drop of oil will ever be developed in Indonesia!"

David smiled calmly before replying. "It may come as a surprise, but learning to dance with the devil will soon no longer be a precondition for a sovereign country wanting to develop its oil. My friends and I, in cooperation with the world's private investment markets, are in the process of organizing a fifteen-billion-dollar international energy development fund. Upon its completion, countries like Indonesia will be able to entertain competitive bidding from independent as well as the major oil companies, none of which will require the installation of a colonial government."

David continued, speaking with a sincere passion Natalie

had only seen glimpses of before. "Couldn't all these problems be resolved by an agreement which calls for the Dutch historical petroleum interests to be recognized and protected by the new Indonesian government in return for both the British and Dutch governments agreeing to recognize the legitimacy of Indonesian independence?

"At the heart of the agreement would be the separation of political interests and petroleum interests. Provided the Indonesian government is prepared to pledge all of the legal and military protection necessary, I fail to comprehend why the installment of colonial rule is necessary. The Dutch garrison is no longer needed and should be free to leave."

As the discussion continued, the Dutch stood firm on their desire to retain political control. They understood they would have the opportunity to compete with any other company for the development rights to future reserves, but ensuring the protection of their historical petroleum interests without having the benefit of government control remained a central concern. Recognition of their rights by a new provisional government wasn't good enough. Something else needed to be added to the agreement.

For two more days the debate continued. Arguments were thrown back and forth, everyone frustrated by being so near the conclusion without being able to reach it. Then, late on the second day, Cecelia spoke up, giving her idea as if it were an afterthought. "Why not create some sort of draconian measure that could be exercised if the new government fails to fulfill its side of the bargain?"

Unprepared for the introduction of such a good idea from a woman, particularly one who had no previous experience in the oil industry, the Dutch were caught by surprise. Acting as if he were annoyed by the question, the oil company negotiator asked, "Such as what?"

Responding immediately, Cecelia said, "In the event of a breach, why not require the Indonesian government to transfer the title to any remaining undeveloped oil fields?"

A final dinner was prepared for the night following the execution of all the necessary agreements. Cecelia, who was sitting at one end of the long table, was unusually quiet. She offered no stories about her tour, no explanation of where she came up with the idea of the Indonesian government forfeiting future oil development rights if it failed to live up to the agreement.

Finally, the lead Dutch negotiator said, "Miss Chang, you seem preoccupied! May I inquire why you don't appear to share our excitement at achieving such a breakthrough agreement?"

When she looked back on it later, Cecelia would never be certain what prompted her answer—the wine, her fatigue, or her irritation over the idea that she, David, and the rest of the Sentinels were making it possible for the Dutch to achieve the control they sought over their historical petroleum interests. The new Indonesian government would become the future recipient of millions, if not billions, of dollars of oil revenues, and the threat to Indonesia's new government had been eliminated. Despite all that, no one had paid attention to funding of the International Energy Development Fund.

"What good will the new agreement accomplish if the energy development fund doesn't become a reality?" Cecelia said, her eyes darting around to each face at the table. "Rather than celebrating, I'm sure that I and a lot of other people would be a lot more comfortable if we were discussing how we are going to complete its funding!

"With all the wealth that has been created, and with the need for a civil war eliminated, why hasn't there been one word said about completing the funding of our plan! Without funding, all our hard work will go up in smoke!"

Shaken by the veracity of her statement, the lead negotiator asked, "Just what is it you would have us do?"

"Somebody should be figuring out how to purchase some of our bonds!"

Chapter 48

HENRI DEMAUREUX

Claudine couldn't wait to inform the other Sentinels that Jacques was well enough to resume traveling. The news couldn't have come at a better time. All of the Sentinels had been performing their own calculations. Although none of them wanted to say it, they understood the American shortfall was placing an even greater burden on all of them. They were being polite about the matter; none of them wanted to make Mike feel any worse.

For Claudine, the added pressure made the hard work of traveling from meeting to meeting seem even more difficult. One morning, watching Jacques add to his lists and draw his diagrams, she heard him say, "I'll be damned if I'm going to allow those oil companies to defeat what we're doing! There must be something happening we don't see."

Despite the seriousness of their assignment, working and traveling together brought back fond memories and made their task seem a little less onerous. *How long had it been since Jacques first came back to Europe to help me sell my gold bearer bond concept?* thought Claudine. *Six years? I wonder how different our lives might have been had we not been so afraid of ruining a good friendship and working relationship? What would have happened had either of us yielded to our secret affection for each other?*

―――

Between engagements, they would sit on the trains and dissect their previous meeting, make notes, and then prepare for the next. During these quiet times, Claudine would study Jacques very carefully. If she saw any signs of trouble, she was prepared to stop their tour and return to Chamonix. Jacques's health and recovery were much more important than any of the meetings.

But rather than showing signs of fatigue, Jacques seemed to be improving. Hesitant to bring the subject up with her husband, Claudine privately wondered what accounted for his marked improvement.

Claudine and Jacques toured the financial capitals of Western Europe one by one and met with the owners and executive managers of each of the larger banks, insurance companies, and private investment houses. After each meeting they would each write down a range of numbers, estimating how much money the bankers might contribute. The disappointments of one meeting were offset by pleasant surprises of another. Although their estimations would vary from meeting to meeting, their totals always seemed to agree, staying at right around two billion dollars. Although it seemed like a lot of money, they suspected it still wouldn't be enough.

Following their meeting with the last company they had on their A-list, Claudine and Jacques were sitting quietly in the comfort of the private compartment of the train that was returning them to France. Both of them were lost in thought, making their own tabulations of how much money they thought they had raised.

Jacques was the first to speak. "No matter how I count it, I'm reluctant to think we have succeeded in raising more than two and a half billion dollars. Even though that total is equivalent to our original quota, I'm worried that it's not enough to overcome the difficulties Mike appears to be having in the United States."

"I've been making some calculations of my own," said Claudine. "For the sake of argument, let's assume Cecelia's report from China is accurate and she has raised two billion dollars. Let's also assume Natalie and David get lucky and raise another billion. When I add those numbers to your estimate of two and a half billion dollars and Mike's current total of three billion dollars, I arrive at a grand total of eight and a half billion dollars. That's a hell of a long way from the fourteen billion dollars."

Eager to take advantage of Claudine and Jacques's sporadic presence in Chamonix, Henri was a frequent guest at the chalet. He had timed his current visit to coincide with their return. He waited until they had finished breakfast on the morning after his arrival to bring up business matters. "Before talking to my friends in Geneva," said Henri, "I asked myself, if I were in the position of the Oil Club's banks, what would I fear most? The conclusion I kept coming up with is that the one thing they can't afford to jeopardize is their ability to participate in the financing of the development of new oil fields.

"In addition, the oil companies may have a problem of their own. Now that their fraudulent treatment of a sovereign, oil-producing county is becoming known, they are going to have to be a lot more respectful in how they treat their present and future partners. Since their operating in good faith can no longer be assumed, and the grip of the Oil Club will likely be broken by our project, the major oil companies have to face the possibility that oil-rich nations could emerge as dominant players. If their efforts to prevent independent oil companies from competing were to be seen in an improper light, they could suffer some very damaging repercussions.

"Then there is the question of funding new development. Not even the seven major oil companies have enough money to finance fifteen billion dollars without the cooperation of the U.S. money-center banks and the Federal Reserve. If I were Hardy or any of his fellow oil company executives, I wouldn't want to test the goodwill of Roger Malone and his board of Federal Reserve governors."

"Papa," said Claudine, "when we last talked at La Garoupe, you mentioned arranging a poker game with your Swiss banking friends in Geneva. With all the excitement, we haven't had the opportunity to hear about the results."

Henri's facial expression gave no clue as to what he was thinking. Finally, after a sip of coffee, he smiled and said, "Like everything else, my friends believe that our commitment must be based, in part, on a 'higher issue.' Your efforts are being received in much the same fashion as when you and Jacques first approached many of the same people in 1940, when you were developing a market for your gold bearer bonds, and again in 1943 with your German funds transfer problem.

"Interest in warehousing money in non-interest-bearing gold deposits appears to have run its course. Now that the threat of worldwide war is over, there is a growing need for secure, liquid, interest-bearing financial instruments to replace gold. My friends share the opinion that your energy bond fund represents a good early precedent. That is the good news."

"And what's the bad news, Papa?" asked Claudine.

"Well, while there are large gold deposits in Swiss and American banks, owned by a diverse group of private members of the European financial community, these depositors' investment involves a wide range of difficult demands. Accordingly, they can be expected to be very careful in how they invest. Although nobody is talking numbers, I would be careful not to raise my expectations too high.

"But Pierre and I have been talking. Once you finish your tour and know the extent of your subscriptions, it might be a good idea if you come to Paris and talk to us. By that time we will have had an opportunity to discuss your investment proposal with these private investors."

Chapter 49

AUSTRALIA

David and Natalie were on board their return flight to Sydney, trying to fathom what had just happened in Jakarta. Natalie spoke as she poured hot coffee for both of them from a thermos. "In my line of work, I thought I'd met some surprisingly strong personalities, but never anybody like Cecelia. Could you believe what she said—or more important, how everyone reacted? You wait and see, when the Dutch and the Indonesians figure out what she was suggesting, I'd be very surprised if we don't see the color of somebody's money!"

"Not that I would question anything you have to say," said David, "but how can you expect the British and the Dutch oil companies to support our bond fund? Have you forgotten that they're part of the group trying to prevent the fund from happening?"

"Don't worry," she said, "they'll find a way. This could be one of the first examples of how the fund can work to everyone's benefit."

Once Natalie and David reached Australia, the intensity of the meetings grew with each stop. In Sydney, the bankers asked different questions from the ones asked in Melbourne. In Perth, the bankers were prepared with an entirely new set of questions. When it became apparent that the various bankers never asked the same question twice, Natalie and David speculated that they were sharing their questions and answers with each other.

In Adelaide, the questions reflected the fact that the biggest coal mines in Australia were located nearby. "How certain are you that the proceeds from your International Energy Development Fund will be available to pay for the development of new coal deposits?" they asked.

David enjoyed answering the question. "Interestingly enough, your friends at the Royal Bank of Scotland raised the same issue before we left. And I doubt there was a single meeting in Canada when the same question wasn't raised. We have already discussed the situation with our lead bankers. If you care to take the time, you might want to review paragraph 13.b of the offering memorandum. I think it contains all the protection you need. But if you aren't completely satisfied with the language, I will obtain a specific opinion for you."

Having finished the last of their meetings, David and Natalie were preparing to return to Sydney when they received a call from the chairman of Australia's biggest bank.

"David, can you and Natalie stop by the bank one more time before you leave?" he said. "We have something we'd like to discuss with you."

The next twelve hours were among the longest in Natalie and David's lives. Cautioning themselves not to become excited did absolutely no good. Exhausted, nervous, and hopeful, the pair walked into the bank's main conference room. The chairman and three other men were waiting to greet them.

"David, let's get right down to business," the chairman said. "Have you received the written confirmation we requested confirming that the proceeds from the fund will apply to alternate forms of energy?"

Trying not to register any reaction to the question, David reached into his coat and withdrew a plain white envelope that he handed to the chairman. While he was watching the chairman read the contents, he could sense Natalie's growing frustration. Without reacting, the chairman handed the letter to one of the other bank executives standing near him, saying, "Maybe you should read this."

Natalie reached over, gripped David's arm, and whispered, not altogether quietly, "Do you mind telling me what's going on?"

Smiling, the chairman answered for him. "I don't think that will be necessary. We've talked to our friends in Scotland, London, and Canada, and subject to our receiving this confirming cablegram from Roger Malone, we are all in agreement. First, we feel it's in our best interest to support your program. As you have correctly discerned, we believe it's important that we try to encourage the creation of a more diverse and competitive energy supply. Second, we are hopeful the success of your program will assist us in making a very clear statement regarding our intentions of becoming independent of British authority and our desire to be regarded accordingly. And finally, we see your plan as the only obstacle to preventing the Oil Club from consolidating an enormous amount of power in a very small number of hands."

David and Natalie looked at each other and smiled, almost involuntarily.

"Your collective efforts," the chairman went on, "have reminded us that there are problems of great importance that fall beyond government and corporate means. We regard this energy situation as one of those problems. There is absolutely no doubt in our minds that if your effort to break the Oil Club's grip on the financial resources required to develop our energy supply should fail, we could find ourselves under the influence of seven ruthless and incestuous oil companies."

Pausing to reach into the inside pocket of his suit coat to extract a long manila envelope, which he handed to David, the chairman continued. "David, enclosed in this envelope is our collective commitment for two billion dollars. That amount comprises half a billion dollars from the Bank of Scotland, the Roth Bank of London, and the London Bank of Commerce; one billion dollars from your friends in Canada; and a half billion dollars from Australia. You have just received the largest single financial commitment that we have ever made in our collective history. On behalf of all of us, we would like to congratulate you both on a job well done. You've made a lot of new friends who truly respect what you're doing. We wish you and your friends the best of luck with the rest of your endeavor and look forward to working with you on a regular basis."

Caught by surprise by the generosity of the commitment, Natalie and David were stunned into temporary silence.

"Oh, I almost forgot," said the chairman. "There is just one condition. Should Miss Cummins ever decide to return to the stage, we would appreciate tickets for her opening night performance. David, no disrespect intended, but it's been a very long time since we met such a beautiful, intelligent, and talented student of the world's energy industry. Natalie, meeting you has been a wonderful experience for all of us. Judging by your ability to answer all of our questions, we can't wait to see what you can do on a more familiar stage."

It wasn't until they'd been served their second cocktail after take-off that the reality of what they'd accomplished hit them. "Natalie, can you imagine a two-billion-dollar commitment? That's a billion dollars more than our original estimate! Somehow we've got to get this good news to the Sentinels straight away."

"I can't wait to tell them!" said Natalie. "I hope everyone else has been able to get such generous commitments."

"I really mean it when I say I doubt very much that I could have made this happen without your help. How can I express my appreciation for all that you've done?"

Sitting there side by side, leaning against each other, Natalie reached for David's hand and said, "I'm beginning to think I've been your research assistant long enough, David. How would you feel about our amending the terms of our travel arrangements? I've been told that New Zealand can be a very romantic country."

Chapter 50
NEW OPTIONS

Each night, sitting in a different hotel room, Mike would write down his best estimate of the money he thought he had attracted that day. He carefully added that number to the previous day's total, watching with satisfaction as the total began to rise—five million here, ten million there. Slowly the numbers began to add up, inching above the three-billion-dollar mark.

Knowing Cecelia's China trip was going to be extended, and despite his growing fatigue, Mike wanted to take advantage of the extra time to call on more community banks. *It's becoming clear that I'm not just raising money*, he thought. *I'm organizing what could be the first step in developing longer-term relationships with these banks.*

When Mike's flight landed at San Francisco International Airport, he called the apartment. He was surprised when Cecelia answered the phone and suggested they meet at Perry's—one of their favorite restaurants in San Francisco—for a late lunch.

Cecelia was sitting at their usual table when Mike walked

through the entrance. One quick glance told Mike he was seeing a different Cecelia. She looked rested, healthy, and excited to see him. Then he thought he saw something else. *Something's changed. She seems even more self-possessed. There's a quiet confidence in her eyes.*

Almost before they had separated from their welcome hug and kisses, Cecelia began talking. "Oh, Mike, you wouldn't believe it! During our meeting with Chairman Wang, the full impact of what we're trying to do finally occurred to me. Not to belittle the importance of selling the oil bonds, but how would you feel if suddenly you realized you were being asked to help preserve a significant portion of the capital of an entire country? As much as I would like to believe our bonds produce a good financial outcome, their use as a substitute capital source serves a far greater purpose. Once China's gold has been converted into our bonds, the Chinese government can transport its national treasury out of harm's way, make it interest-bearing, and create the liquidity needed to preserve its current banking obligations."

In her excitement, she failed to realize that she hadn't given him an opportunity to respond. "Do you realize," she continued hurriedly, "that your father and Pete Ferrari have committed their banks' balance sheets to cover the option position for the Chinese people? Half a billion dollars is one hell of a commitment for two banks to be making. And that is on top of one and a half billion dollars that will be presented by letters of credit issued by the three Hong Kong banks. The Chinese commitment could be as high as two billion dollars—and that's before we hear anything from Indonesia."

"That's incredible, Cecelia!" said Mike. "Do you realize you have exceeded your quota by a least a billion dollars? I wish I could say the same thing about the American contribution. Without some drastic change, it won't be more than three billion dollars, or less than half of our original quota. I know Jacques,

Claudine, and Juan Pablo are trying their very best to make up for the shortfall, but the gap is so large, I don't see how they can make up the difference."

Mike was sitting alone in their apartment; Cecelia had left for her office at the bank. It was one of those raw, foggy days in San Francisco when the cold seemed to permeate even the most tightly sealed rooms. He had talked with Jacques. *Four billion dollars short—where are we going to find that kind of money?*

The ringing phone startled him. Answering it, he was surprised to hear the voice of his father. "Mike, have you heard from Pete in the last twenty-four hours? Both of us have been receiving some very curious calls from our old friends who run the big money-center banks—the same ones who have been making your life so difficult. Apparently, they've heard about Cecelia and David's success. They may also know about the progress Jacques and Claudine are making in Europe, although they don't know about your commitments from the community banks. Somebody must be getting nervous. I'm not sure I understand their logic, but it appears I never have.

"Here's a list of the people who've called me, and I'm sure Pete has another list. It might be a good idea if you called them. Good luck, son, and keep me posted."

When Mike started returning the calls, he found the tone of the conversations had changed. Gone was any mention about the approval of the loan committees, a review of the documents, and so forth.

Instead, he was hearing, "Mike, the bank has reassessed its

position and we are wondering if there is still room for us to revise our offer."

Mike knew the question could be a trick designed to provide the calling bank with the information it would need to more accurately assess his position. If these banks became suspicious of the actual amounts of money they had in commitments, they could be in real trouble. Mike knew he had to be very careful and precise as he answered their questions.

"We have a half-billion-dollar, unfunded commitment from the National Chinese government," he told each of them. "It is contingent on their ability to transport their funds out of China to Hong Kong. If you like, I'm certain the Fed would be willing to accept backup offers, providing they don't collectively exceed five hundred million dollars and you are willing to produce the required unconditional letters of credit. For them to count, they have to be presented before the close of business on Friday, December seventh, 1946, to Treasury Secretary Ainsworth."

That Friday was their deadline for presenting their funding.

After explaining the calls to Cecelia, she asked, "Mike, I don't understand your logic. Why can't you accept multiple offers from different banks? Why limit yourself to half a billion dollars? We need all the support we can generate."

"If I indicated I was prepared to accept more than five hundred million, in conversation between themselves they might conclude our need is far greater. That's a risk I don't think we should be taking."

With the scheduled showdown meeting between the Sentinels and the Oil Club banks only five days away, Cecelia and Mike were on the St. Louis-to-New York leg of their trip, enjoying a glass of white wine and a light lunch, when Mike turned toward Cecelia and said, "There's something we need to discuss."

Instantly alarmed, she said, "This isn't going to be one of those relationship talks, is it?"

Laughing, he said, "No, this is just career talk. You know that Jacques and Claudine have committed themselves to moving back to Europe. Father is suggesting that I return to New York and resume my career at the bank as an executive vice president. Apparently, he wants me to start preparing to assume the presidency within the next five years. He also thinks it's very important for me to continue cementing my relationships with all the regional and community bankers I've been meeting lately.

"Naturally, if I accept this position, I will be expected to move to New York. Since I'm not going without you, the question then becomes, would you consider moving to New York?"

"Congratulations, Mike!" said Cecelia. "I know you secretly wanted to be asked to succeed your father. Do you think he's really serious about starting the process of stepping down? You would be the fourth Stone to serve as president of Stone City Bank. How does it feel?"

"That's an interesting question," said Mike. "As much as I have been hoping this would happen, now that is has I'm not really certain how I feel. Naturally, any decision I make depends upon what you want to do."

"Knowing the opportunities Morgan's invitation could create for you," said Cecelia, "I'm impressed that your first thoughts were of me. I didn't know I had you so well trained!"

"Cecelia, you know the only way I would consider accepting his offer is if you were willing to move to New York."

"Interestingly enough, it just so happens I've been thinking about my own career since my return from Hong Kong. Pete Ferrari has talked to me about what needs to be done to preserve all the new relationships I've developed in China. Partly for health reasons and partly because I think Ted can do a better job servicing those new accounts from Hong Kong, I have recommended they find a way to merge the Asian operations of the two banks. Naturally, I've offered to remain involved on a consulting basis until all the problems are ironed out, but my active role should be coming to an end."

"Don't you want to do something else at the bank, though?" asked Mike. "Your work there has represented a big part of your life for a long time. Are you certain you are ready to end it?"

"It's almost ten years since I first joined the bank, Mike. That's a long time and I have had the opportunity to do a lot of interesting things. Maybe there is something else I would prefer to do. The time has come for me to head in a new direction, find something that will leave a more permanent mark on the world.

"Mr. Stone, don't think you can use that old excuse of moving to New York to drop me! Wherever you go, I go. You can't get rid of me that easily."

Chapter 51

A PROPOSITION

The series of long flights, flying against the sun, made travel from New Zealand to America seem even longer. The sun came up earlier and set later. It was confusing; the only thing that was predictable was the constant serving of cocktails and meals.

It was late afternoon of the third day when they reached their hotel atop Nob Hill. The San Francisco Bay fog was beginning to roll in. Watching Natalie hang up her dresses, David said, "Why don't we take a nap? I'll set the clock for nine and then we can order room service. Then, there is a special jazz joint I want to show you. Do I have a treat for you! There is a musician—he's an institution around here—who plays banjo and writes and sings his songs. His name is Clancy Hayes, he's a friend of mine, and he plays at the Tin Angel down on the Embarcadero. I can't wait for you to see him sitting on top of an old bar stool, singing his songs and plunking his banjo. If we're lucky, maybe I'll be able to introduce you."

It was 12:30 a.m. when they entered the dimly lit, smoke-filled bar. The crowd from the early show had left, and a bigger crowd for the late show filled every table. Forced to stand near the entrance, David was trying to get the attention of the headwaiter when Clancy recognized them. Bending over, he asked a passing waiter to set up a table for his guests, right down in front of the small stage.

They had been seated for only a moment when Clancy motioned for Natalie to join him onstage. It was as if they had been performing together for years. David couldn't believe what he was seeing. Watching Natalie, he saw a woman totally abandoning the cares in life. *But how the hell does she know Clancy?* he thought.

When they finished the first song, she turned toward the banjo player and asked, "Can we do another? How about 'Long Gone from Bowling Green'?" Then came "A Huggin' and a Chalkin.'" And they finished with the locals' favorite, "Spin a Silver Dollar."

The audience, sensing they were witnessing something special, stood, clapped, and whistled their approval after each song.

Natalie was engrossed in what she was doing. It wasn't until they had performed their fourth song that she glanced at David. She noticed the pained look on his face at just about the same time that she saw the three empty glasses on the table. *Something must be wrong. I've never seen David have more than one or two drinks . . .*

Finishing the song, she bowed to the crowd, thanked Clancy, and excused herself.

Clearly upset, David had left money on the table and was standing, holding her coat. It was obvious he was ready to leave.

Sitting in silence in the back of the cab, Natalie was confused by what had happened. Finally, in a strangely tight voice, David said, "Natalie, not that I am ever totally surprised by anything you do, but would you mind telling me how you and Clancy know each other?"

"David, if I didn't know better I would think you're jealous! All you saw was a couple of old friends having fun. It's no secret:

two or three years ago, when we were touring my last play in Chicago, before our New York opening, I found myself in the bar one night where Clancy was singing and playing. Chicago's Tin Pan Alley is like Soho in London; there is great jazz and the bars close late. I liked his music so much that I returned for the next three nights. I introduced myself, and here we are."

"But that's not what upset me. Watching you up on the stage gave me the impression that you had left me and were returning to your former way of life. I know it sounds silly but I have become so dependent upon your company and support, the fear of losing you is more than I can stand."

"My dearest David, you haven't lost me. One night of a little fun certainly doesn't mean I'm returning to the stage. Just remember, you can take the girl away from the theater, but you can't take the music out of the girl!"

The next morning, knowing that there were no more flights, meetings, or information to prepare, David and Natalie slept late. It was eleven o'clock when they left the Fairmont Hotel, boarded a cable car, and headed toward Fisherman's Wharf. The ride down Hyde Street helped clear David's head, but his new image of Natalie was there to stay. *She is so special; I wonder if there's any way I can make her a permanent part of my life . . .*

He was still thinking about her as they climbed down off the cable car, crossed the street, and entered the Buena Vista Café.

The maître d' recognized Natalie immediately. "Good morning, Miss Cummins, it's so nice to see you again. If you don't mind waiting for a few minutes, I can give you your old table in front of the picture window."

"May I assume that your play also came to San Francisco?" David asked.

Sensing the explosive potential of the situation, Natalie chose not to answer. A faint smile was to be her only response.

Returning from the ladies' room a few minutes later, Natalie found David at the table, seemingly lost in thought. *He's apparently forgotten his habit of standing up and holding out my chair when I return to the table. Something is definitely wrong!*

Two Ramos gin fizzes had already been placed on the table. Sitting down and picking up her glass, Natalie said, "Okay, David. Tell me what's going on."

Shifting in his chair so he could look directly into her eyes, he said, "Natalie, this last month we've spent together has meant more to me than you can possibly imagine. Until recently, it's been all about you helping me. Watching you perform with Clancy last night made me realize, in a different way, how much I've enjoyed your support. If I didn't love you so much, it might not be so important for me to me tell you how I feel."

Caught totally off guard by what David had just said to her, all Natalie could do was look into his clear blue eyes and search for the true meaning behind them. There was no doubt he was being serious.

"For the last few months, I've watched a very intelligent woman apply her considerable skills to an entirely new field and earn the respect of some of the finest minds in the industry. I've seen you rise to the pinnacle of success in the theatrical world. I've seen how you can captivate a musical audience. And, now I've seen how you can apply those same skills to help support me and capture the attention and respect of a totally different group of people.

"You once told me that I failed to see beyond the surface of a celebrated actress. I hate to admit it, but you were absolutely correct. I hope you believe me when I say that's a mistake that I will never make again. We've known each other for years, we've been friends, and now I hope we can be lovers, but as if I am truly seeing you for the first time."

"David, I sure hope you mean everything you just said," said Natalie, searching his face. "You have no way of knowing how important those words are to me. If I didn't care for you so much, I doubt that I would have ever learned how important it was to me to be regarded and cared for as a human being, as a friend—not just as a sexy musical actress.

"After we broke up, I knew I was still in love with you. That's probably the real reason why I was so anxious to change my life. If it meant learning something about the energy business, then that's what I needed to do. You have no idea how much it meant to me to be able to discuss your work with you and your friends. After a while, I was beginning to feel that all my research and hard work was making your projects *my* projects, and your friends *my* friends."

David said, "But there's something even deeper. I've seen you when you're bearing down on a new script or a new song—you were no longer willing to merely learn the scripts, the music, and the dance routines. Whether it's learning a new play or learning the energy business, that's the girl I have learned to love and want to be with."

"David, what does all this mean, what are you trying to say?"

They had been so engrossed in each other that they had lost track of the time. They were surprised when the waiter asked, "May I bring you another drink, and have you had a chance to look at the menu?"

"Hell, it's almost time for lunch!" said Natalie. "Would you mind bringing the new non-actress a cheeseburger and a beer, please?"

"And for you, sir?"

"I'll have the same, thank you."

"Natalie," said David after the waiter had left, "ever since you walked into Claridge's that night, my life has changed. You've become my best friend, and I treasure sharing my work with you. But watching you last night, I realized that you are truly an independent spirit. As much as I might be tempted, I understand that I can't box you up in my life. Just the opposite! I realize that I must learn to become as supportive of you and your interests as you have been of me and mine."

Smiling, she said, "David, you are a rich and powerful man. How can you give all that up? Not only would I never ask you to do such a thing, but I would always be worried about you growing restless and wanting to return to your world."

"There may be some options we haven't considered," said David. "First of all, my life in London, as I have known it, is probably over. I can't oppose the entire British Oil establishment and expect to be treated as if nothing had happened. In certain circles, I'm already regarded as *persona non grata*. The time has come for me to sell my company and move on."

"What would you do?"

"The one thing that I don't want to give up is working with Mike and Juan Pablo in the Middle East. It's important to me that I have the opportunity to keep working on what we've started. It's the same way I feel about our work in Great Britain and the Commonwealth countries. It seems to me that I need to find some new kind of work that allows me the time to continue my other work."

Noticing her look of alarm, he said, "Don't worry. Several universities have expressed interest in my recent experiences in the Middle East and my investment experience in the oil industry. I've been offered a teaching fellowship at the University of California at Berkeley, right across the Bay. I understand there is a very fine school of music there. How would you feel about the idea of teaching music and living with dear old Professor Marcus?"

Totally unprepared for the question, her mind raced. *Natalie, you'd better think before responding. What David has just said requires your full attention. Is what happened last night, when he wasn't the center of my attention, a preview of what's to come? What is all this business about what I want to do and what I don't want to give up? What about my interests? Am I supposed to become a music teacher so that he can keep me all to himself? What happens if I should develop new interests of my own?*

"David," she responded at last, "I'm not sure I understand the full implications of what happened last night, and I certainly don't want to lose you over my concerns about a single event or a possible misunderstanding. On the other hand, before I answer your question, I feel I need to explain to you how I feel.

"In my heart of hearts, I know I love you, I enjoy sharing in your life, and I can't think there is anything that would please me more than to be part of it. But not if that means that I have to subordinate who I am to please you. If I have to worry every time I get up to sing or enjoy performing with an old friend. Pursuing my personal interests is a lot of what my life is all about. If it is going to result in your getting upset, that is a risk I'm not willing to accept."

"Natalie, I understand and appreciate everything you have just said. If I were you, I wouldn't want it any other way. The problem is, I don't know if I'm capable of changing. All I know is that I love you very much and I'm willing to try, but no guarantees."

"Living together is a process that takes place one day at a time," said Natalie. "I don't know about marriage, but I am willing to try living with you at Berkeley, or any other place of your choosing, as long as we both understand that we're taking it one day at a time."

Chapter 52

PATERNAL ADVICE

Claudine and Jacques were on their way to Paris for a meeting with Pierre Roth and Henri Demaureux. The meeting had been scheduled as their last so they could provide Pierre and Henri with an accurate picture of their position.

As much as they needed their fathers' assistance, the idea of discussing a five-billion shortfall was not a happy thought.

The two experienced bankers were surprised when Claudine and Jacques failed to register excitement as they relayed the news that the Sentinels had been able to raise nine billion dollars.

Pierre was the first to speak. "I don't understand your reaction. I would have thought you would be elated by what obviously has been one hell of an expression of confidence and support. Have you been so focused on raising the fourteen billion that you've overlooked what an incredible accomplishment raising ten billion dollars really represents? You have accomplished much more than anyone ever expected. Had your minimum standard not been arbitrarily set at fourteen billion dollars, everyone involved would have been delighted with what you've accomplished.

"Now that we understand the size of the shortfall, it's time for the rest of us to do what we can to ensure all of your fine work isn't sacrificed.

"Henri and I have been discussing what we can do to help you," Pierre continued. "Maybe it's time to test the long arm of the Oil Club. Unfortunately, four billion represents a bigger shortfall than our two banks and our private clients can handle. We can add an additional half billion dollars and hope we succeed in sending the proper kind of signal of support to all the other people who want to see your plan happen.

"In selling your program, I'm not certain whether you have given yourselves enough credit for the excellent investment opportunity you have created and the endorsement you have received from the world's investment community. It's important you realize we aren't talking about some failed proposal; we're talking about what happens before the 'nervous sisters' have finished studying their hole cards.

"This isn't the kind of situation where we want to test the strength of our will against the will of the Oil Club. It's been our experience that when the fog finally lifts and the sun begins to shine, the power of a better idea will trump threats and intimidation. All we have to do is create the proper example and provide the right people with more time to digest what has been happening. Give it some time and you might be surprised by what happens."

THE SENTINELS: CRUDE DECEPTION 307

Despite Henri and Pierre's encouragement, the atmosphere in the Roth plane en route to Geneva was anything but euphoric. Claudine was thinking out loud. "Even if Venezuela does contribute a billion dollars, where in the world are we going to find three billion more at this stage of the game? Surely, by this time, we haven't overlooked any significant investment source capable of making a material contribution in the remaining time frame. With the meeting scheduled for next Friday in New York, we only have one week left to pull some very big rabbits out of a very small hat."

Sitting in the back of the plane, Jacques was reviewing the long list of names he had been assembling. "There has to be some source of capital we've overlooked," he said. "This situation is way too tight."

As the plane taxied toward the terminal, Claudine became suddenly aware of the change in the look on Jacques's face. "I think I may have come up with an idea that will relieve some of the pressure," he said. "If you don't mind, I will leave you in Geneva. I need to catch to first plane to New York. If all goes well, I'll plan to meet you at the Plaza in New York no later than next Thursday night—the night before our showdown with the Oil Club."

Chapter 53

SHOWDOWN IN NEW YORK

When he arrived at New York Municipal Airport, Mike placed calls to his office, Cecelia's office, and the switchboard operator at his old apartment building in the city. Still no messages. While he and Cecelia were checking into the Plaza Hotel, the desk clerk said, "Excuse me, Mr. Stone, we received a message for you this afternoon."

Mike opened the envelope with excited anticipation. After scanning the note, he handed it to Cecelia.

Dear Mike,

Leaving Caracas, arriving late tonight. See you at breakfast. I bring good news. The Venezuelan government wishes to participate. I will be bringing a certified letter of credit in the amount of one billion dollars.

Juan Pablo Perez

David and Natalie had arrived in New York late the previous evening. They had made a reservation for ten at Le Veau d'Or, a fine French restaurant within easy walking distance of the Plaza Hotel.

Cecelia continued to place calls to San Francisco and Hong Kong. No one had heard anything about her father or Ted Lee. Well aware of Tai-Pan's penchant for punctuality, she suspected that something might have gone wrong.

Claudine arrived in New York and checked into the Plaza, hoping Jacques would have already arrived. Disappointed to learn that he hadn't checked in, she asked for messages. There were none. Sad and worried, she went up to their room and began to dress for dinner. She forced herself to think of reasonable excuses. *He must have traveled on to some other place and is planning to return to New York. Maybe he's been delayed; he might be waiting at Le Veau d'Or.*

Most of the others were seated at the restaurant when she arrived. Still no Jacques. There were four vacant seats: the one next to Claudine; the two next to Cecelia; and the one at the end of the table, for Señor Perez. The four missing people could only mean bad news. Their realization that they were still three and a half billion dollars short destroyed any effort to make humorous conversation. What had been planned as a joyous affair had turned into a very somber occasion.

The next day at breakfast there were only three vacant seats, and a smiling Juan Pablo Perez was sitting at the end of the table. Everyone in the room could feel his pride as he explained his conversation with the Venezuelan government.

"Juan Pablo," said Mike, "how did you know it would be safe for you to return to Caracas? What changed? I just assumed you would be public enemy number one down there."

"Well," said Juan Pablo, "the whole situation has changed. It appears, as a result of the finalization of the government's agreement with the oil companies, the balance of power and influence has shifted back to the state. Not only have the companies paid three billion dollars to the Venezuelan government, but new clauses have been inserted into each of the new agreements that control any unusual oil company behavior. There's a new sheriff in town, to use a phrase I learned at Castle Dome Ranch."

Beaming, Mike reached over and gave the Venezuelan oil minister an enthusiastic pat on the back.

"The actual conversation regarding the one billion contribution was interesting," said Juan Pablo. "The President told me that, although some might think Venezuela's participation represents a reciprocal reaction to all the money we helped generate for the oil companies, they know they have a much better reason for investing than simple gratitude. He told me their decision was made on matters of trust, and that they had learned it is no longer a sensible proposition to be linearly dependent on members of the Oil Club. He told me he hopes Venezuela's participation in the fund will be regarded by the world as an indication of the importance of making the oil industry more diversified and competitive."

Despite Venezuela's contribution, the funding gap still remained at three and a half billion dollars. Mike knew they were still in real trouble.

The minute they entered the conference room, the Sentinels could sense the Oil Club executives and their attorneys were somehow aware of their dilemma. They looked ready to attack.

The meeting started promptly at ten o'clock. As previously scheduled, Henry Ainsworth and Roger Malone were present to preside.

A confident Jack Hardy and three other oil company chief executive officers, along with their chief legal counsels, sat along the far side of the wide conference table.

The three chairs reserved for Jacques, Ted Lee, and Tai-Pan were conspicuously empty.

Secretary Ainsworth opened the meeting. "I think we need to establish some ground rules before we start. It is my understanding that the terms of the recently passed bill require proof, satisfactory to the chairman of the Federal Reserve, seated to my left, and myself, that sufficient letters of credit have been issued for a minimum of fifteen billion dollars. It is also my understanding that the terms of the bill include, among other things, clauses that stipulate that the proceeds from the development fund are to be made available to all qualified Big Oil and independent oil company applicants.

"Anyone wishing to make an offer has until today, five o'clock p.m., Eastern Standard Time, December seventh, 1946, to submit any offer they wish to make. If there aren't any questions, Mr. Stone, I suggest that you proceed. Do you have a bid that you wish to enter at this time?"

Standing up and pausing for what seemed an inordinate length of time, Morgan Stone replied, "No, sir, we do not wish to enter a bid at this time."

Rising as though he had been shot out of his chair, the lead counsel for the major oil companies announced in his customarily arrogant style, "Mr. Secretary, since there are no competing bids, we respectfully request that bidding be closed."

Responding in his typically calm and respectful manner, Morgan said, "Mr. Secretary, I'd like to remind counsel that according to the rules just accepted by all parties, we have until five o'clock to complete our submissions."

Standing once again, the lead counsel said, "We have it on good authority that Mr. Stone is not authorized to bid more than ten and a half billion dollars. At this late stage, a four-billion-dollar shortfall suggests that our esteemed friends are wasting our time. That being the case, we see no reason why this process should be delayed. Why don't we call it a day and all go home?"

"Mr. Stone, is your current authorization limited to nine billion dollars—or ten billion if you include the one-billion prototype fund?" Secretary Ainsworth asked.

"No, sir, that is not quite accurate; we have recently received two additional offers in the amount of a half billion dollars from the Roth Bank in Paris and the Demaureux Bank of Geneva and one billion dollars from the Venezuelan government. In aggregate, they raise my current authorization to eleven and a half billion dollars."

The lead counsel rose once again. "We have it on reliable authority that the major money-center banks' contribution was limited to two billion dollars. Examining the exhibit Mr. Stone has been kind enough to provide us, we find he has listed the total contribution of the U.S. banks as three billion dollars. That represents a one-billion-dollar discrepancy. Aren't we entitled to some explanation?"

Turning toward his son, Morgan said, "Mike, would you mind enlightening these gentlemen?"

Rising out of his chair, Mike said, "You are quite correct in your assumption. Originally, the national banks were willing to commit only two billion dollars and that amount is reflected by the line item 'Master Bank Agreement.' Since then, however, regional and local community banks have committed another billion dollars."

"Pardon me, Mr. Stone, but you have us confused," said the lead counsel. "How were you able to convince the smaller banks to participate?"

"Oh, we didn't. You did."

"*We* did? What the hell are you talking about?"

"It has to do with your presumptive use of power. Knowing that the day is coming when they would have to increase their dependency on the big money-center banks, the owner-managers of these local banks have been closely following the Oil Club's exercising of its influence. When they completed their economic analysis of the bond offering, community banks made inquiries regarding their possible participation. These requests were met with determined denial.

"Do you really believe, when left alone, that these independent banks would choose to be dependent on the same money-center banks that allow them to be controlled by a consortium of large oil companies? From that point on, raising the extra money only required good old-fashioned elbow grease."

Shifting his stance so he could look directly at Jack Hardy, Mike continued. "You might be interested to know that once the word got out that my colleagues and I were enjoying some success, your money-center banking pals began inquiring if there was any room for them to reconsider their position.

"Since I had no way to determine what was what, I simply told them we had an unresolved position of half a billion dollars in an option agreement with the Chinese government and that we would entertain the idea of accepting backup offers as long as they were unconditional and secured by enforceable letters of credit. Once we received the half billion dollars of commitments, we would cease to accept additional offers."

"Wait a minute, are you telling us that you deliberately misled our major money-center banks by telling them you were only half a billion short, when in reality, you knew, at that time, that you were more than four billion dollars short? Haven't you just admitted you have engaged in a material breach of ethics? Are we expected to agree, in light of your behavior, that you haven't violated the ethical standards of the U.S. Treasury and the Federal Reserve?"

Roger Malone intervened. "Learned counsel raises a good point, Mike. I think we are entitled to an explanation."

"Mr. Chairman, what I told the major bank representative was and is, to this day, entirely true. There were two questions I wasn't asked. The first was whether or not the Chinese failure to fund the last half billion dollars of their commitment would have changed the outcome. Whatever conclusion they reached resulted from their perception of the significance of my answer. It is a matter of record that American West and Stone City Bank had issued a callable backup letter of credit that we can exercise in the event that the Chinese fail to exercise their option."

Turning toward his trusted friend, Roger said, "Morgan, is what Mike has just said true?"

"Not only is it true, I have brought with me the original letter of credit."

Pausing to extract a document from his briefcase, Mike handed the document to the chairman.

"Mike, what about their claim that you deliberately misled them about the money you had raised? Would you be kind enough to elaborate?"

"Yes, sir. That's the other question I wasn't asked. No one at any time asked me to state the magnitude of our enforceable commitments. Frankly, I was surprised. I just assumed they were obtaining their information from some other source. But I will tell you, had they asked, I would have refused to answer."

Turning toward the Oil Club's side of the table, Ainsworth asked, "Do any of you have any evidence to refute what Mike Stone has just said?"

Pausing to provide ample time for response, the secretary then said, "Let the record show that in the opinion of the Secretary of the Treasury and the Chairman of the Federal Reserve, we have found no discernible reason to believe that Mr. Stone has acted in any manner that violates the law or any covenant of professional ethics."

Chapter 54

THE LATECOMERS

Jacques was sitting in Morgan's office when Morgan, Mike, and Claudine entered, on break from the meeting. "Where the hell have you been?" asked Claudine. "Why weren't you in that conference room taking your beating along with the rest of us?"

Reaching into his briefcase, Jacques extracted a letter of credit drawn on the Stone City Bank in the amount of one billion dollars. He passed it to Claudine, who carefully studied it before passing it to the others.

"Jacques, is this the result of the idea you were talking about in Geneva? Perhaps you wouldn't mind explaining to us where you happened to find a billion dollars?"

Morgan stepped in. "Claudine, maybe I should explain. The idea was Jacques's. He correctly assumed our old friend Erhart Schmidt and his co-investors would jump at the opportunity to convert part or all of their two-billion-dollar gold bearer bonds into interest-bearing energy bonds.

"The problem he faced was that of determining whether the Fed would agree to the exchange. Resolving the financial issues was not the problem. Determining what legal authority was required to execute the agreement was much more difficult. Finally, we concluded there was no precedent that set this authority. Obtaining Presidential approval was our only remaining option.

"Interestingly enough, securing the President's cooperation was the easiest part of the process. It seems he was more than willing to assist Cecelia and her colleagues in completing her mission, provided we maintain some semblance of control over the Germans by limiting the exchange to half of their gold bearer bonds, or one billion dollars.

"Once we were able to arm Jacques with the necessary authority, there wasn't much time remaining for him to travel to South Africa, obtain Schmidt and his other investors' consent, and return in time for this meeting."

"Wait a minute, Morgan," said Claudine. "You knew about this and didn't inform the rest of us?"

"Until we knew that he would make it back in time, Jacques, Roger, and I all agreed it was best for us to remain silent. In fact, his plane didn't land until eleven o'clock this morning. I had a team waiting for him, and apparently they have been busy completing the documentation required to produce that letter of credit."

Mike, who had been patiently listening to the conversation, finally said, "I don't know why we're getting so excited! With Jacques's contribution, our total commitment's only total thirteen billion dollars—we're still two billion short!"

———

At four o'clock, the meeting was reconvened. With Jacques seated at his designated place at the table, only two chairs remained unoccupied.

The Treasury Secretary noted his presence. "Good afternoon, Mr. Roth. Glad you were able to join us. Do you bring any new information?"

"Yes, sir," said Jacques. "I would like to add another billion dollars to the pot. Here is a letter of credit; I think you will find everything in order."

"Wait a minute," learned counsel said. "Do you expect us to believe you can come breezing in here and calmly introduce another billion-dollar letter of credit? How can we be convinced this isn't some sort of internal Stone City Bank trick that can be unraveled once the deal has been closed?"

The brazen nature of the lawyer's charge not only surprised Morgan and his friends but also embarrassed the Oil Club members sitting at the table.

Attempting to mediate, Malone asked, "Do I interpret your comment to mean you would like to review the underlying documentation before we accept this offer?"

A prepared Jacques laid out each of the supporting documents required to trace the note conversion, the Treasury Department agreement, and Stone City Bank's step-by-step documentation, executed contracts, and notary public stamps and signatures.

As they waited for the lawyers to complete their examination, Morgan Stone's executive assistant entered the room. "Excuse me, Mr. Stone, but Mr. Chang and a Mr. Lee are in the lobby asking to see you."

Before anyone else could react, Cecelia pushed back her chair and disappeared through the door. A few minutes later she returned.

"Gentlemen, I would like to introduce my father, Ivan Chang, the honorable Tai-Pan of the House of Chang. Accompanying him is Mr. Ted Lee, president of the Bank of Hong Kong. They have something to say that I think you will find of interest."

"Mr. Secretary," Tai-Pan began, "please forgive our disheveled appearance. We have traveled a long way, and we didn't have time to change. I have in my possession a one-half-billion-dollar letter of credit drawn on the Bank of Hong Kong. Mr. Lee, president of the bank, has accompanied me in the event that any of you have questions regarding the authenticity of this document."

The time required for learned counsel and the rest of the attorneys to examine Ted Lee's documents gave Cecelia an opportunity to consult with her father in hushed tones. "Father, you and Ted nearly scared us to death. Mike and I read an article in the *San Francisco Chronicle* about a military-escorted gold train that had been organized to transport people and their possessions from Nanking to Shanghai. Then, a few days later, another article described a flotilla of a thousand junks that unexpectedly sailed into the Shanghai harbor. That's when I developed the suspicion that you two might have taken your 'special' junk and sailed for Shanghai to help rescue the Nationalist Chinese gold bullion."

"Cecelia, my dear daughter," Tai-Pan replied, "we were nowhere near Shanghai. When it appeared that the Communists might move on Nanking, we had to move quickly. It's true; a thousand junks sailed to Shanghai. The trains arrived, with their heavy crates. Once they were placed in the junks, the diversionary plan was in place. The Communist navy must have opened the crates on the first forty junks before they convinced themselves that the crates contained rocks, not gold. By that time, the Nationalist gold was already being transported from Nanking to Hong Kong and Taipei."

"If the crates were just full of rocks, how were you able to smuggle all that gold out of China?" asked Cecelia.

"Immediately following Chairman Wang's decision to invest in your bonds, we were approached by Chiang's personal pilot, George Liao. He suggested that we consider moving the gold by air. He convinced us there were still thousands of old DC-3s left over from the war that were still floating around China. People in the United States are not generally aware of the massive airlift that was organized to supply American, British, Indian, and Chinese troops, intent upon preserving Burma's back door into India. Tens of thousands of DC-3s were organized to fly what was called 'the Hump.' It's a little known fact that more planes were lost in the Burma operation than were lost in the entire European campaign.

"Well," continued Tai-Pan, "Liao, working under a shroud of secrecy, managed to organize ninety-seven of these old DC-3s still in private charter service to move the gold. Have you ever calculated how much one billion dollars of gold weighs? At thirty-two dollars per ounce, one ton of gold is equivalent to thirty-two thousand ounces, or one million dollars. That means a half billion dollars of gold weighs 488 tons. A DC-3 was designed to carry approximately five tons of payload. Ninety-seven planes, making one trip, were required to carry the half billion dollars of gold from Nanking to either Hong Kong or Taipei.

"To minimize their risk, each plane departed Nanking at random times. The flights were equally divided between Hong Kong and Taipei. The first plane to land in Hong Kong was Chiang's personal DC-3, flown by Liao. We watched as he made his final approach and our trucks went out to meet him. You should have seen the look on his face when he climbed down from that plane. You talk about pride; he knew his plan had helped to preserve the future of their country.

"As soon as the gold was safely deposited in the Bank of Hong Kong vaults, Ted and I were on our way to New York with letters of credit in hand. Our biggest concern was whether we would get here in time."

This time it was Jack Hardy who was on his feet. "Mr. Chairman, Mr. Secretary, it's four thirty and all of the seats have been filled. By the official count, Mr. Stone's group is still two billion dollars short of meeting its minimum stipulation. Unless there are any more offers, I respectfully request you rule that the stipulations of the bill have not been satisfied."

Chapter 55

NOT SO FAST, MR. HARDY

Rising out of his chair to directly face Jack Hardy, Roger Malone said, "In my capacity as chairman of the Federal Reserve, I have been asked to submit two additional bids. The first offer, in the amount of half a billion dollars, comes from the sovereign government of Indonesia."

Interrupting the chairman before he could finish, the lead counsel for the oil companies asked, "Where is a pissant of a country like Indonesia going to find that kind of money? Before inspecting the documentation, I think we are owed an explanation."

Up to this point Cecelia had been sitting quietly, absorbing the progress of the meeting. She wasn't certain whether the arrogant attitude of counsel or his derogatory reference to Indonesia upset her more.

Everybody in the room was startled when this petite, seemingly quiet scholar burst out of her chair. "Now, Mr. Know-It-All attorney, have you ever considered there might be a few things in the world you don't understand? For example, how would you react if you learned that the Dutch and British oil companies operating in Indonesia have authorized the Fed to submit an offer in the amount of half a billion dollars on behalf of the world's newest populace government? This 'pissant' country to which you refer is about to became the world's newest hundred-and-fifty-million-person democracy, where the Oil Club's historical oil interests will no longer have the protection of a foreign colonial government!"

Hardy could no longer restrain himself. "Wait a minute, why would sister companies help fund a program they are committed to defeating?"

Smiling, Cecelia responded, "The Dutch loans represent their effort to build and preserve a more constructive working relationship in the event that new oil development concessions are put up for competitive bidding."

"I still don't get it," Hardy said. "Since the Dutch have stationed more than a hundred thousand troops in Indonesia, why would the oil companies and the colonial government agree to such a proposal when they could simply take over the country and have it all?"

"Because the President of the United States has said they can't," exclaimed Cecelia.

As everyone sat in their seats, stunned, Secretary Ainsworth said, "Well, if we have resolved that issue, maybe it's best we permit Chairman Malone to submit his second offer."

Reaching for a file that had been lying prominently on the conference table, the chairman continued. "Member banks of this country's Federal Reserve system have authorized me to submit an additional bid of one billion dollars, which when added to all the other offers raises the total commitment to fourteen and a half billion dollars. Mr. Hardy, if you would be so kind as to have learned counsel inspect these documents, I believe he will opine they are all in order."

"*What* member banks?" demanded Hardy. "Where does it say you are authorized to make an offer on behalf of your member banks? What about the terms of our master agreement? I protest!

They were deceived! Who informed them, despite all we have heard, that the Sentinels were way short of achieving the stipulated minimum?"

"Mr. Hardy, I've been waiting for a long time to answer your questions," Malone said as he rose to his feet. "I did. When Mike Stone correctly decided to limit his remarks regarding the opportunity for banks to increase their bids, the chairmen of certain money-center banks began to call me and the regional Fed governors. Complaining about the restrictive nature of your master agreement they had been encouraged to execute, they were inquiring as to whether they had any alternative means by which to make complementary offers.

"We explained we didn't know of any reason they couldn't submit their offers through their supervising regulatory agency. Once we gave them a more complete progress report, the banks seemed less concerned about the Sentinels completing their task and more concerned about their fellow money-center banks' desire to independently buy up the unsubscribed shares for their own investors. They were more afraid of being left on the proverbial dock than incurring your wrath. Contingent upon our agreeing to not disclose their identity, their offers began to flow in. By the time we finished receiving their orders, they totaled another one billion dollars."

Hardy was livid. "How can you do this? It violates our master agreement! Under what authority can you represent your member banks?"

"Mr. Chairman, if I may be allowed to respond?" said Mike. Malone nodded.

"Mr. Hardy," Mike began, "if memory serves, it wasn't very long ago that many of us met in the executive conference room of Stone City Bank. At that meeting, you and your colleagues tried to impose your tactics of intimidation on the ABA. I watched while my father attempted to counter your threats and intimidation with factual information. This time I would like the privilege of responding.

"Do you really believe that those of us who are relied on by so many people to exercise good judgment were going to be stampeded into a decision? Do you believe a world threatened by the proposed concentration of ninety percent of its oil production in the hands of seven companies could be manipulated by slick legal tactics and financial intimidation?

"You keep bringing up this master agreement, but rather than rely on its enforceability, I would suggest you start worrying about defending yourself against restraint of trade, complicit violations of laws involved in your employment of Samson, investigation for further existence of fraudulent pricing and transportation practices, and dozens more crimes you have most likely committed. You are all going to be very busy defending yourselves.

"In case you still don't get it," Mike continued, "let me further explain. There are those of us who look forward to the day when large concentrations of wealth and influence are no longer allowed to pursue agendas of self-interest at the expense of the public interest. It's not the companies themselves we object to. I'm certain they are composed of many fine men and women. It's your leadership that is in question. When you and your fellow managers deliberately attempt to subvert prudent limits required to preserve and enhance your companies' capacity to best serve the public, you step over the line.

"You and other management leaders like you should be regarded as arrogant dinosaurs. Your presence tarnishes all of the other fine companies who, every day, responsibly strive to better fulfill the public's needs. Mr. Hardy, you are an embarrassment to our system of democratic free enterprise!"

Wanting to prevent any further altercation, Secretary Ainsworth interrupted. "It's now 4:45 p.m. Since we have already agreed to the five o'clock adjournment of this meeting, and according to my calculations, you are still one-half billion dollars short, I would like ask if there are any more bids."

"Point of clarity?" Morgan asked. "Does the additional Chinese commitment of one-half billion dollars replace the Stone City, America West backup position or add to it? Do I infer, from your statement, we are one-half billion short and that you have assumed our offer has been replaced? Should that be the case, I would like to resubmit our half-billion-dollar pledge."

"Accepted. Unless anybody else has anything to say, I declare the minimum stipulation has been satisfied and this meeting is adjourned," announced Secretary Ainsworth emphatically.

Chapter 56

VICTORY

P.J. Clarke's, the same bar where Walt and Jacques had previously met, had been selected for the Sentinels' victory celebration. By the time the celebrants began to filter in, the bar leading from the entrance to the back room was already filled with its normal array of neighborhood patrons and members of the working press.

Henri and Pierre had flown in from Paris unannounced. Pete Ferrari had arrived earlier in the day from San Francisco. They were waiting in the back room when Morgan Stone and Roger Malone arrived. This was the first time the five original ABA bankers had gathered together since they had convened to pay homage to the Sentinels for their work involving the transfer of the German industrialist funds.

"I have to admit," said Roger, "when Jacques and Mike first approached us and explained their concern over the consequences of seven oil companies controlling the world's oil supply, we listened to them out of respect for their former achievements. We never believed this small group of admittedly talented people could successfully challenge the Oil Club.

"They've been able to do something the American government was never able to accomplish. When we discovered, during wartime, that Titus Oil was selling oil to the Germans, the American government was forced to withdraw its lawsuit or risk Titus reducing oil shipments needed to support our own war effort. Do you have any idea how humiliated we were to learn one company could be so powerful that it could blackmail the federal government? If one company can exert so much power and influence, can you imagine what seven companies controlling that much of the world's oil production could do?"

"I'll tell what has fascinated me the most," said Pete Ferrari. "How can it be that a small group of friends, independent of the government, without the benefit of corporate resources, can solve such an important problem? Maybe there is more than one lesson to be learned here."

"What amazed me the most was their ability to develop so many relationships in five totally diverse investment cultures," Henri said. "Even the Swiss banks have never succeeded in tying so many markets together. Do you realize how broad their base of support really is? Imagine what they are capable of doing should another problem arise that requires their attention?"

"You have no idea of the number of calls I've received from the community bankers Mike called upon," said Pete. "If there was any doubt, we can be sure the wide chasm that has historically separated money-center and community banks has been bridged. Morgan, I hope you appreciate that Mike accomplished much more than the raising of money; he has succeeded in organizing an informal network of local banks that have expressed their interest in forming longer-term relationships with our banks. If we allow him to complete what he has started, he could very well develop a cooperative system of interstate banking."

"Pierre, Henri," said Roger, "I think the turning point of their entire mission must have hinged on the meeting in your office. The combination of the money the Sentinels had raised on their own and the added support and further endorsement of your half-billion-dollar investment created the spark that was needed to encourage the extra cooperation."

———

The older generation of bankers was so intent on discussing the Sentinels that they failed to notice the arrival of Sir David Marcus and Natalie Cummins. The patrons sitting at the bar noted the man with the striking red hair, but none of them recognized the celebrated star of the New York and London musical stage, adorned in her Yankees baseball hat and big dark glasses.

Fascinated by all the people who had congregated in the back room, the curious members of the working press began to watch the entrance, hoping to recognize one of the new arrivals. No one paid any particular attention when Mike and Juan Pablo entered or when Cecelia and two men of Oriental extraction escorted her along the length of the bar.

Some of them recognized Jacques from the many pictures and stories that had appeared in the New York newspapers, but they all noticed the tall, exquisitely dressed, beautiful woman with the silver-blonde hair who accompanied him.

The already-suspicious members of the working press became even more curious when their fellow newspaperman, Walt Matthews, entered the bar, said hello to his friends, and disappeared into the back room.

Out of professional respect for the privacy of their respected colleague, they resisted their reporter instincts, remained at the bar, and began to speculate among themselves about what could be happening. They didn't have to wait long. Walt soon reentered the main bar area and invited them to join him and his friends. In uncharacteristic fashion, with the aid of a chair, Walt climbed up and stood on one of the tables in the back room.

"Ladies and gentlemen of the press, my friends, and the

Sentinels, I would like to read you a story that will appear above the fold in tomorrow morning's *New York Times* and the thirty-two other papers where my column is syndicated."

December 8, 1946

CRUDE DECEPTION

By Walt Matthews

Tonight, the citizens of the world can rest more easily knowing another cycle of unbridled greed has been avoided. The presumed authority of the "Oil Club" has been successfully challenged; the efforts of seven major oil companies to perpetuate their control over 90 percent of the world's petroleum supply has been prevented.

The formation of a $15 billion international energy development fund will assure the world of a more diversified and competitive oil industry capable of supplying the world with a reliable supply of affordable oil.

In May of this year, a group calling themselves the Sentinels learned of a secret meeting organized by seven major oil companies to be held at a remote hunting and fishing club in Wyoming. The purpose of this clandestine meeting was to discuss and approve a plan to control 90 percent of the world's future petroleum production.

Concerned about the effects of so much power becoming concentrated in such a small number of hands, the Sentinels developed and executed a plan to break the grip of the Oil Club. To implement their plan, the Sentinels were required to mobilize public awareness and concern, to create and pass new legislation, and to fund an unprecedented $15 billion energy development pool from the world's international investment community.

"I hope you will join me as I tip my hat to these courageous, motivated, and talented young people," said Walt when he was done reading. "Without them and their efforts, our world could be a far different place."

After a long round of applause, Matthews hopped down from the table and led the crowd of newspaper reporters away to file their own reports. The remaining people raised their glasses in salute of a job well done.

Tapping his knife against his glass, Mike indicated he wanted to say a few words. "Jacques," he began, "it wasn't so long ago that a very brave lady and your friends felt the need to express their feelings when you appeared lost. To a person, none of us thought you were actually lost; we just didn't know where you were. In our hearts we knew we would need you to return and assist us in completing our mission. We just didn't understand you would choose to help us in such a dramatic fashion! Would you honor us with a few words?"

"It's all Claudine's fault," said Jacques, standing. "It's not that I would ever recommend getting smashed in the head or losing one's memory, but if it has to happen, being nursed back to health by Claudine is one hell of an experience. She has some very interesting ideas about recuperative medicine!"

All faces turned to Claudine as the group chuckled together.

"But seriously," Jacques continued, "one of the most difficult things for me to endure was watching her go off, by herself, and make all those calls on the European bankers. As it turned out, she didn't need my help, but waiting for her to return was always excruciating.

"With all that time, I went clear back to 1935 and started making a list of everyone we had met who either possessed or represented the kind of capital we needed. Next, I started to check off all the people we had already contacted in our more recent quest.

And guess what, Schmidt was the only one we hadn't contacted. Identifying him required no genius, just a lot of hard work.

"Let us not forget, making up a four-billion-dollar shortfall represents a lot of work on the part of many people. What do you suppose might have happened if Cecelia hadn't lost her temper in Jakarta, or Mike hadn't organized all those community bankers? Who in their right mind would organize an air force to fly nearly five hundred tons of gold out of China, right under the noses of the Chinese communists?"

Claudine then spoke up. "Given all that, the question I want to asked Henri and Pierre is, how could you be so certain there would be a second wave of follow-on interest?"

After exchanging a conspiratorial grin with Henri, Pierre answered, "Oh, we weren't sure—it was the only thing we could think to say that might rekindle your enthusiasm!"

After waiting for the group's shock to fade, Henri said, "I would like to believe the collective efforts of all of you were sufficient to play on the bankers' suspicious nature. I am beginning to think they had become alarmed by the possibility that their fellow American bankers might independently decide to complete the balance of the funding.

"Remember when I told you that one of the risks a major money-center bank could not afford to take was the possibility of the transaction being consummated without them as a major participant? In a way, Pierre and I were correct, but not for the right reasons. Maybe the lesson to be learned here is to never underestimate the greed and the suspicious nature of a money-center banker."

Chapter 57

CECELIA AND MIKE

Over breakfast the following morning, served in the smaller dining room of the Morgan Stone mansion, Morgan turned to Tai-Pan. "My old friend," he said, "how would you like to join me for a tour of our bank? There have been a lot of changes since you last visited us. There are a number of people I would like you to meet."

During their tour later that morning, Morgan—eager to be a congenial host—asked his guest, "Is there anything special you would like to see or do while you are in New York?"

"Could we go to Yankee Stadium?" said Tai-Pan. "I've always wanted to see the New York Yankees and Joe DiMaggio play baseball."

Thirty minutes later their taxi pulled up in front of Yankee Stadium for the Wednesday afternoon game. The Yankees were playing their American League rivals, the Cleveland Indians. Both clubs were fighting for the pennant. Bob Feller was pitching for the Indians, and Joe DiMaggio was playing center field for the Yankees.

As the usher was escorting them to Morgan's box, Tai-Pan kept stopping and looking around. The stadium was filled; the place was in a state of bedlam. It was the bottom of the first inning and DiMaggio was coming to bat.

Once they were seated, they took off their ties and coats, rolled up their sleeves, and ordered their first hot dogs and two bottles of beer. By the third inning, each was eating a second hot dog and drinking another beer. By the fifth inning, the two men were enjoying another beer; they had become just two more Yankee fans yelling for their team.

By the seventh inning, they had spilled beer on themselves, spots of mustard covered their shirts, their hair needed combing, and they were hoarse from yelling. Before they knew it, the game had gone into extra innings and DiMaggio hit his game-winning home run in the bottom of the twelfth.

As they left the stadium Morgan said, "Why don't we go directly to my house? We don't want to keep everyone waiting."

"What about the way we are dressed?" Tai-Pan protested. "I need to shower and change my clothes. This is a very important night for Cecelia and Mike; I wouldn't want to disappoint them."

"Tai-Pan, my friend, I'm quite certain they are going to be a lot more concerned about how we feel about their relationship than how we are dressed."

Hoping his comment would encourage Tai-Pan to say something, Morgan patiently waited for a response. When, after an appreciable period of time, he realized that the wily trader from Hong Kong was not prepared to say anything, Morgan motioned for his car.

The rest of the Sentinels were taking advantage of Tai-Pan and Morgan's absence to have a meeting of their own. In his new role as their team leader, Mike was speaking to the group. "Not to minimize all we have accomplished, but it's important we appreciate that our job isn't finished. In certain respects, it's just beginning. I have no great confidence that, left to its own devices, the fragmented independent oil industry will succeed in forming the kind of well-organized and competitive effort required to compete with the Oil Club. We have only swatted it on the ass.

"Having access to development capital is one thing; beating the Oil Club to the punch could be another matter. With Claudine and Jacques returning to Europe, and Cecelia and me being pinned down here in New York, who is left to make certain the implementation of the independent oil plan doesn't get dropped?"

Claudine was the first to respond. "You haven't said anything about the University of California's newest redheaded addition to its graduate school faculty. Who among us knows more about the oil industry, and enjoys the trust and confidence of Middle Eastern leaders, than David? And who enjoys the support of the god-damnedest research assistant the industry has ever seen?"

"Wait a minute," David protested, "there's someone in this room who has the best set of oil credentials I've ever seen. If this conversation is headed where I think it's headed, I think you'd better ask the gentleman from Venezuela how he feels about becoming involved."

With everyone's attention focused on him, the one man who in his own quiet way had probably done more than anyone to change the landscape of the world's contemporary oil industry measured his words before speaking. "Nothing would please me more than to continue to work alongside David, and to be able to call on the support of all of you. I think we have started something that we need to finish!"

Everyone had already arrived at the Stone mansion when the two disheveled, slightly inebriated men, who seemed to be new best friends, came through the front door. Without acknowledging the other guests, they made their way to Morgan's bar for a spot of twelve-year-old Macallan scotch, served neat.

Properly served, Morgan and Tai-Pan turned to the other guests and family members, who were all staring at them with their mouths open in astonishment. Cecelia couldn't believe her eyes. She had never seen her noble and notoriously formal father so relaxed and having so much fun. She turned to Mike and asked, "Where do you think they've been?"

"Judging from the mustard stains on their shirts, I would think they've been to a ball game," he said. "It seems we're seeing another side of our fathers!"

Before anyone could say anything, Mike's mother went up to Cecelia's father, gave him a small kiss on the cheek, and said, "Welcome, Tai-Pan. It's a privilege and a pleasure to have you and your daughter as guests here in our home. I have reserved the seat next to mine for you at the dinner table, and Morgan has arranged for Cecelia to sit next to him. I'm looking forward to our having a nice chat."

Everyone knew it was the kind of evening when things could go very right or very wrong. The adrenaline and the wine were freely flowing. Dinner was delayed twice. When the dinner chime rang for the third time, the Stones' crusty maid of thirty years announced, "If you people aren't going to sit down, I'm going to throw a magnificent dinner in the garbage can and go home!"

The waiter, moving around the table, filled the glasses with a special white wine that had been selected to complement the first course. The guests waited before taking their first sip, thinking that one or the other of the fathers might want to make a toast. They needn't have waited. The first course came and went. White wine glasses were replaced with red wine glasses. Everyone was telling stories.

Neither Morgan nor Tai-Pan indicated any intention of

proposing a toast. The tension was building; the stories were becoming a little less cavalier. The laughter was not quite so loud.

After the dessert had been served, the waiter began to fill the champagne flutes. At just the right moment, Morgan stood up, somewhat shakily, to make his toast.

"To Tai-Pan, my new-old friend and America's newest baseball fan. You have given new meaning to the phrase, 'When in Rome . . .' I can't remember when I've had such a good time at a baseball game, eaten so many hot dogs, or consumed so many beers!

"On a more serious point, I want to talk about what a valuable lesson Mike and Cecelia have taught Mike's mother and me. Before we met your beloved Cecelia, we had always hoped Mike would marry some nice Jewish girl from a prominent New York family. God knows we introduced him to enough of them.

"When we learned that Mike was dating a girl of Chinese descent, we found ourselves afraid of things about which we knew little. Ignorance can be a terrible weapon. For years, we asked ourselves why Mike was so determined to perpetuate his relationship with Cecelia, particularly when it meant having to work out so many problems that are involved in maintaining a coast-to-coast relationship.

"All those things occurred before we had the opportunity to meet Cecelia. Once we got to know her, we could see her lovely ways, her intelligence, her beauty, and the love she and Mike shared for each other. When we learned of her kidnapping, we, like everybody else, held our breath during all those scary months before she was rescued.

"I hope all of you will join me in a toast to Mike and Cecelia. May they have a long and happy life—and lots of healthy children."

After Morgan completed his toast, all eyes turned toward Tai-Pan. After what seemed a very long time, he slowly rose to speak. Despite his wrinkled clothing, Tai-Pan's formal and powerful character was evident. His posture was controlled and he stood erect.

Smiling, he said, "Morgan, thank you for your very gracious remarks about my Cecelia. Even now, I am having a difficult time not seeing her as the little girl who sat on my lap and asked all those questions. It took a long time before her mother and I accepted the fact that she needed to leave home and seek a life in a bigger world. For a long time, it's been very important to us that she understands she has our love and support in whatever course in life she chooses to pursue. We are sorry it has taken so many years for all of us to understand how we really feel.

"Like you, we were concerned about the harm that might come to Cecelia in her relationship with Mike. For people of an orthodox, privileged Chinese heritage, the thought of a daughter leaving home, pursuing an education, and leading a career in a foreign country can be very confusing. Adding the knowledge that she was in love with an American, not a man of Chinese ancestry, only increased our curiosity and concern.

"Even though I had the pleasure of meeting Morgan on more than one occasion, Cecelia's mother and I had never had the pleasure of meeting Mike, nor did we know anything about their life in America. Naturally fearing what we didn't understand, we hoped that with the passage of time their infatuation for each other might fade.

"All that ended the day Mike called me in Hong Kong. As you can imagine, his revelation about his relationship with Cecelia came as quite a shock. After listening carefully to him, I could feel his concern and his love for our daughter. What I didn't know was how she felt about him. For reasons I have only just begun to understand, I misinterpreted her not telling us about him and their relationship for such a long time.

"Cecelia, you once asked me to come to San Francisco and meet Mike. I knew how much you loved this man and that you needed my approval before you would feel truly comfortable marrying him. I would like to apologize to you for making you believe I was so unapproachable. Please understand that you are the true love of my life and your vitality and happiness will always be my brightest beacon."

Tai-Pan then turned toward Mike and looked him straight in the eye. "Twelve years ago, Cecelia needed my support and understanding before she could embark on a new life beyond the barriers of Hong Kong. Although it is apparent that she loves you and wants to marry you, I am very proud that she still thinks my support is important."

Bending over to pick up his champagne flute, Tai-Pan raised his glass and said, "I wish to make it as clear as I possibly can that her mother and I are very pleased that you will be her partner in the remaining adventure of her life. Both of you have our complete approval to get married. Here's to the two of you. May the path of life be plentiful, loving, and produce lots of grandchildren."

The guests remained silent, spellbound by Tai-Pan's eloquence.

Taking advantage of the brief moment of silence, he continued. "There is one matter for clarification, however." Everyone stiffened in anticipation. Smiling, he asked, "Morgan, do you think we could go back to Yankee Stadium tomorrow? I didn't have the opportunity to ask Joe DiMaggio for his autograph!"

EPILOGUE

Sixty years later, in the year 2007, the world's daily demand for oil had increased to approximately ninety million barrels, twenty times greater than the consumption in 1947. In the intervening period, control over 90 percent of the world's production shifted from seven major oil companies to seven sovereign nations. The price of oil had risen from fourteen to more than seventy dollars per barrel, an increase of more than 500 percent.

A READER'S DISCUSSION GUIDE

The Sentinels: Crude Deception, a World War II–era thriller that combines politics, business, and history, has relevance for our world today. One of its themes is the issue of unbridled greed and how secret circles of a handful of wealthy individuals—in this case, as part of a monopoly of oil conglomerates—run the world.

A group of six graduates of an elite American doctoral program, with ties to the global financial community, the Sentinels learn of this "Oil Club" and its plan to perpetuate its control over 90 percent of the world's future oil production. To prevent this dangerous concentration of power in the hands of seven incestuous companies, the Sentinels develop a plan to break the club's grip. That plan requires the cooperation of some of the world's most powerful private investors, government officials, and Middle Eastern leaders, plus the help of grassroots America.

To implement their plan, the band of six econ wizards/friends must rally support over four continents—in the jungles of Indonesia, the corporate boardrooms of America, Europe, and Asia, and the desert of the Western frontier—all the while eluding the constant threat of ruthless assassins hired by the Oil Club. Together they take on a Goliath of skyscraper proportion—and prevail.

QUESTIONS AND TOPICS FOR DISCUSSION

When the novel opens in 1946, the world's seven biggest oil companies—united in what the Sentinels dub the "Oil Club"—secretly plan to perpetuate their control over 90 percent of the world's future oil production. How do *we the people* protect ourselves from the secret agendas of concentrated wealth and influence in their quest of unbridled greed?

Author Gordon Zuckerman has said, "Americans should be concerned about the consequences of nine-tenths of the world's oil supply being concentrated in the hands of a limited number of oil companies and sovereign countries." Do you share his concern, and what do you think should be done about it?

Are their aspects of the Sentinels' plan that you think need to be implemented today? Who would you trust to solve the problems?"

Were the Sentinels' efforts to garner the cooperation of powerful private investors, government officials, and Middle Eastern leaders plausible?

Do you feel that the Sentinels' efforts to generate grassroots support for constructive legislation are required in today's political environment?

What role do you think the "national press" should play in informing the public of the real story behind the story, as the *New York Times* journalist Walter Matthews did in the book?

What other industries do you see where power is concentrated in just a few individuals or nations?

Who do you think will step forward in our modern world in the way the heroes of *Crude Deception* do?

What happens when government and big business can't provide a solution to a pressing problem? Should the void be filled by an independent group?

Did you take away ideas from this thriller that could actually be applied to help you move away from a dependency on oil for your energy needs?

How would you describe the relationships among the six Sentinels? Do you agree that it was necessary for that band of economics wizards to invite new members from the UK into their circle to achieve their goal of foiling the Oil Club?

Which character best represents your attitude toward the Oil Club? Did you agree with his/her proposal for preventing the monopoly from attaining world domination?

AUTHOR Q&A

1. **Why have you chosen to write historical fiction? Is it more challenging than writing science fiction or a totally fictitious thriller, do you think?**

   With an ever-increasing exposure to life and my growing experience, I couldn't help believing that there is a need to better understand the circumstances and the significance of some of the more important events of our times. Having been exposed to the influential power of the oil lobby, I decided to study the general concept of hidden power. The more I learned, the more convinced I became that I wanted to find a way to tell the stories behind the stories. The idea of using the evolving lives of the main characters as fiction vehicles to tell what I regard as serious stories just evolved.

2. **Does your academic background and work history specifically drive your creation of characters and plots and alternative outcomes?**

   Unquestionably, the stories, the plots, and the composite makeup of my characters have been derived from observations along the way on my life's journey.

3. Have you always been telling stories or writing them since childhood, or is writing a craft you've been drawn to in retirement?

   I always found my former life to be so active and demanding, with the exception of being a lifelong student of history, I never had the time to do the applied research and the writing required to pursue my other curiosities. Following my retirement, I have the time to pursue hidden interests that seem to be bubbling to the surface.

4. How do you go about researching the little-known details regarding extremely familiar topics, such as World War II, that can capture your readers' interest and surprise them?

   A new idea can pop to the surface from almost anywhere. Some result from things I've encountered and experienced in an active life filled with diverse interests and interesting people. Of particular interest, I have been fascinated by the general subject of responsible and able leadership. I find it difficult to talk about personal leadership without becoming involved in a person's career and his or her emotional and personal development.

   With the availability now of extra time, coupled with all the wonderful resources offered by published books, the plethora of Web-based information, and travel and continued interaction with interesting friends and new acquaintances, I find I'm provided with more information than one person can possibly absorb.

5. Are the goals for your stories to forewarn society not to repeat history? Simply to entertain? To actually offer ideas

for solving contemporary problems in the business world and in world economies?

The more I read and learn, the more impressed I have become by and convinced that our great gift of democratic free enterprise represents a special and delicate opportunity. In America, it can be used to create great wealth as a result of better fulfilling public need. It can also be used to create wealth at the expense of the public's best interests. The presence or absence of responsible and competent leadership can determine whether the quest of free enterprise produces another constructive brick in our country's great house or provides the next great challenge that must be overcome.

6. Your novels feature characters from the United States, Europe, the United Kingdom, and the Far East. Have you traveled to all of those regions to collect details about language nuances, customs, art and culture, and business practices to add authenticity to your characters and story lines?

There are some people who have accused me of living a life of anecdotes to support my writing of books.

7. Are there aspects from different stages of your career in business and finance that emerge in one or more of the characters you've created?

When I look back over my life, I sometimes think of it as a series of different kinds of speed bumps, each of which required the achievement of some special learning experience.

The composite characters, the problem solving, the evolution of their lives, their observations, their reactions, and the reactions of others have been drawn from the challenge of the ever-increasing size of life's obstacles and challenges.

8. **What genre(s) do you pick up for leisure reading? Who are your favorite authors and what are some of your favorite books?**

    There are highly capable historians who make history as exciting as any mystery: William Manchester, James Michener, Ron Chernow, Daniel Yergin, and Aron Sorkin. Likewise, there are historical novelists—Herman Wouk, Wilbur Smith, Tom Clancy, Leon Uris—who have learned to illustrate history through the lives of their main characters. And, there are the mystery writers Ken Follett, Fredrick Forsyth, and Fletcher Knebel, for purely great reads.

9. **Do you think this nation is on the right track regarding alternative sources of energy so we are not as oil dependent as we were, say, at the end of World War II?**

    In a world of managed energy scarcity, he who owns the energy can fix production costs, pursue power, and wage war. In a shrinking world of growing environmental concerns and expanding energy needs, it's not a question of replacing historical forms of power with cleaner power; it's learning how to use all sources of power on both an economic and an environmentally sensitive basis to meet our needs of reliable sources of affordable power.

10. If you had one word of advice for recent college graduates today, what would it be?

Take a more active and objective interest in the world that is evolving around you. Never in the course of history have we been more susceptible to irresponsible agendas of concentrated wealth and influence, nor have we been faced with greater challenges. Constantly question what you can do to become one of life's "rainmakers."

ABOUT THE AUTHOR

Gordon Zuckerman, a graduate of Harvard Business School, has studied banking, international finance, and history extensively, focusing on how wealth and governmental machinations can advance private agendas that conflict with public interest. He lives with his wife in northern Nevada.